THE EXPERIMENT

I0682221

A linear story horror anthology hosted by **Zach Cole**

Including the talents of: **Christofer Nigro**, **Dustin Dreyling**, **Alex Dumitru**, **Breyden Halverson**, and **Robert Galvin**

Cover Art: rizkynugraha

https://www.fiverr.com/rizkynugraha

Title Logo and Cover Embellishments: Lungga Creatives

DEDICATIONS

To the mystery lights of the sky: May you always tantalize us with your mystery, for without you, there would be no such thing as mystery.

--Breyden Halverson

For Jacquelyn Gonser, my beautiful girlfriend who has stood by me through this dark time in my life and supported my writings. Happy one year, baby!

--Zach Cole

To my grandpa George, who introduced me to Godzilla and Science Fiction; and my dad, who introduced me to movies that scared the crap out of me but are forever my favorites because of it.

--Dustin Dreyling

This one is for Jake. Just like all of them.

--Alex Dumitru

This is for my maternal great-grandfather, Sebastian "Sibby" Anastasia, and my great-grandmother Stella

Anastasia, both of whom loved me as much as any great-grandparents possibly could.

--Christofer Nigro

Table of Contents

THE ESCAPE

Zach Cole

1

Mark Hudson hopped from the Black Hawk helicopter he arrived in, ducking under the rotor wash as he made his way across the tarmac toward the entrance to Area 51. Once he reached the entrance, a soldier wearing futuristic battle armor opened the door for him, granting him access.

He nodded to the soldier as he stepped through the door where two more soldiers, dressed in the same battle armor, waited for him in the hallway beyond. They escorted him to the elevator that sat at the end of the corridor. After they entered the elevator, one of the soldiers pressed the button for the lowest point of the facility.

He was Mark Hudson, director of operations at Area 51, which meant he oversaw every project conducted at the facility. His current interest, however, was Project Hydra; a biological weapons project.

The elevator doors opened, and they made their way down the hallway it opened into. Hudson stopped at the door labeled: Project Hydra and swiped his ID across the scanner next to the sealed entrance. The door clicked, and he pulled it open. The room beyond was vast, containing six clear domes, each occupied by a horrific beast.

The biological weapons.

The intent of Project Hydra was to create living weapons to replace soldiers on the battlefield; or, at the very least, give the U.S. soldiers an upper hand.

A lone man sat at a desk in the middle of the room. He glanced up from whatever papers he was looking at, noticing Hudson and his two bodyguards. The man stood from the desk as the director of operations approached, his bodyguards following close behind.

"It seems our subjects are doing quite well, eh, Doctor," Hudson said.

"Indeed. They've grown rapidly since their... births," Doctor Alicio Brice said with a nod.

Brice's hair stuck at odd angles, his clothes were ruffled, and his eyes were bloodshot.

Hudson raised an eyebrow at Brice. "Have you been getting enough sleep?"

Brice shook his head and motioned to the domes lining the room. "They go nuts when I leave. And if I try to sleep here, they make an ungodly amount of noise to keep me awake."

Hudson glanced at the creatures in their domes, their eyes locked on him. He had read that a bunch of different DNA went into the beasts. Mostly culled from animals that were known to be efficient killers. Predators. But something else went into their genetic structure. Something from a creature very not from this world. They found it buried in Antarctica, frozen and very much dead. Its corpse was brought to Area 51 for study. Its genetic properties were extraordinary.

Eventually, Hudson, as director of operations for Area 51, gave the greenlight to use the alien creature's DNA in Project Hydra. The result was the six different creatures occupying the domes. The alien DNA made their behavior unpredictable, so it was hard to tell their thinking for torturing Dr. Brice.

"But, they are ready?" Hudson asked.

"I've not observed any more growth in them, so I'd say they are fully grown," Brice said.

Hudson frowned. "Are they ready?"

Brice sighed. "Yes. They're ready."

"Good."

Hudson looked at each creature in turn, their appearances horrifying and deadly.

That was the intent, Hudson thought, proud that they accomplished their goal.

Now to test them in the field…

Hudson turned his back to Brice and the creatures, making his way toward the door. A blaring klaxon stopped him, a red light flashing through the room. Hudson whirled around, giving Brice a questioning look. Brice sat behind his desk, tapping away at his laptop. Brice looked up at Hudson, his eyes wide and full of worry.

"What is it?" Hudson asked.

"Someone has hacked into our systems," Brice said, his voice shaky.

"What are they accessing?"

"The domes."

The two body guards took up position in front of Hudson as hissing emanated from the domes, the airlocks unsealing. Brice scurried away from his desk, scuttling behind the two armed guards.

"Director, Dr. Brice, get the hell out of here!" one of the guards said as the beasts closed in on their now open domes.

Brice pulled on Hudson's arm. He allowed Brice to guide him to the exit, watching the creatures step from their domes and turn in their direction. The door shut as the creatures charged and the soldiers opened fire.

Hudson followed Brice down the hallway, the screams of the soldiers following them. Brice made it to the door first, repeatedly jamming his finger down on the call button. Sweat rolled down his forehead as he nervously looked back the way they came. The soldiers' screams had stopped.

A ding turned him back to the elevator. Hudson and Brice jumped inside, the elevator doors closing as the door to Project Hydra shuddered from a blow.

"Do we have countermeasures in place in case of an escaped subject?" Brice asked, his breathing heavy, his voice shaking.

"Of course, we do," Hudson snapped. "They should already be in place."

With a ding, the elevator doors opened into a vast room filled with computers, screens, and people frantically working them. Hudson stepped into the security room, armed soldiers nodding at him with helmeted heads, their faces obscured by silver visors. Hudson returned the nod, making his way toward the consoles at the front of the room and the people operating them.

11

"Someone give me a sitrep," Hudson barked.

"The concussive turrets designed for this very situation are keeping the creatures at bay," one of the techs, a blonde-haired woman, reported.

Hudson sighed in relief at that. Hopefully the creatures would return to their domes. That was the intent of the concussive turrets. To give them an incentive to return to their encapsulated vaults, which they would lock from the safety of the security room.

"Any idea who unlocked the domes?" Hudson asked.

"No, sir," another tech, a man with dark hair, said. "But we ran a trace. Whoever did it… it was an inside job, sir."

"Fuck," Hudson muttered. "Keep on it. Locate the exact point in the facility the hack came from. I want them found and I want a goddamn explanation! Two men are dead because of them…"

"Yes, sir," the tech said, tapping away at his keyboard. "It might take a while, though."

"Understood."

"Sir!" a third tech shouted. "You need to see this."

Hudson made his way over to the tech, a red-haired woman, finding each of them monitoring the security cameras in the Project Hydra room.

"Shit," he muttered.

The creatures weren't backing down. Instead of retreating from the devices hanging from the ceiling, pelting them with sonic blasts, they were advancing toward the weapons, withstanding the assault.

They really are the perfect weapons, Hudson thought, cringing.

Subject Two, a horrifying quadrupedal beast that was covered in white-grey fur, leaped at the turrets, ripping one of the four from the ceiling and crushing it in its powerful jaws.

The numbers were the creatures' codenames. It was simpler than giving them actual names. Each creature had a tattoo of their assigned soubriquets on various parts of their body.

Subject Five, a nightmarish tentacled beast, grabbed ahold of two more of the turrets with its long arms and ripped them from the ceiling. Its snake-like limbs coiled around the turrets, crushing them in its grasp.

Subject Four, a creature that looked like a cross between a yeti and a demonic being, reached up with one of its thickly furred arms and pulled the last turret down, crushing it in its fist.

"Get a team down there stat!" Hudson ordered. "Have them armed with heavy weaponry. Rocket launchers and high caliber rifles."

"You want to destroy them?" Brice asked, stepping up next to Hudson. "After all the money and resources we put into them?"

Hudson frowned. "We have no choice. We can't allow them to escape."

Brice mumbled something but said nothing more.

"Relay the order," Hudson said to the operations tech, a younger woman with raven black hair and sharp, green eyes.

The tech nodded, getting ahold of the security team and conveying his order.

"They're on their way," the tech informed the director of operations.

2

Captain Jack Snyder pulled the charging handle back on his M249 light machine gun, also known as a SAW (Squad Automatic Weapon), chambering a 5.56 millimeter round from the STANAG 150 round drum magazine. He wore standard issue Area 51 body armor, complete with a teched out helmet that hid his face behind a silver visor. A heads-up display (HUD) was projected on the inside of the visor, in front of his face, feeding him tactical information. The armor was designed to be bullet and knife proof, giving the wearer a sense of invincibility.

But will it hold up against the creatures we are about to fight? Snyder wondered.

He looked to his four other teammates, all wearing the same armor as him, two of which were equipped with SAWs, the other two with M141 anti-fortification rocket launchers. The launchers fired 83 millimeter rounds and were known as 'bunker busters.'

The only thing they'll be busting are monsters, Snyder thought with a smirk.

They all had .50 caliber Desert Eagle hand guns strapped to their hips, just in case. They were a backup, but he doubted they'd need them. He had confidence the weapons they were carrying would take care of the targets.

"Let's move out," Snyder said, getting a nod from his teammates.

They made their way out of the armory, heading for the elevator at the end of the hallway.

"They're trapped on the lowest floor. So as soon as the elevator doors open, be prepared to fire," Snyder commanded.

"And if our weapons have no effect on them?" Fredrick Smith, one of the M141 wielders, asked.

"Then... we fall back, regroup, and come up with a new plan," Snyder replied. "We need to keep them contained to the lower levels."

"Easier said than done," Charles Michaels said, holding one of the SAWs.

"I know," Snyder noted, pressing the button to call the elevator.

When he elevator arrived, the five-man team squeezed inside. Snyder pressed the button for the lowest floor and the doors closed. They readied their weapons as the elevator descended toward their destination. The elevator doors opened, and they rushed into the hallway, weapons raised, the three with SAWs up front, the two with M141s in back.

Snyder's brows furrowed in confusion at the sight of an empty hallway.

"Uh… where are they?" Elizabeth Collins, the other M141 wielder, asked, just as befuddled as Snyder.

The team advanced down the corridor, weapons leading the way. They stopped at the door labeled 'Project Hydra.' Snyder reached for the door.

"Wait!" Gabriel Watson hissed. "It could be a trap."

Snyder raised an eyebrow at him, though he was unable to see it because of the mirror-like visor obscuring his face. "You think they're that smart?"

"It's possible," Watson replied.

Snyder nodded. "Be ready then."

He grasped the doorknob. Collins and Michaels pointed their SAWs at the entrance. Watson and Smith took a step back, launchers ready, but wary about firing them in such an enclosed space. And for the right reasons.

Snyder twisted the knob and yanked the door open. He expected one of the creatures to charge out of the doorway and tear into them, but no attack came.

Snyder rounded the door he opened, sweeping his light machine gun from side to side. There was no sign of the creatures, besides the crushed turrets lying on the white, tiled floor. The desk in the middle was also overturned, its contents scattered across the floor. The laptop that sat upon it appeared to have been stepped on by something very heavy. The domes that previously contained the creatures were still empty; the beasts had not retreated to them.

"Where the hell are they?" Collins asked, stepping up beside Snyder.

"I'm not sure," Snyder said with a shake of his head. "But stay alert. They could still be in here somewhere."

"But where?" Michaels asked. "There is no place for creatures as large as them to hide."

Snyder scanned the room, frowning. Michaels was right. The room was very open, sporting no hiding places for the beasts.

"Can they turn invisible?" Smith asked nervously.

Snyder opened a file on his HUD, showing him all available data on the creatures.

The team leader shook his head. "I don't see anything about them having adaptive camouflage capabilities."

A sudden shout turned them around. Snyder's eyes widened in horror at the sight. Watson was floating in the air, flailing around in an attempt to free himself. Snyder's HUD alerted him to Watson's finger tightening over the trigger of his M141.

"Get to cover!" Snyder shouted as he dove toward the overturned desk.

The resulting explosion sent him flying, right into one of the domes. The armored team leader slid down its surface, toppling to the ground. He pushed himself up with a moan, having been severely jarred by the impact with the hard transparent surface.

A snarling to his right called his attention. Snyder slowly turned his head toward its source, finding himself face to face with Subject Two. It bared its teeth and opened its jaws wide. The soldier ducked as Two lunged. Two's jaws snapped closed with a crack where Snyder's head was located a second previous. Snyder rolled to the side, away from Two. He jumped to his feet and lifted his twenty-two-pound SAW, taking aim at Two.

The creature snarled as Snyder pulled the trigger. The M249 bucked wildly in his grasp as it spat hot lead at the beast at a rate of 100 rounds per minute.

The armored security leader's aim had been the creature's face, but it shifted to the side, the rounds striking its shoulder. Grey hair flew away, but no blood or flesh. After about thirty rounds with no effect, he cut off his assault.

Snyder glanced to his team mates, some facing off against the monsters they were sent to stop, others already dead. Watson was blown to bits by the blast of his M141 at such close range, having fired it at the floor. The creature that picked him up, the one known as Subject Four, however, was fine, its fur only singed.

I guess the armor doesn't protect against explosives, Snyder thought.

It was a quick glance, but when he turned his attention back to his adversary, it was lunging at him, its mouth opened wide. The creature's maw enveloped Snyder's helmeted head. He could feel its teeth digging into the armor protecting his neck. Panic coursed through him as he felt Two's teeth slip past the armor and dig into his flesh. With a jerk of the unholy beast's head, Snyder's own popped off.

The soldier's brain still functioned for a few more seconds, seeing himself fly from his own body with a spray of blood the neck. He saw the other experiments slaughtering his team mates.

Then… he saw nothing at all.

3

Hudson watched in horror as the experiments slaughtered the team sent in to deal with them. The weapons they wielded had no effect. Not even the powerful rocket launchers. Sweat dripped from his forehead as the creatures finished their ghastly work, regarding the bodies for a moment before turning toward the door that the soldiers entered through.

"Get another team down there!" Hudson ordered.

"It'll take too long," Brice said in a sing-songy voice.

Hudson growled. "Then get teams at every exit. We can't allow those things to get out of this facility!"

"On it, sir," the operations tech said.

Hudson cringed as the creatures slipped out of the Project Hydra room and into the hallway. They set their eyes on the elevator, heading for it.

"Oh, shit," Hudson muttered.

The director of operations spun around, relieved to find four armed soldiers in the room with them. He frowned at the weapons they held. KRISS Vectors were small caliber firearms. They fired .357 SIG pistol cartridges. Not powerful enough to stop the creatures bearing down on them.

He pointed to the elevator. "Make sure nothing gets through there!"

The soldiers nodded, taking up positions in front of the elevator.

Hudson turned back to the camera feed. Subject Four, the biggest of the creatures, was forcing the elevator doors apart. The other five hopped and barked excitedly.

"Call the elevator!" Hudson ordered.

The soldiers complied, one of them hammering his finger on the call button. A few seconds later, the doors slid open, the cart empty.

"Just leave it go," Hudson said to the soldiers.

The doors slid shut, the cart staying put with no destination point. Hudson turned back to the screen in time to see Four slide apart the doors.

"Most of them might be able to climb up the elevator shaft, but Four and Three are entirely too big to make it," Brice said, watching the screen thoughtfully.

"We've underestimated them enough today," Hudson said.

"True. They've proven to be a force to be reckoned with. But... wasn't that what they were designed for?" Brice flashed Hudson a fiendish grin.

Hudson frowned. "Unfortunately."

Hudson's pulse quickened as Subject Two disappeared into the elevator shaft, the rest filing in one at a time, ending with Four and Three.

"Are the teams at the exits like I asked?" Hudson queried.

"Yes, sir," the operations tech said. "All exits are covered by security teams."

"Status on the creatures?"

"Slowly making their way up the elevator shaft," a tech monitoring the motion sensors, a man with light, unkempt hair and dark brown eyes, said. "They've climbed past the bottom three floors."

"They're coming here," Brice muttered.

Hudson turned toward the operations tech. "Get two personnel from each team up here now!"

The tech nodded and spoke softly into her mic. After she was done communicating with the teams, she turned to Hudson. "They're on their way."

The director of operations nodded to the woman, his eyes continuously flicking to the elevator. At any moment, the creatures could peel apart the doors and slaughter them all.

Minutes passed.

Hudson could feel the sweat pouring down his forehead, drenching the expensive suit he wore. It was by no means hot in the security room. The whole facility was set to just the right temperature. The perspiration was from his fear. Fear of the creatures he created.

A bang sounded from the elevator. Then another. And another, followed by the sound of wrenching metal.

A clawed hand slipped between the doors, followed by another.

"They're here," Brice said, his voice trembling with terror.

All eyes in the room were on the elevator, eyes wide with fear. The soldiers raised their KRISS Vectors, fingers in the trigger guards.

The doors slowly slid apart, revealing the horrific face of Subject Two. It slammed the doors to the sides, shattering the mechanisms that operated them in the process.

Gunfire filled the room as the soldiers opened fire, the hot lead pelting the creature's chest, shredding its fur, but not doing much else. Two snarled, showing his curved fangs to the attacking soldiers.

Hudson ducked under a desk as Two lunged from the elevator shaft, tearing into the security officer he landed on. The soldier's gun flailed around the room, his finger jamming down the trigger as he tried to free himself from Two's grasp. The bullets pinged around the room, some finding unarmored techs and killing or injuring them.

The other three soldiers made the mistake of turning toward the attacking monster and firing on it. Tendrils snaked from the elevator shaft, wrapping around two of the soldiers, lifting them in the air, and slamming them against the walls on either side of the doors. It smashed them against the walls two more times before releasing them, and their lifeless bodies tumbled to the floor.

The horrifying face of Subject Five emerged from the darkness of the elevator shaft. It sneered at the two men it pummeled. Five pulled itself from the elevator shaft, making way for the next terrifying abomination.

Subject Six, a nimble, skeletal, almost insectoid creature, slithered into the security room from the elevator shaft. It hissed, baring its fangs as it made its way around the room, tearing into the injured lying on the floor.

They seem intent on picking us all off... but why? Do they resent their creation? Or are they just compelled to kill?

Hudson shook his head, deciding not to waste his time trying to figure out the mindset of monsters he knew nothing about, even if he did create them. They used DNA from an alien creature that was a complete enigma to the team. They only focused on the military possibilities it offered.

A stupid mistake...

Hudson made eye contact with Brice, who hid under another desk several feet from him... before he was pulled from under it.

Six held Brice aloft by a leg. It sneered at him, bringing his face up to its own grotesque visage. Hudson watched in horror as Six bit Brice's face off. The monstrosity then dropped to all fours, its head tilting to the side as it spotted the director of operations.

"Fuck," Hudson muttered.

4

Hudson pressed himself deeper under the desk as Six stalked toward him. A high-pitched noise pierced the air that gained the attention of the six nightmarish experiments. They seemingly followed the sound, heading for the exit that'd expel them into the outside world. There was nothing Hudson could do, so he stayed put. The mysterious noise had saved him.

Four sent a fist into the metal door, denting it. Its second punch dented it further. Its third punch sent the door flying from its frame, clanging on the concrete tarmac beyond. Hudson anxiously watched as the creatures made their way into the world beyond the facility.

Once he knew it was safe, the director of operations shuffled out from the desk he hid under. Death surrounded him. Two of the soldiers laid dead at his feet, their armor torn open, their insides ripped out. The two that were pummeled by Five began to stir. The tech that ran the facility were all dead, killed either by stray bullets or from the creatures themselves. Hudson gagged at the sight. He pitched forward and vomited his lunch onto the already soiled floor.

"Nasty."

An unfamiliar voice suddenly spun Hudson around. His hidden handgun was drawn and leveled at the man's chest. The strange man wore a leather jacket with a black shirt beneath, and jean pants. He had the face of a younger man, despite the beard. The intruder raised his hands as Hudson pointed the firearm at him.

"Woah now, partner. No need to get violent," the man said.

Hudson glared at the man. "You're the hacker."

The man gave the director a lopsided grin. "Correct Mundo. The name's Logan--"

"I don't give a fuck about your name," Hudson growled, poking Logan's chest with the barrel of his handgun. "I want to know why you did it."

Logan grinned. "I was ordered to."

"By who?"

Logan's smirk widened. "You're only Director of Operations. One step below the big boss."

Hudson's eyes widened. "Are you telling me the Director of Area 51 ordered you to release Project Hydra into the world?"

Logan nodded. "This is the beginning of the true experiment."

Hudson, gun still aimed at Logan's core, turned to the soldiers that had stepped up next to him. "I want teams after those things!"

The soldiers nodded, running off to gather the surviving security team members.

Logan chuckled, and Hudson's attention turned back to him. "Good luck catching them before they slaughter innocents."

Hudson was tempted to kill the man, but he refrained, knowing he worked for the director. The director of operations leveled his angry gaze at Logan.

"They've already killed innocents," Hudson growled, motioning to the dead that surrounded them.

Logan pursed his lips but said nothing.

Hudson pushed the barrel of his handgun into Logan's chest a little more. "Now… you're going to tell me everything."

Logan grinned.

5

"You'll lose your job for this."

Hudson sat across from Logan in the interrogation room. The chamber was dimly lit and sparse on details. What an interrogation room should look like.

"I very much doubt that," Hudson said, arms crossed.

Logan shook his head in frustration. "You don't believe me, do you?"

"Of course not," Hudson growled. "I think you're some animal rights hippy that found out about the creatures and thought it cruel, so you set them loose."

Logan snorted. "You're nuts."

Hudson smirked. "Maybe a little. But you're even crazier for setting those things loose. They're dangerous. Killers. *Monsters.* They're weapons."

"And weapons must be tested," Logan said.

Hudson frowned deeply. "You expect me to believe my boss ordered the release of living weapons for …for …*testing?*"

"Yes. Because it's the truth."

Hudson shook his head. He didn't believe it. *Couldn't* believe it. Director Stenze was a respectable man. A kind man. He didn't think the Director could hurt a fly, let alone make an order that could result in the deaths of who-knows-how-many civilians. It wasn't possible.

But what if it was true?

The thought couldn't help but cross his mind. People weren't always what they seemed; that was an uncomfortable truth he had come to know very well in his life.

Hudson's answer came bursting through the door.

"What in the hell is going on here?" Stenze growled.

It was all true…

HORROR AT STONE HILL

Zach Cole

6

Stone Hill was a small town in Nevada, about thirty miles from the military base known as Area 51. It wasn't a very big town, set up a little like depictions of Atlantis. In rings. Three. The innermost ring was comprised of businesses: a bar, a hardware store, the police station, and a few others. The other two rings were the residents' houses and a school, which was located on the north side.

In the center of it all was a great big stone slab, looking a great deal like a hill, with strange symbols carved in it: the source of the town's name.

Stone Hill was roughly forty miles across and supported about three hundred and fifty people (a quarter of that kids and teenagers). It was small and quiet.

And that was just how Gabriel Gregory liked it. But sometimes, he found himself looking forward to the day he came of age and was able to leave the small town to start his life. He was only seventeen, a year (give or take a few months) away from that day.

Gabriel sat up groggily from his bed, waking for the morning.

But first I have to finish school, he thought, rubbing the sleep from his eyes.

The teenager slithered from the comfort of his bed and glanced at the digital clock that sat on his TV stand, just under the twenty-inch flat screen his parents bought him last Christmas. They got him the newest Xbox as well. They were not rich in the slightest, but they did what they could for him, and he didn't ask for much. So, he appreciated when they got him what he asked for and understood if they couldn't.

A scratching at his door drew the young man's attention. Gabe made his way across the room and opened the door. Scout, the family's German Shepard, bounded into his room, tail wagging madly, tongue washing his exposed legs. Gabe smiled, kneeled, and began to pet Scout vigorously.

"Good morning to you, too, buddy," he said, giving the dog a final pat on the head.

With a final lick, this one on his cheek, Scout bounded out of his room. Gabe wiped the dog drool from his face, his visage twisted with disgust yet still bearing a smile. "Gross!"

Scout was his best friend. No one understood him quite like the dog. Not even his parents. Most kids at school avoided him or made fun of him. He was what people called a nerd. Maybe even a geek. He was smart. Got good grades. Great grades, actually. But the thing that interested him were… unusual.

Science fiction and horror were his favorite genre of movies. In a small town like Stone Hill, they didn't get newly released movies, but he scrounged what he could from the local hardware store. The first that interested him was an old monster movie. *Mothra vs. Godzilla.* He instantly fell in love, hoping the store would get more monster movies like it in the future.

And they did.

Godzilla. Gamera. Jason. The Thing. Freddy Kruger. The Deadly Spawn. Critters. Gremlins.

Monsters are awesome! he thought.

Every month, he arrived at the store, with money he raised by either doing work for neighbors or around his house. The allowance from his parents further helped him in purchasing a new movie or three.

One day, a few kids from his school were at the store when Gabe arrived for the newly stocked films. They were rooting through the movie section themselves when he noticed them. He slunk back, waiting for them to leave. Once they finally did, he rifled through the films, relieved to see the ones he wanted were still there. He held one up with a smile. *Ghidorah, the Three Headed Monster.*

"Godzilla, huh?" one of the kids said, startling Gabe, having suck up behind him to peer over his shoulder. The kid snorted a laugh. "I always thought you were a bit off. I see why now."

Gabe turned toward the kid, the movie clutched in his hand. "What do you mean?"

The kid squinted at him. "Godzilla's for babies, don't you know? Are you a baby?"

Gabe shook his head.

With a scoff, the kid turned away and walked off with a muttered, "Nerd." He then joined his friends, laughing as he told them something. Something, Gabe knew, about him and his liking of monsters.

The insulted teen clutched the movie tighter, determined to not let that jerk tear him down. He could like whatever he wanted.

Gabe shook the memory by the time he awakened the following morning. The young man stood and opened his closet, picking what he wanted to wear for school today. He dressed himself and slipped on his sneakers. Before departing he took one last look around his room, which was decorated with movie posters and figures that he was able to procure via special orders from the local store.

Gabe made his way out of his room and into the living room. It was empty. A few steps took him out of the living room and into the kitchen where he found his mother sitting at the table with a coffee mug in hand. Her hair was ruffled, and she was still in her pajamas. He realized she had just woken up not long before.

Gabe's mother smiled at him and said, "Morning, hun."

He returned the smile. "Morning, Mom."

She pointed to the counter where a paper bag sat. "Your lunch is ready to go."

He gave her a hug. "Thanks."

Her only reply was a smile and a sip of her coffee.

Gabe retrieved the bag from the counter and headed for the door with a "Love you, Mom!"

School went as usual. Classes. Lunch time. More classes.

But there was something different about that day. There was a new girl who had just recently moved to Stone Hill. He couldn't fathom why anyone would want to move there. He wanted to get out, yet people were moving in. The new girl seemed timid, as if not sure how to react to the change. She had wavy brown hair and sparkly blue eyes and was overall a very pretty girl.

Gabe had never had a girlfriend. Most of the girls his age were uninteresting to him, and the ones he was interested in rejected him.

All the boys at school are going to be all over her, he thought solemnly.

Gabe returned to doodling in the corner of his math worksheet when a movement to his right caught his attention. The new girl had taken the empty desk next to his. It wasn't the only empty desk in the room. Most were farther away from him, too. He was near the back of class, away from everyone else.

Is she like me? An outcast? A nerd? A weirdo?

He knew he wasn't a weirdo. People just thought the things he liked were weird.

The class started as their teacher began his lesson. Gabe couldn't help but glance over at the new girl every once in a while. She noticed him looking at her, and he quickly looked away, embarrassed. He saw her smile out of the corner of his eye, however.

Once she knows about me, she won't be smiling at me anymore. Or sitting by me, he thought with a frown.

The class passed slowly, but it finally did come to an end, along with the school day. Gabe stood from his desk, putting papers in his bookbag. A presence next to him called for his attention. He looked, surprised to find the new girl standing there, looking at him with a smile.

"I'm Alaina," she said with a wave.

Gabe's eyes dropped to the floor, trying to find something to say. A giggle brought them back to Alaina.

"I'm guessing you're shy," she said, still all smiles.

Gabe's eyes dropped back to the floor. "Not a lot of people like me here."

"So, that's why you're sitting back here by yourself."

Gabe nodded.

Alaina stepped closer.

"Why don't they like you?" she asked.

Gabe hesitated, reluctant to say why.

Alaina's smile shifted from happy to sad, seeing the pain on his face.

"Here," she said, taking out a piece of paper and writing something on it. Once it was finished, she handed it to him. Gabe looked at it, then back at Alaina.

"Why are you being so nice to me?" he finally asked, unaccustomed to the hospitality of another human being besides his parents.

They knew their son was being bullied and had even spoken to the school about it. Not everyone hated Gabe or thought of him as a nerd. Most didn't care. He knew, yet he didn't try to make friends with them, as he felt he was better off on his own.

"You're different than those other guys that were ogling me when I was introducing myself to the class," Alaina said, her smile widening. "Plus, you're cute."

Gabe watched her turn and leave, his chest warming.

He looked down at the paper with Alaina's phone number written on it. *Maybe this town isn't so bad after all…*

Little did he know it soon was about to be.

7

Gabe stared at a poster on his wall that depicted a woman reaching out of the dirt, a grotesque hand pulling her into the earth. Beside the scene was written *The Evil Dead*. The poster wasn't his focus, however; that was taken up by thoughts of his earlier encounter with Alaina.

The boy looked down at the paper with her number in one hand, his cellphone in the other. The phone was unlocked, the messenger app opened, a blank text message ready.

"What should I do?" he asked Scout, who laid on the floor at his feet. The dog looked up at him and tilted his head in response.

The sound of someone shuffling through the grass outside Gabe's window suddenly caught his ears. He tiptoed to his window and peeked through the blinds. It was late enough that it had gotten dark out. There were no lights to illuminate whatever was outside. He could, however, discern a large shadow as it made its way along the fence that separated his house from the neighbor's. It was much too big to be a person. It almost looked like a bear to him.

Gabe shook his head at the absurdity. There were no bears in Nevada. Not to mention Stone Hill was in the middle of the desert. They didn't have any of the kinds of animals they did in other cities around the state. He knew the night played tricks on the mind, so that was what he chalked it up to. He was seeing things.

The teen turned his attention back to the cellphone in his hands and tapped out a message that read: "Hey. It's Gabe."

He had his doubts about getting a reply, but after about a minute, his phone dinged. Gabe was delighted to see it was Alaina's reply and not some Facebook notification.

"Oh hey! How's it going?" was her reply, followed by the smiley face emoji.

"I dunno. Kinda weirded out," he replied.

"Why's that?" came her response a minute later.

"I thought I saw something walk past my window. Something big, like a bear. That's crazy, I know. There are no bears here," he tapped out.

"Maybe it was a monster," she wrote, followed by a winky face.

Gabe's heart fluttered, a scowl adorning his face as he tapped, "So you know?" followed by a frowning face.

"Those guys I told you were ogling me came up to me after class, saw I was talking to you, and told me how you were a 'monster obsessed weirdo.'"

The words stung more than he thought they would. Maybe it was because he was hearing --reading-- it from the only girl that had shown any interest in him.

He almost didn't reply.

Gabe's fingers worked over the touchscreen keyboard, tapping out the reply, "Do you think the same?"

"Maybe you are obsessed with monsters. I saw the doodle you did on your math worksheet. Pretty cool, actually. But I have yet to see you as a weirdo. People like what they like, and everyone has their obsessions."

A wide smile spread across Gabe's face. His cheeks flushed. His stomach swirled. His heart beat faster. He may not have known Alaina long, but he knew this was the start of his crush on her.

He hesitated on his reply, trying to find something to say. Then he found his words.

"Thank you for not being as judgmental as them," Gabe wrote.

Alaina replied with a smiley face followed by, "I'm going to go to bed now. Catch you tomorrow?"

"Definitely. Night," he tapped, followed by a smiley face of his own.

"Night," she said with another smiley face.

Gabe frowned, wanting to continue talking to her. Then he glanced at the clock, saw the time, and realized he needed to get to bed himself.

He dressed in his pajamas, rolled into bed, and pulled the covers over himself. Scout hopped on the bed, curling up at the foot. With a smile, Gabe drifted off to sleep.

8

Alexander Bowers seethed. Alaina chose the monster freak over him. He was the cool kid in the school, not that nerd. His anger bested him. He kicked hard, sending sand flying through the air. The irate teen walked just outside of town, where asphalt and grass turned into open sand. It was dark out, but it wasn't late at night.

The events of that day replayed in his head. He'd seen the cute new girl talking to the monster-loving nerd after class ended. He waited until she left the room to approach her.

"Hey there cutie," Alex had said, his most charming smile on his face.

Alaina raised an eyebrow at him.

"Whatcha doin' later? Wanna come over to my place and watch a movie?" he asked, the charming smile still adorning his face.

Her brows furrowed. "You broadcast your intentions loud and clear, dude. I'm not interested."

His smile faltered. She'd turned him down. That was something no girl had ever done before.

Alaina went to walk away, but Alex caught her arm. "You think that monster-obsessed faggot can do you better than me?"

She turned toward him, a sneer on her face. "At least he doesn't ooze douchebag. As for you, its running out of every orifice."

He really wanted to sock her one. To teach her she couldn't talk to him like that. If only they weren't in a hallway full of students.

Alex let go of the girl's arm, glaring at her as she made her way down the hall.

The memory renewed the young man's rage. He kicked again and again until he fell on his ass, breathing hard.

"Just let it go, man," Kenneth Scott, Alex's best friend and partner-in-crime, said.

"I'm not losing to the monster freak," Alex growled, getting to his feet.

"If you ask me, she's out of our league. Everyone at that school," Mark Watson, the third in Alex's little gang, opined.

Alex shot him a glare. "Maybe, but I'm gonna teach monster boy not to take what I have my eye on…"

The other two boys grinned mischievously. They found it fun to pick on young Gabe. They didn't despise him, however. Unlike Alex.

The trio walked along the edge of town, hatching out a plan for getting back at Gabe.

A growl sent a hush over them.

"What was that?" Mark asked, his voice a whisper.

Alex looked around, trying to find the source. His eyes were adjusted to the dark, allowing him to see through it. The moonlight helped, too. His gaze fell upon a cave dug in the sand, about twenty feet away from the edge of town.

"The hell…?" he muttered.

Alex unconsciously started toward the cave. Mark and Kenneth followed close behind him. The closer they got, the more reluctant he could feel his friends becoming. He wasn't, though, being more curious than anything.

They stopped about five feet from the cave. Kenneth grabbed Alex's arm, causing the latter to spin around.

"What the fuck are you doing?" Alex growled.

Kenneth shrunk back, but his grip didn't waver. "I've got a bad feeling about this. We should go back."

Alex shook his head with his eyes clenched shut in exasperation. "No. Go back if you want, you friggin' wussies."

They didn't budge.

That's what I thought. Alex turned back to the cave and considered its dark entrance. "What do you think is in there?" he asked.

"Looks like an animal burrow," Mark replied.

Alex observed the burrow. It was at least ten feet from one side to the other.

"What made it? A friggin' bear?" Kenneth said.

Two glowing yellow orbs appeared from with the burrow, the sight of which caused the three boys to stumble back.

35

Lights? Is there a person down there? Could a person have made the burrow?

"Who's down there?" Alex queried into the dark portal.

A growl coming from within the burrow was the only answer they received; an *inhuman* growl. It certainly wasn't a person that sound.

Alex let out a laugh, thinking he had figured it all out.

"I see now," Alex said. "I know that's you, monster boy. Trying to get back at us for picking on you by giving us a little spook? Not gonna work."

The yellow orbs just stared at him, unmoving and unblinking. It was unnerving. But the leader of the trio wouldn't let it show.

"Get your ass out here, so I can teach you not to fuck with me," Alex demanded.

The orbs remained where they were.

"Get out here!" Alex yelled.

The yellow orbs rushed forward, the body they were attached to cloaked in shadow… for a moment. What they saw was not Gabe. It was a horrifying beast beyond their wildest imagination.

They tried to run, shrieking in fear, but the beast caught them... and began to feed.

9

Gabe's eyes fluttered open, his mind waking, not to the sound of his alarm, but to his parents' hushed, ominous voices. He slid from his bed, Scout raising his head at him. He put an index finger to his lips and said, "Shhh." With a whine, Scout laid his head back down.

Good boy, Gabe thought.

He crept across the floor, toward his door. The voices grew clearer. A third voice registered in his ears.

"--ies were so mangled, identification was not easy," came the voice of the town sheriff, Dustin Dreyling.

"That's horrible," he heard his mother gasp. "So, are we dealing with some kind of animal or just some deranged person?"

"Honey," he heard his dad say in a soothing voice, "Don't worry. It's probably some animal. The dumb kids got too close to it. It's a travesty, but incidents like that happen."

Gabe cracked open his door, peeking out. His parents were at the door, their backs to him. His dad was in his uniform. He was the Deputy, second hand man to Sheriff Dreyling, the guy who stood between them in the open doorway.

After saying good bye, he stepped through the door to join Sheriff Dreyling, shutting the door behind him. His mother turned around, spotting him.

"Gabe. How… uh… how much did you hear?" she asked.

Gabe stepped from his room and said, "Not a lot. Something about mangled bodies and some animal."

She shook her head and put on a smile. "Don't worry about it." Her smile faded. "I don't think you should go to school today. Too close to the edge of town."

Gabe's heart sank. He was looking forward to seeing Alaina today.

Seeing the sad look on her son's face, she put a hand on his shoulder. "I know you hate missing school. Most kids would be happy, you know."

A chuckle escaped his mouth.

"I'm not most kids," he said.

Gabe's mom patted his back. "I know. You're unique. One of a kind."

The boy's smile widened.

He then returned to his room, planning on going back to bed. The teen looked to his bed, finding Scout gone.

Must've slipped out while the door was open.

A ding sent him scrambling for his phone. He smiled when he saw the message was from Alaina. It read: "Mom said there was an accident. Something about a wild animal. Doesn't want me going to school today. Wanna hang out in town later?"

Gabe couldn't help but smile like an idiot as he typed "Sure," followed by a smiley face.

"Great. Let's say noon?" was her reply, followed by a smiley face of her own.

"Sounds great," he typed back.

"Great. Meet you by the stone," she replied.

Gabe laid back in his bed. Sleep didn't come. All he could think of was the day ahead of him. He'd never been so happy in his life.

A few hours later, Gabe leaned against the stone, which hovered about ten more feet above his head, waiting for Alaina.

"Been here long?"

The voice startled him, his foot slipping out from beneath him and sending him sprawling to the hard asphalt ground.

"Oh shit," Alaina offered her hand to him. "Didn't mean to startle you."

Gabe smiled and took her hand. "It's fine."

Once on his feet, he took in the sight that was Alaina. Like him, she was dressed for the fall weather, in a hoody and jeans. Her wavy brown air laid on her shoulders. Her blue eyes sparkled in the sliver of sun that peeked through the cloudy sky. A smile spread across her face, releasing Gabe from whatever trance she had on him.

"What?" he asked.

"You're staring," she said, her face dubious.

Gabe looked away, his cheeks warm. Alaina giggled.

"Did you hear what happened?" she asked, changing the subject.

Gabe nodded his head. "Something about a wild animal and a body."

"Two kids were found dead. Their bodies ripped to shreds and partially eaten. Another is missing. I couldn't tell you who, though."

Gabe's face shifted through a multitude of emotions.

"What could've done that?" he asked.

She shrugged. "An animal is possible. But it'd have to be a *big* animal. Like a wolf, bear, or lion. And as you so eloquently put it last night, there are none of those around here."

"Then what could it have been?"

Alaina frowned and then smiled. "Something... not natural?"

Gabe frowned. "Monsters may interest me, but I don't believe they are real. Maybe a bear or wolf just wandered into town. The kids foolishly approached it, it felt threatened, and it attacked."

Alaina raised an eyebrow at him. "I'd have thought you'd be open to the idea."

"Are you?"

She smiled. "It'd be pretty cool."

"Not when it came for you."

Gabe was being serious, but Alaina must've though he was making a joke, because she let out a laugh. Gabe couldn't help but smile himself.

"So," he said, "what do you want to do?"

"Well," she said, "I was just thinking we could hit the town, yah know."

Gabe motioned to the businesses set in a circle, the inner ring of Stone Hill. "This is the town."

Alaina looked around, disinterest in her eyes. "Well... what else is there to do?"

Gabe frowned. "Nothing. It's so boring here. Why'd you even move here?"

It was Alaina's turn to frown. "I had no choice. My dad got a job on the SHPD, and my mom agreed to it because she always feared dad'd get shot or die. It's safe here."

Gabe scoffed. "Safe? It used to be. Now we got some mad animal running around and three kids are dead."

"Coulda been a one-time thing."

"Coulda. We can hope."

A silence fell over the two teens as a sense of foreboding washed over them. As if something bad was coming and the murder of Alex and his cronies was just the beginning.

"Wanna go back to your house? Watch a movie or something?" Alaina asked, breaking their silence.

Gabe was taken aback by the question. He debated whether he should say yes or not. But he feared that if he said no, they'd go their separate ways for the day. And he wanted to continue hanging out with her.

"Sure," he said, a shy smile on his face.

As they walked to Gabe's house, they noticed a black SUV. It was out of place, but they didn't give it too much thought as they continued on their way.

The dead kids were the first sign of a coming catastrophe. The SUV was the second.

10

Gabe took a deep breath as he opened the door to his house. He knew his parents were at work; his dad at the police station and his mom at the bar. Yet, even being saved from the embarrassment and teasing from them, his heart pounded. Scout didn't greet them, meaning he was out in their fenced-in backyard.

A single question repeated over and over in his head: *Is this a date?*

They made their way from the door, through the living room, and into his room. He watched as Alaina looked around at the posters on his walls, the figures atop his book case, the TV sitting on the stand, and his movie collection. Gabe expected her to turn tail and run. Instead, she smiled and made her way over to his bed, sitting down.

"What you wanna watch?" he asked, seeing her eying his movie collection.

Alaina stood from the bed and crouched in front of the TV stand, looking at the stack of films. After a minute or two of scanning the row of movies, she slid one out and said, "I love this one."

She stood, waggling it at him. Gabe smiled at her choice. *King Kong.* The three hour long, 2005 version.

"Your parents aren't gonna flip at you being gone so long, are they?" he asked.

The pretty brunette smiled. "Nah. Told them I'm hanging out with a friend all day. They're just jazzed I already have a friend."

Gabe returned her smile. "Just didn't want you to get in trouble."

"I appreciate it," she said, thrusting the movie in his hands.

Gabe popped the disc in the Xbox, turned on the TV, and started the movie. Alaina was scooted with her back against the wall that the bed sat against. He joined her there, sliding up next to her. But not too close. Nervousness flooded through him.

41

They sat watching the movie. Gabe kept his hands in his lap, but he wanted nothing more than to hold Alaina's hand. He'd never held a girl's hand before and wanted to know what it was like.

About an hour into the film, which he unconsciously got too into, Gabe jumped from a pressure on his shoulder. He craned his head to the side, surprised to find Alaina's head leaning there. Her eyes flicked toward him, a smile spreading across her lips.

She moved her head upwards, lips puckered. Gabe leaned in, his own lips furrowed. He'd never kissed a girl, either. Well, besides his mom. But that was different.

Their lips were millimeters away when he jumped back, hearing the front door open. Gabe caught a glimpse of her disappointed face.

"Sorry," he said, his tone sincere.

Alaina smiled. "It's fine. I get it. You've never done this. You're nervous. Doesn't help that one of your parents came home."

Gabe shook his head but said no more. He strained his ears, tuning out the movie and listening to the sounds outside his room. He heard two voices. They belonged to his mom and dad. The teen looked to the clock situated just below his TV.

They're home early, he thought.

Gabe slid from his bed to the door, cracking it open. They were in the living room. His mom sat on the couch. His dad stood, looking down at her. Both were in their work uniforms.

"--wers isn't missing anymore. They found his body dumped at the edge of town an hour ago," his father said. "I'm going to spare you the grisly state he was in. We're definitely dealing with some kind of animal, though."

"I had Gabe stay home from school," she said.

"Why? Is he here?"

"Last I knew, he said he went into town. I had him stay home because that damn school is too close to the edge of town. Too close to where those kids were killed. I couldn't

42

stand it if something happened to him. I can't imagine how the parents of those boys feel. But if I – *we* -- lost him…"

The woman burst into tears. His dad went over to his wife and wrapped his arms around her.

Gabe shut his door, turning around. For a moment, he forgot Alaina was in his room. That is, until he looked up from his staring match with the floor.

"You alright?" she asked, her voice low and worried.

Gabe started to nod, but it turned into a shake. She stood and walked over to him, wrapping him in a hug like his father did with his mom.

Then his door opened, and he felt his heart leap into his throat. Alaina still had him wrapped in a hug, his parents standing in the doorway to his room. Alaina pulled her arms away and tucked them behind her back.

"Oh, Gabe. I'm sorry. Didn't realize we were interrupting a date," his mom said with a proud smile.

Gabe shook his head, his cheeks flushed, his hands up in a defensive posture. "I-i-it's not a date! We're just hanging out."

"But coulda been a date," Alaina said beside him, a fiendish grin on her face.

Gabe's cheeks grew white hot.

It was *a date,* he realized, berating himself for not figuring it out.

"You must be James's daughter," Gabe's dad said, offering her his hand.

Alaina took his hand and gave it a shake. "Yeah, that's my dad."

"Well, welcome to Stone Hill," he said with a friendly beam.

Alaina returned his smile. "Thanks."

Gabe's dad patted his wife's shoulder and they both departed the room, closing the door behind them.

"Go easy on my baby boy," his mom said before the door shut all the way.

Once the door was closed, Alaina got close to Gabe, her eyes staring into his. She smiled. "I think they gave us permission."

Gabe's eyes creased in confusion. "For... what?"

Alaina leaned in closer and whispered in his ear. "To do... *it*."

Gabe's eyes widened, beads of sweat forming on his forehead.

Alaina pulled back, letting out a laugh that relaxed him. "I'm just messing with you."

Gabe giggled, trying to act confident. "I knew that."

She motioned toward his bed, their previous seat before they were interrupted. "Shall we continue our date?"

Gabe smiled. "Yeah."

The rest of the date went well. They didn't kiss, but they did hold hands. That was enough for Gabe. They finished the movie and had some dinner with his parents. Afterwards, Gabe said bye to Alaina with a hug. It was about six o' clock when she left.

A few hours later, he laid in bed, the day's event replaying in his mind.

Today has been the best day of my life, he thought with a smile.

Until a rustling from outside his bedroom window erased that smile.

It's back...

The teen slid from his bed, peeking through his blinds into the darkness beyond. Scout whined as a shadow moved in the opposite direction from the last time Gabe saw it. He knew it was the same thing he saw the night before. And somewhere, far in the back of his mind, he knew he was looking at the thing that killed those three boys.

It was closer to his window this time. His room was dim, so his eyes were adjusted to the darkness. He couldn't see much of the creature, but it was definitely not a bear. And as it craned its head around toward his window, its eyes glowing yellow, the teen knew the creature wasn't natural.

44

Maybe Alaina was right… maybe we are dealing with a monster instead of an animal.

Gabe shook the thought away.

No… there is no such things as monsters. I'm just dreaming.

The glowing eyes turned away from him, the creature skulking away into town. The boy's curiosity almost overcame him, but he shook it away. Dream or not, he had seen enough horror movies to know following that thing would result in his death.

So, he slid back into bed, cuddled with Scout, and, eventually, fell asleep.

11

Gabe's alarm clock awoke him the next morning. He rolled out of bed and dressed himself. He grabbed his backpack and stepped out of his room, Scout at his side. His mom sat on the couch watching the TV with a mug of coffee in her hand. Her head swiveled toward him, her tired eyes going wide. Then she suddenly stood up.

"No, no, no," the woman said to her son. "You're not going to school. Too close. Too close."

Gabe's eyebrows creased in confusion. "Because of those three boys, still?"

His mom hesitated.

"No," she eventually said.

Gabe's slowly waking mind was suddenly in full gear. "Something else happened, didn't it? Another animal attack?"

His mother's silence was confirmation enough.

Without another word, Gabe strode back into his room with Scout following him and closed the door behind them. Such was his frustration that he could barely restrain himself from slamming it How long was she going to keep him from school? Too long, and he'd get behind. Then it'd be longer before he could leave.

Gabe slipped his backpack off, allowing it to fall to the floor. He kicked it, sending it flying into the side of his bed. Scout cowered at the outburst. The flustered boy stood in the middle of his room, breathing hard with his brows furrowed and his teeth clenched.

Then his cell phone dinged, relaxing him. He fished it out of his pocket to see who had texted him. The message was from Alaina.

"Another killing last night. Staying home from school again. I'm starting to get scared," it read.

"Wanna do something today?" he replied.

"Yeah. When?" she wrote back.

"In an hour? Meet you by the stone?" he replied.

"Sounds good," she said, followed by a smiley face.

A smile stretched across Gabe's real face, his stomach swirling, his chest warm and fuzzy.

An hour later, Gabe sat at the base of the stone. He stared down at his feet, noticing every scratch on his shoes, every pebble on the ground, and every crack in the concrete.

A pair of sneakers stepped into view. He looked up to find himself gazing into the twinkling eyes of Alaina. He smiled. It faded when she didn't smile back. Gabe stood, and she threw herself into his arms, startling him. He wrapped his arms around her when she began to sob violently.

"W-what's wrong?" he asked, his voice cracking.

Gabe was patient as he waited for her answer while the girl controlled her sobs. He held her, rubbing her back.

With a sniff, her voice quivering, Alaina finally answered, "L-last n-night... m-my mom was out late, watering her f-flowers. I w-was asleep. I didn't hear anything. D-dad found her when he came home from work. It... it got her!"

"The animal?" he asked.

Alaina pushed away from him. "It's not an animal. My dad's screams woke me up. I..." she clenched her eyes shut. "I saw her body. No animal could do something like that."

Gabe reached out and took her hands. He knew what she was telling him. The thing that killed three boys and her mom was a supernatural beast. A monster.

He couldn't say that he believed monsters existed. It was a scary thought. They were fun when they were fictional...

Gabe didn't know what to say to her, so he just stood there, holding her hands in his. They stood like that for long minutes, tears threatening to food from Alaina's eyes again. Then she spoke. A question. One that caught Gabe off guard.

"Can..." Her voice was shaky, almost indiscernible. She clenched her eyes shut, controlling her shaking voice. Or, perhaps, mustering the question to ask such an awkward question. "Can I stay with you tonight?"

Gabe's eyebrows shot up. "L-like in my room? All night?"

Alaina croaked a laugh. "Yeah."

His hormones conjured up inappropriate scenarios that might unfold with her in his room, but he chased them away. He was better than that. She was upset. It wouldn't be right. However, he wouldn't let her be alone tonight.

"What about your dad?" he asked.

She frowned. "I have a feeling he will be spending the night at the station, or out looking for... my mother's murderer."

Gabe nodded. He let go of one hand and led her by the other towards his house. The boy didn't think his parents would mind, especially with what she was going through. He was her only friend in this town, it seemed.

Gabe opened the door to his house and led Alaina inside. Scout bounded over to greet them but sensed something was wrong as he sat and waited for them to pet him. His mom still sat on the couch when they walked in. Her head swiveled away from the TV towards them. She stood up and looked at Gabe, then to Alaina, where her eyes filled with tears. She strode over and took the girl in her arms.

"I'm so sorry, my dear. I heard what happened," his mother said to Alaina.

Gabe felt his eyes tear up as well but held it back. He needed to be the strong one. For Alaina, who was also sobbing.

The sobs soon came to a stop, and the girl stepped back. She wiped her eyes and nose and put on her best smile.

"Is it alright if I stay here tonight?" Alaina asked.

Gabe's mom smiled. "Yes, of course. I'm sure we can find a spot to accommodate you."

"If it's alright with you. I'd like to stay close to Gabe," Alaina said while grabbing his hand.

Gabe's mother looked concerned at first as she looked into her son's eyes. But, seeing no ill intention in them, she nodded. "Alright then."

With a smile for his mom, Gabe led Alaina to his room. They sat together, watching movies all day. But soon, it was time for bed.

12

Gabe laid on his floor, hands behind his head, looking up at his ceiling. Blankets lay beneath him, providing more cushioning than the bare carpet. Another blanket lay over his midsection, with a pillow beneath his head. Scout was curled up next to him. The dog was weary of the stranger that had taken over his usual sleeping spot as Gabe let Alaina have the bed.

Having a girl in his room wasn't as weird as he thought. His hormones conjured up fantasies, but it was easy to ignore them.

But he couldn't sleep. He was too worried about Alaina. He didn't know how he could help her, as he didn't know the pain of losing a parent.

"Hey."

Alaina's voice pulled him out of his thoughts and toward the bed he laid beside.

"You should get some sleep," he said.

"I've tried," she replied. "I can't."

Gabe sat up. "Want me to get you something? A glass of water?"

Her hand rested on his shoulder, sliding down his arm and wrapping around his bicep.

"Lay with me," she said, her voice quivering.

The sound of her shaking voice broke his heart. He may not have known her long, but he knew what was becoming of them. They were friends. Maybe even more. And he cared about her.

Gabe stood from the floor. Alaina scooted against the wall, allowing him to slide into the bed with her. Scout whined, but eventually settled taking Gabe's mess of blankets on the floor. They laid face-to-face, their noses just inches from each other's.

"Better?" he asked.

She smiled and slid closer, their noses now touching. "Yeah."

Her arms wrapped around him, pulling herself closer yet, curling her body so that her head found his chest.

"So much better," she said, her hands grabbing fistfuls of his shirt.

Gabe put his arms around her and smiled. The last few days have been full of new experiences, but this one, lying in bed, holding each other... it didn't feel weird. Even though he would have thought it would.

The two of them laid like that for an hour. Gabe still couldn't fall asleep. Alaina, however, had drifted into slumber as soon as she curled up to Gabe. By then, however, he was starting to feel sleepy. His eyes fluttered and finally closed.

Then they snapped back open.

The sound of shuffling grass, just outside his window, caught his ears.

It's back...

Gabe eased himself out of bed, careful not to wake Alaina. Scout looked up as Gabe peeked out the blinds covering his window to once again behold that horrible shadow. As it lumbered by his window, the boy's fear was replaced by anger.

The creature, whatever it may be, was the reason Alaina was in pain. Gabe wanted to go after it; to end its life. But what could he do? He was a seventeen-year-old kid. He wasn't strong or athletic. He wouldn't stand a chance against it.

Gabe stood there for minutes after the creature passed, staring into the darkness. He jumped as another shadow passed by his window. That one he recognized as human, with a rifle in its hands. Another figure ran after the first, that one armed as well.

They're chasing the animal.

A thought crossed the boy's mind, and he hoped it wasn't true: that the people chasing the creature weren't who he thought they were.

"Gabe? You okay?"

Alaina's tired voice startled him.

"Uh... yeah. Everything is okay," he replied.

He laid back in bed, Alaina curling up to him.

"You sure?" she whispered.

"Well, this is all a first for me," Gabe said. "I've never been on a date. I've never held hands with a girl. Never kissed a girl. Not to mention, I've never had a girl spend the night in my room."

Alaina giggled. "I've been on dates before, had a few boyfriends, kissed a few guys, but I'll admit, this is a first for me, too. I've never stayed at one of their houses before."

"Probably a good thing," he said.

"Yeah. They were all horny bastards."

Gabe let out a laugh, cringing at its volume.

"You're different, though," she said. "You've not once tried to make a move on me."

"I just know how to keep my hormones in check.".

Her head appeared in front of his, a smile on her face. He smiled back.

"You're a good guy, Gabe," she said, sending his stomach swirling. "Those other girls don't know what they're missing out on."

Gabe's smile widened. He was about to say something more when a gunshot made them both jump. Scout whined.

"The hell was that?" Gabe wondered aloud as he rolled off the bed with Scout bounding to his feet.

"Sounded like a gunshot," Alaina responded as she stood beside him.

They must've found it.

"What do you think is happening?" Alaina asked.

Gabe fought against his curiosity. If he went to investigate, Alaina was sure to follow. Whatever was happening, it wasn't worth risking his or her life on finding out.

"Nothing we should concern ourselves with," he said.

Another gunshot.

Alaina moved for the door, but he caught her.

"It's dangerous. It could be some gun wielding lunatic," Gabe lied.

"Or it could be someone trying to fend off that creature," she countered.

51

Gabe raised an eyebrow at her. "And just what do you think you can do to help?"

The girl lowered her head, conceding his point.

"Let's just... go back to bed," he suggested.

She nodded, and they laid back down with Scout actually hopping into the bed with them.

A third gunshot came, making them flinch.

Neither of them could sleep, but they said nothing to one another and didn't move for the rest of the night.

13

Dustin Dreyling, the Sheriff of Stone Hill, chased after the newest member of the Stone Hill Police Department, James Phillips. Dustin noticed the man wandering around town until he saw something and took off. What prompted Dustin to follow was the fact that James was armed with a rifle. The man may have just lost his wife, but the sheriff wasn't about to let him run around with a gun, doing who-knew-what.

Dustin's lungs burned after a few minutes of pursuing the deputy, but he noticed something weird. James seemed to be chasing something.

Is it the animal? Dustin wondered.

The sheriff followed James from the inner ring to the middle, after which he continued to the outer ring and eventually out of town. Dustin stopped just before the edge of town. He crouched behind a bush at the back of a darkened house with the residents inside asleep, careful not to alert the deputy to his presence.

James stopped before what looked like a burrow, aiming his rifle down at its dark opening.

"Come out!" James yelled into the burrow.

Dustin glanced back, relieved to see that the house behind him was still dimmed out. He turned his attention back to James and the burrow… and his eyes widened.

Two yellow orbs shone from the hole. James had taken a few steps back, as their appearance had startled him. The deputy's hands shook, his trembling fingers squeezing the trigger of the rifle he held. The thunderous report echoed through the night air, followed by a sound he had never heard before. A horrifying sound. Yet, it was distinguishable as a roar of pain. Or, maybe just annoyance.

James stumbled back as a large form emerged from the burrow. The orbs glowed downwards at him, radiating menace. Those orbs, Dustin realized, were eyes. The creature raised a thick arm, the clawed fingers at the end hooked, ready to disembowel James. Dustin's hand went to the side arm holstered on his hip.

A second gunshot stopped him. It wasn't from James. Whatever was shot at the creature, it caused the beast to stumble. Its wide head shot to the side, and the glowing orbs became slits as it squinted or glared at something.

That was when Dustin noticed the man approaching James and the creature, large rifle in hand. The monstrous beast dove back into its burrow as the new arrival ran for the hole. The creature was already gone, though.

The man whirled on James. They became immersed in a furious conversation or argument. It was hard to tell, because Dustin couldn't hear what they were saying. Their tone, however, was frantic.

After a while of conversing, the man walked away from James, arms at his sides, body language oozing frustration. What happened next startled Dustin. He had to cover his mouth from shouting out.

The man produced a hand gun from a holster on his leg, leveled it at James, and pulled the trigger. The deputy's body fell to the ground, his blood staining the sands.

The man stood next to James's corpse, peering into the dark burrow. He kicked the sand and stalked off back the way he had come with a a hand going to his ear. Dustin could hear the man speaking.

The sheriff clenched his eyes shut, squelching his anger. When he opened them again, about a minute later, the man was gone.

Who the hell was that guy?

The lawman doubted he'd ever get his answer.

Once he was sure it was clear, the sheriff stood from his hiding spot and made his way back to the police station. Deputy Thomas Gregory, Dustin's right hand man, greeted him upon his return.

"The hell was that about?" Thomas asked.

Dustin shook his head. "I'm not sure. But something seriously fucked up is going on."

"What happened?"

Dustin looked his friend in the eyes. "Honestly? You wouldn't believe me if I told you."

14

Gabe disabled his alarm the night before, knowing he wasn't going to school yet again. He'd managed to fall asleep hours after the last gunshot echoed in the night.

Voices tickled his ear, stirring him from sleep. He jumped at the sight of a face in close proximity to his own. Gabe beamed when he saw whose face it was. His smile faded when the memories of the previous night crept back into his brain.

The boy started to wiggle out of bed when his father's raised voice, not quite a yell, stopped him: "They killed a cop, for Christ's sake!"

His mother hissed at her husband to be quiet. "They're still sleeping," she said, "and that's how I'd like to keep it. They don't need to hear this. Especially Alaina."

Their voices faded as they walked into another room.

A cop is dead? he thought. Stone Hill was a small town. There were only three active officers, because nothing *ever* happened in Stone Hill. They were just there to keep the peace. If his dad was okay, that meant either Sheriff Dreyling, or...

Gabe clenched his eyes shut. *Please, no... she's been through enough with losing her mom.*

He opened his eyes, surprised to be staring into Alaina's. Tired bags hung beneath them, but they shone like twin blue moons. A smile spread across her lips at the sight of him. He managed a smile back, though it felt unconvincing.

"You alright?" she asked, seeing the strained nature of his smile.

Gabe didn't want to lie to her, but he didn't want to alarm her either. Especially since he didn't have all the facts.

So, he did lie, saying, "I'm fine."

Gabe felt her breath, warm yet sweet on his lips. He could see what she wanted in her eyes, and he wanted it too.

But it wasn't the right time.

She was hurting from the loss of her mom. And if Gabe's suspicions were correct, she was going to be hurting even worse soon enough.

However, he couldn't bring himself to get away from the situation.

Their faces inched closer. Gabe's lips twitched with anticipation. When his met hers, it was like a surge of energy radiated throughout his form. Their bodies pressed against each other as their lips mingled.

Gabe pushed away. Alaina looked hurt.

"I'm sorry," he said, rolling out of bed and alerting Scout, who had moved back to the floor at some point during the night. "I like you, I really do. But, you're hurting. I honestly can't imagine what you're going through. I feel you're trying to drown out the pain. It wouldn't be right."

Alaina nodded. "You're a good guy, Gabe. Most guys would've taken advantage of such a situation."

A smile twitched onto Gabe's face. "I'm not most guys."

Before the moment could go any further, the door to Gabe's room opened, revealing his parents. Their faces were solemn.

"Did we interrupt something?" his mom asked.

Gabe shook his head, relieved that they hadn't walked in a few moments earlier, or that that he decided to cut off what was about to go down before they decided to waltz in on them.

"What's going on?" Gabe asked.

Alaina's face went grim. "It claimed another victim, didn't it?"

His dad's nod was nearly indiscernible, but Gabe noticed it. He already knew the animal had struck again and had claimed the life of a deputy. He feared he even knew the identity of that cop...

Alaina buried her face in a pillow. "Please tell me it wasn't him. Please tell me he didn't go after it..." in a muffled voice.

Tears formed in Gabe's eyes as his dad said, his voice cracking with grief, "I'm sorry."

Alaina's body shook as she sobbed, and her pain increased tenfold as she officially became an orphan.

Everyone was quiet, letting Alaina cry out her sorrow and pain. Gabe's nails dug into his palms and they curled into tight fists. Minutes passed before she started to calm. Blood ran from the boy's palms and dripped off his fingertips by the time he uncurled them.

"We…" his mom started, swallowing hard, "we want to take you in… if you'll let us."

Alaina slowly raised her head, looking toward the woman with a weak smile. Then she looked to Gabe, her smile gaining strength. "I think I'd like that."

Gabe smiled back. But inside, he was determined to put his life on the line for her. To destroy the source of her pain and suffering.

He was going to kill the monster that killed her parents and left her an orphan.

15

"Damn idiot!"

Arnold Robinson's fist came down like a sledge hammer on the table of the hotel they stayed in with a thunderous bang. The two other men looked in his direction, saying nothing.

"We know where the creature is, now. We didn't need an inside man anymore," John Wilson said.

Arnold nodded. "You're right. But James was a good man."

"He almost compromised our mission, though," Chris Wayne said.

"And I acted accordingly," Arnold rejoined. "If anything, I did him a favor."

"And left his daughter an orphan," John said solemnly.

Arnold frowned. *Did not think of that... shit.*

Arnold now felt worse about the situation, but he shook it away. He had a job to do, and he wasn't about to let anything get in the way of that.

Not even the death of James Phillips.

Arnold picked up the rifle in front of him, inspecting it.

"And we now know where the creature is, thanks to the tracking device you shot it with," Chris said.

Arnold smirked, sliding a laptop in front of him. He opened it and the screen blinked to life. A few taps of the keys and he was looking at the location of the creature, codenamed "Subject One."

"It seems to become active at night. We can't move in the day without drawing too much attention," Arnold said, his face thoughtful.

"I guess we'll just have to move in on it at night," John noted.

"We'll use the suits. They'll help us blend in with the night and... more," Arnold said, closing the laptop. "I've sent the creature's location to their HUDS."

The rest of their day was full of weapon and equipment checks, with continual monitoring of Subject One's location.

The perks of being an Area 51 operative was having access to high tech gadgets and weapons. The suits were standard issue for these soldiers. They were integrated with the most advanced situational awareness tech and even gave the wearer a strength boost. It was closely related to the TALOS that was also created at Area 51.

Arnold smirked as he picked up another of his toys. An AA-12 fully automatic shotgun loaded with frag-12 HE explosive shells. The frag-12 shells were designed to penetrate a target and then explode. Hopefully they would be more effective against their prey than the high caliber rounds used against them back at Area 51, when they escaped.

We'll find out tonight, he thought.

16

Gabe and Alaina spent the day sitting around and watching movies to take their minds off their troubles. Soon, night was upon them and they curled up in bed together. Gabe waited for Alaina to fall asleep before he carefully slid from the bed and tiptoed to his closet. The boy frowned as he scooted aside the clothes dangling from the hangers to reveal a gun case.

His dad planned to take him hunting next month. They were going to take a trip up to Montana, where some of their family lived. Inside the case was the rifle his dad bought him for the trip.

I guess I'm going hunting earlier, he thought somberly.

Gabe unlocked the case with a key and retrieved the rifle from within. It was heavy, but manageable. He had a few loaded magazines and stuffed them in his pockets. Then he slid the closet door closed and crept out of the room, softly closing the door behind him. He snuck across the living room, slipped on his shoes and a jacket. Gabe was startled as Scout sat in the living room staring at him. He put a finger to his lips and said "shhh." The loyal dog whined but laid down as Gabe left his house.

The teen wiped the sweat away from his forehead, relieved that he didn't get caught. He took off toward the edge of town, rifle in hand. As much as he liked monster movies, he never though he'd be living one. But there he was, rushing off to face something that was clearly not natural. Something that was able to rip people to shreds with its bare hands and had teeth sharp enough to cleave flesh from bone.

For Alaina, he kept repeating in his mind. It was the only thing keeping him from turning tail and running away.

Gabe skidded to a stop, looking out at an endless expanse of sand... and a hole that resembled an animal burrow. He knew there was a number of burrowing species in Nevada, but the burrow he was looking at was too big to have been made by any of those animals.

It's the creature's...

Gabe took a step toward the burrow, trying to peer beyond the blackness, to see the monster within. But it was too dark. He feared the creature had gone out for a snack.

He went to take another step forward but stopped upon feeling a presence. It wasn't like feeling the eyes of a person staring at him. It was the presence of something much worse. Something radiating an aura of what he could only describe as… evil.

Two orbs of yellow light flicked to life in the dark warren. Gabe stumbled back, raising his rifle. He knew exactly what he was looking at.

The creature's eyes.

A clawed hand rose from the burrow, grasping one side. Another hand rose, grasping the opposite side of the hole. The creature's head emerged next, its brows furrowed, yellow eyes squinting at him, wide jaws agape, sharp teeth glinting in the moonlight. Boney protrusions extended from the side of its head, and just above its eyes. Gray hair flowed from the head, down its back.

The creature pulled itself further from the burrow, revealing a broad, muscled body. One of its thick, toned legs emerged, the five obsidian claws at the end digging into the sand as the creature pulled itself out of the tunneled lair.

The creature stood above Gabe, glaring down at him from its ten-foot height. His eyes flicked to an abnormality on the creature's shoulder. A tattoo, it looked like. Of the number one. It was a weird thing for a monster to have, Gabe thought. But he quickly forgot about it.

A name popped into his mind.

Snallygaster.

Being a monster fan, Gabe had heard of the mysteries creatures that have been sighted known as 'cryptids.' These were creatures, both natural and supernatural, whose existences have yet to be proven. The Snallygaster is one such cryptid. It was known to have features of sirens, demons, and ghouls. It was very close to what he saw before him. A creature of nightmares.

THE EXPERIMENT

Gabe raised his rifle toward the Snallygaster's face and, with a twitch of his finger, pulled the trigger.

17

Sheriff Dustin Dreyling stepped out of the warm police station and into the cool night air. He let out a breath. His mind was a mess, continuously replaying the events of the previous night. The creature. James's death. And the man that killed him. He knew he had to get a handle on things before they got worse… and they were going to get worse. He could sense it.

Dustin looked around the business ring of the town, his eyes landing on the motel… and the three men armed to the teeth exiting a room. One of them was the man that killed James. He was sure of it.

The men sprinted toward the edge of town, moving with the speed of an Olympic runner. Dustin didn't hesitate. He ran after the men, not caring whether they noticed him tailing them or not. The sheriff of Stone Hill didn't know who the men were, but after witnessing the events of last night, he was certain they were connected to the creature.

It occurred to him about halfway to the spot where James was killed that the men he was chasing were going after the creature again.

Should I sit this out? Just let them kill the creature and look the other way?

Dustin was about to stop pursuing the men, to let them take care of the monster in the town's midst… when he saw the creature, out of its burrow, hovering over his deputy's son.

Shit!

Gabe raised a hunting rifle, firing a round into the creature's face.

"Stupid kid!" one of the soldiers he was chasing said.

With a snarl, the creature raised its arm, its hooked claws ready to rip and tear.

One of the armored men dove, tackling Gabe to the sand, the creature's claws slicing through the air where they were a mere second ago. The two other men raised their weapons, AA-12 shotguns, and pulled the triggers. Two thunderous booms echoed through the night as their pellets punched into the creature's skin. The monster stumbled back, roaring in pain when the exploding pellets threw chunks of flesh away from its chest.

Gabe rolled away from the armored man that saved his life. He was thankful for the soldier's effort, as the boy almost had his head lobbed off.

The sound of the Snallygaster's pained shriek pulled his head up. It was then Gabe saw the chunks of skin blown away from its chest by the impact of the soldiers' exploding projectiles. Flecks of its blood speckled the teen's cheeks.

Gabe was amazed that they were hurting the creature. His memory of firing a bullet straight into the beast's forehead, with the round having no effect, flitted through his mind.

The Snallygaster snarled, revealing its long, curved fangs. It spun around and leapt back into its lair.

"Fuck!" the tallest of the armored men -- the plate on his chest identifying him as 'Robinson' -- hollered, as he stomped towards the burrow.

Another of the men, his plate reading 'Wayne,' grasped Robinson's arm and said, "What are you doing?"

Robinson turned his helmeted head toward Wayne. "Going after it. Tonight is the night the Experiment One ends."

Experiment One? Gabe wondered.

Wayne said nothing more, his helmeted head dipping in a nod.

Wilson, the man that tackled Gabe, rose to his feet and said, "So, we going down there after it?"

Robinson's helmet nodded an affirmation.

"And him?" Wilson said, hitching a thumb at Gabe.

The teen's heart thumped madly. He didn't know who the men were, but they were shady. Probably government agents. And if the creature he just attempted to kill on his own was some experiment of theirs, and he wasn't supposed to see it, then there was a strong possibility they'd get rid of witnesses.

The men whispered among themselves. Gabe's heart beat harder. He knew he should run. To get the hell out of there.

But something told him that if he ran, they'd shoot him just the same. He didn't want to die.

The whispers stopped, and the armored men turned towards Gabe. The teen gripped his rifle tighter, ready to fight for his life if he had to. Robinson, who Gabe figured was the leader, stepped forward.

"Taking on One by yourself was brave. Stupid, but brave," Robinson said, his face concealed behind a reflective silver visor. "I don't know your reasons for taking it on, but I can see the fire in your eyes. The determination to kill it."

Robinson paused, as if hesitant to say more.

"Wanna help us kill it?" the team leader finally asked.

Dustin Dreyling watched as the men and Gabe slid into the burrow. He didn't know what to do. Should he follow them? Back them up?

He couldn't entrust his friend's son to a bunch of teched out strangers.

So, the sheriff ran over to the burrow and peered into the darkness within. After a moment's hesitation, he dove into the tunnel.

18

The inside of the burrow was dark, but the night vision goggles the men let him borrow turned the darkness into shades of green. The tunnel was narrow, forcing them to walk single file. Gabe, being the final member of the team to enter, was last in that line.

He had traded his hunting rifle for a spare KRISS Vector submachine gun armed with explosive rounds one of the soldiers carried. He had never used such a weapon before. In fact, the first time he handled a gun was when he faced down the Snallygaster with his hunting rifle.

I'm going to have to learn fast.

A hand on his shoulder spun him around. Gabe's finger tightened on the trigger of his Vector. The person thrusted his weapon up as it went off. The explosive rounds punched into the roof of the burrow, the rifle report loud in the enclosed space. The soldiers spun around, their pieces raised.

"Don't shoot!" Dustin Dreyling said, hands elevated to show he wasn't a threat.

"The fuck are you doing here?" Robinson growled.

Dustin lowered his hands, his brows furrowing. "Following strangers skulking around my town is my job. I'm Sheriff, after all. And when they take a child down into the burrow of a monster, I wasn't just going to stand by and let you lead him to his death."

Gabe lowered his head. He knew what he was doing was dumb. Suicidal, even. But he was doing it for a good cause. For Alaina.

"So, what? You're here to stop us? Or to take the kid?" Robinson asked.

"As much as I'd like to take the kid and leave, I have to make sure this creature dies. I can't have any more of my townsfolk killed," Dustin replied, drawing his high caliber revolver and waggling it in his hand.

Robinson's helmeted head tilted to the side as he said, "Fine. Let's just get this over with."

Dustin replied with a nod.

They continued on their way through the burrow for ten long minutes.

How long is this burrow? Gabe wondered.

The long tunnel opened into a vast space that the Snallygaster had dug out.

This must be its lair…

His assumption was proven true when he spotted the creature huddled in the far corner of the den. It uncurled as they entered the space, glaring at them with its menacing, glowing yellow eyes. The message they conveyed was clear: intruders weren't welcome there.

Fresh blood flowed as the Snallygaster flexed its chest, the wounds inflicted by Robinson and his team reopening. It stood to its full height, glowering at them.

Gabe resisted the urge to raise his weapon, seeing that the others hadn't yet.

"You didn't wander very far from home, eh, guy?" Robinson said, raising his shotgun.

The Snallygaster roared, knowing the weapon's deadly potential. Robinson pulled the trigger, the report deafening in the enclosed space.

The monster dove to the side, the explosive shells punching into the burrow wall where it stood a moment before. The pellets detonated, throwing chunks of dirt away from the burrow wall and triggering the Snallygaster's attack.

The Snallygaster charged, its feet thumping against the dirt floor. Robinson and his team opened fire. Most of their shots missed the creature, but the few that found their mark sent the beast reeling.

Gabe raised the KRISS Vector he held with shaky hands. He took aim and squeezed the trigger. The weapon hardly bucked in his hand as hot lead spit from its barrel. He was surprised and delighted when a few of the rounds hit their target, blowing bits of flesh from the Snallygaster's shoulder. The creature spun from the attack, tripping over its feet and tumbling to the ground.

Wilson gave him a thumbs up and said, "Nice shot, kid."

Gabe offered a nervous grin in reply. It faded when the Snallygaster bucked suddenly, jumping to its feet and lashing out with one of its arms. It struck Gabe in the chest, sending the gun flying from his grasp, and him through the air. His head struck something which felt like a rock.

The gun fire that followed sounded distant. As his vison faded, he saw the Snallygaster peppered with explosive bullets. Large portions of its flesh were blown away and blood coated the ground.

Then everything went black.

Dustin Dreyling cradled Gabe's head as he watched the dead monster's body twitch. After a few more of these convulsions, its torn and bloodied form fell still.

He felt eyes on him. The lawman looked up to find the three soldiers staring at him from behind their reflective silver visors. The one with 'Robinson' stenciled on his chest plate leveled his gun at Dustin.

"What are you going to do? Shoot me?" the sheriff queried.

"Sorry," Robinson said. "Orders are orders. No witnesses."

"That's what they said last time."

Robinson's helmeted head tilted to the side, his confusion evident even without being able to see his facial expression.

"This isn't the first monster this town has seen," Dustin elaborated. "The previous Sheriff, Derek Dawson, died fighting it. The previous deputy, before this boy's dad, left town. A few weeks later, I got word that she hung herself. They were both my friends and it killed them. Arachne is what they called it. It came from Area 51, which I assume both you and this creature are also from."

Robinson lowered his weapon, looking from Dustin to the boy in his arms. "It's possible a wound like that could cause memory loss. And I trust you not to say anything. No one else, as far as I know, knew about the creature. It had better stay that way."

The threat was evident in Robinson's voice. If he found out anyone else knew about the creature, he'd kill both Dustin and the person.

The sheriff nodded as he stood with Gabe in his arms. Robinson and his two teammates turned their backs to him, looking at the dead creature. With a nod of thanks, which he knew they saw, the armored soldier and his team turned back the way they came and marched out of the burrow.

Gabe's eyes fluttered open. As soon as the light entered his pupils, his lids clenched shut due to the piercing pain rocketing through his head. The bed beneath him was comfortable, but unfamiliar. The chemical smells in the air told him where he was and why the bed was unfamiliar. He was in a hospital.

Gabe tried to open his eyes again. He fought against the pain, his blurred vision eventually fading. Faces came into focus. His mom and dad. Alaina. Sheriff Dreyling. Their expressions were twisted with both concern and relief. He smiled at the sight of them.

Then his smile faded.

Why am I in a hospital?

"What... happened?" he asked, wincing at the sound of his voice as the noise sent pain through his head.

"You were in an accident," Sheriff Dreyling said. "Found you on the side of the road. No idea what you were doing out that late."

Gabe's brows scrunched as he tried to remember.

Nothing came to him.

He was unable to recall anything after finding out Alaina's dad was murdered by the animal that had been terrorizing the town.

"I don't remember," Gabe said after a few moments.

Dreyling nodded. "Understandable with the knock you took to the head."

"They hit you pretty hard. If I ever find out who did this, I'm gonna--" Gabe's dad was cut off by the calming hand of the sheriff on his shoulder.

"Calm down, Tom," Gabe's mother said. "Everything is going to be okay now."

Alaina crushed Gabe with a hug, sobbing into his shoulder. "I'm so glad you're okay," she whispered. "I couldn't stand to lose one more person I care about."

He smiled, patting the girl on the back.

Gabe was released from the hospital days later. The creature that had plagued the town had gone quiet.

Stone Hill was finally at peace.

FLUFFY FURY

Christofer Nigro

19

Tim Greymountain pushed his flowing black hair from his eyes to get a better view of the lower forest. Though he generally enjoyed the cool breeze from the top of the Goshute Basin, this day he was here for something far more serious than a relaxing commune with nature.

On this particular day, he wanted his acute 20/20 vision to be as sharp as possible, so he could not tolerate his sight getting occluded due to hair blown into his eyes. His intention, as he leaned against a convenient cottonwood tree while scanning the lush forests of the lower elevations, was to spot a sign -- any sign -- of something unusual or out of place in the verdant woodlands he knew so well.

The reason he was on this hunt was due to something very personal and extremely tragic. Less than two weeks earlier his cousin Shaun, a cherished lifelong confidante of his, had mysteriously disappeared in the Goshute Canyon Wilderness along with his friend Marcus, who was also a member of their tribe. The duo was scouting for an area near the cave system where they could set up a small community outside the aegis of the Goshute Indian Reservation, which constituted intolerable living conditions to a minority segment of its residents who chose to live a strongly traditional Native American lifestyle.

The faction of radical Goshute traditionalists to which Greymountain and his missing cousin belonged detested the rampant alcoholism, and the pandering to the white man's world by selling cigarettes and other health-destroying products to both their own people and the white interlopers to make a living.

Not to mention the many other encroachments of the white man's government and culture that forced them to live according to rules and under conditions imposed upon them by what they considered to be imperialistic invaders. To the Goshute traditionalist sect, this invasive culture forced them to follow a system of laws that are anathema to their honored ancestors who inhabited these lands for millennia.

When Shaun and Marcus failed to return, Greymountain was certain it wasn't due to one of the many natural calamities that could befall those who journey into the wilderness. Like all members of his tribe who followed the ancient traditions, these two were skilled outdoorsmen who were well-acquainted with the forest and learned how to survive in its environs from the day they learned to walk. Greymountain knew this because he spent much time in these woods with Shaun and others on sometimes month-long camping jaunts to experience nature as their ancestors did. These summer excursions were among the most cherished memories of his childhood.

Moreover, Greymountain knew for a fact that Shaun and his friend left well-armed and well-equipped for an outing of a few days into that wilderness, and no inclement or unexpected weather conditions had occurred during the duration of their sojourn. Something foul had befallen them, and the tribal police weren't allowed to conduct an official search since it was out of their jurisdiction, as the forest was under the control of the Bureau of Land Management, an ancillary of the white man's government.

Though the local sheriff's department claimed they did a full search and found absolutely nothing, Greymountain wasn't satisfied. His twenty-nine years of life experiences had built up many reasons not to trust the white man's government agencies, particularly those related to law enforcement, and he was determined to look into the matter himself – even if it meant doing so without the permission or assistance of the tribal council.

Greymountain further suspected the too-frequent incursions of white people into these forests for a variety of recreational purposes may have had something to do with the tragic loss, particularly since the local white "rednecks" weren't overly fond of the Native American population, and the antipathy was quite mutual. He "smelled a rat," as the white man's vernacular would say, and he wouldn't let this matter rest until he found out what happened to Shaun and his companion; and after he had definitively identified the perpetrator and saw to it that they paid for what they had taken from his tribe, and from his life in particular.

As he had expected, Greymountain's astute eyes eventually caught a sign of white man presence in the area. He gritted his teeth in anger and slowly pulled his traditional, self-carved stone blade from the sheath that was secured to his rawhide belt and began a slow descent from the canyon. The colorful war paint that decorated his facial skin was not just for show, as the identified culprit behind the murder of Shaun and Marcus would soon learn.

20

Hollis Clemens covered his ears as his good friend Billy-Bob Tyler unexpectedly blasted a thunderous double ought from his 12-gauge shotgun to the left of the trail they walked on.

"Jesus shit fuck, Billy-Bob!" the shorter, slightly rotund man shouted at his BFF. "What the holy fuck you just do that for?"

"I thought I saw a coyote over there!" his rugged, dark-bearded friend replied, pointing to the left with his rigidly extended index finger. "Right there, hidin' in the brush 'tween those two junipers!"

"Couldn't you be right kind enough to tell me before you just shoot like that?"

"And alert the cy-ote along with you? Have some sense, you shit for brains!"

"It's not like the damned fuckin' thing can understand English, ya know!"

"But the 'damned fuckin' thing' *can* understand the tone of a loud scream! It don't need to understand English to know it should bolt off when it hears a person yell from close by!"

"Jesus, I hate huntin' with you." Hollis adjusted his hunting cap and checked the safety on his own hunting firearm of choice, a 204 Ruger.

"Then why the fuck you come with me then? Is it 'cause you get off on complainin' and bitchin' at me all day long?"

"Well, I had nothin' else to do today…"

"Yeah, as usual! What you mean is you got no friends other than me, and your uncle never wants you sittin' around the house in your underwear eating nachos all day long. So, if yer gonna hang with me and hunt, be a man about it!"

"You don't even know if there are any coyotes in these woods."

"Oh, I heard they been seen here."

"And you think there ain't a good chance your skunked over bar buddies got so Jesus fuckin' sauced one day that they mistook a bobcat for a coyote? Never mind they couldn't tell a dick from a twat when they get that kinda shit-faced! Or, did you forget what your friend Lonnie did to your other friend Louie that time he got wasted and actually mistook the guy for his sister Myra?"

"Shut up! You're just all pissed 'cause my friends don't want you around to drink with 'em, 'cause you don't act like a man! They told me they saw coyotes here last hunting season, and I always told my pop that I was gonna bring a few to him before he goes down in the ground."

"And you'll never stop tryin' to prove yourself to him, even if that puts you down in the ground instead! That guy is a douche nozzle! He spent all your life puttin' you down, and all you ever did about it was keep respectin' him and tryin' to do better when he wasn't worth the shit stains on yer boxers!"

Billy-Bob pushed his smaller friend up against a nearby pine tree with the middle of his shotgun while he held it in both hands like a staff. He then thrust both his face and finger into Hollis's stubbled and fear-ridden visage.

"Now you shut it 'bout my old man! You never had no dad, so you don't know what it's like to have that kinda relationship!"

Hollis crunched his face in anger and summoned a rare moment of defying Billy-Bob's usual intimidation, since he believed his friend needed to hear what he had to say, and he was tired of his shit at any rate.

"Okay, maybe my dad didn't raise me, but my uncle sure as hell did, and he was more'n close enough to a father figure. And he's a big douche nozzle too. And I don't waste my time tryin' to please him none!"

"And look at the wuss-bag you turned out to be! That's why I got those drinkin' buddies you're so jealous of and you don't! And that's why you feel the need to put 'em down all the time…"

Billy-Bob abruptly cut off his angry verbal diatribe and turned his head as if something caught his attention.

"What?" Hollis asked while looking over his friend's shoulder into the thickets behind them. "You think you saw a coyote or sumthin'?"

"Naw," Billy-Bob replied while still looking at a certain spot located several yards away. "I done heard somethin', but it didn't sound like no coyote. Hold on for a minute, okay?"

Billy-Bob aimed his shotgun in the general direction of where he was looking, and then sauntered off to the two juniper trees he spotted earlier. Hollis watched him walk up to that vantage point, kneel behind a bush sequestered at the base of each tree, and glare at something that must have been well beyond the wide creek that separated one section of the forest from another.

The less aggressive of the two friends leaned back against the pine tree and began wiping the sweat off his brow, which had accumulated there, as it often did, whenever his best friend lost his temper and pushed him up against the nearest convenient object that would hold their combined weight. He needed the "breather" granted to him by whatever had caught Billy-Bob's. Or so he thought until something strange caught his own attention, albeit in the opposite direction.

Upon hearing a rustling noise and a very odd, deep breathing sound emanating from the thickets located a few yards to his right, Hollis put his hand over his eyes to help him acquire a clear view of whatever might be making it. He caught sight of what appeared to be a fluffy patch of grayish-white fur, and it seemed to be attached to something that was quite large. But the entirety of the creature sporting that fur was obscured by the thick patches of flora surrounding it.

Hollis felt a chill creep up his spine, as if he was experiencing a form of internal frostbite. He suddenly learned what it felt like to have the hair on the back of one's neck raise, even though he was nowhere near a live electrical wire. Could it be a coyote he was seeing? Could Billy-Bob's beer-guzzling buds have been correct after all?

Hollis did his best to resist the eerie feeling threatening to hold him immobile against the tree and tempting him to call out to Billy-Bob. Even though he always berated his friend for trying to prove himself to his never-satisfied dad, he was aware that he too was always out to prove himself. Only in Hollis's case, it was to prove himself to the best friend who was the only person on the planet who had ever been inclined to tolerate his presence and value him as a person to any degree.

As a result, Hollis pushed aside the feelings of both fear and hypocrisy that assaulted his mind and forced himself to advance a few steps towards the incongruous patch of grayish-white fur, and whatever animal it was attached to -- it had to be some kind of animal, right? – and carefully aimed his rifle in that direction as he did so. The lanky but lean man needed to show Billy-Bob that he could handle whatever it was by himself. If he did, then hopefully his friend's negative opinion of his fortitude would go up a notch.

As the slightly trembling man stepped forward a bit more, what was hiding within the thickets suddenly made its full nature known. But Hollis could not, for the life of him, make heads or tails of what that "nature" could possibly be.

Rather than seeing the fierce but distinctly recognizable features of a coyote, what instead thrust its fearsome appearance from the cover of the thickets was that of a creature completely out of his worst childhood nightmares. It had an enormous head that was in no way, shape, or phenotypical form that of a canid. Rather, it looked vaguely if grotesquely simian, but with a gaping maw far larger and wider than that of any anthropoid or even canine on the planet.

The mouth was open wide and filled with rows of sharpened teeth that resembled nothing less than bony knives. It was a mouth that suggested a size that could take a whole human head in its gullet with ample space left over; a jaw strength that could bite a human head clean off in a single chomp; and teeth that looked capable of slicing into bone as easily as flesh.

Its eyes were a dull yellow, with no discernible pupils from that distance, with a bald face that sported a deep beige skin color. It had a barely visible nose but two flaring nostrils that gave it a truly demonic countenance. Its enormous, horrific-looking head was topped by a coating of its characteristic grayish-white fur, almost approximating a human head of hair, despite the follicular strands more resembling an animal's fur.

The head sprung out of the brush at a height that stood nearly six feet off the ground, thus further differentiating it from any known canid or anthropoid. Or any other known genus native to the planet he knew, for that matter. Two extremely large, wickedly clawed hand-like feet with four visible toes – or were they actually fingers? – with razor-sharp nails extending from them could be seen in the bushes below it.

Also, just visible from such a distance was the basic outline of the macabre monstrosity's form, which suggested either a quadrupedal stance, or at least something akin to the typical posture of a great ape.

The fact that its natural stance was apparently of this nature made it all the more chillingly clear how large this creature had to be in order for its head to appear positioned as far above the ground as it was despite not standing anywhere near as erect as a normal human does.

The uncanny beast opened its cavernous mouth to a width exceeding that of an anaconda after unhinging the bones of its jaw to release a guttural sound that seemed like a bizarre combination of growl and breathy exhalation.

Needless to say, Hollis panicked and fired his rifle twice into the brush. He was a fairly good shot and didn't think his long-range mag shells could possibly have missed such a large target, considering they were good for at least 200 yards. However, he didn't see the creature fall to the ground, or even hear it howl in pain, both of which he had anticipated. Instead, he saw just an extremely swift backwards moving swirl of gray before all signs of the horrific beast had disappeared.

Billy-Bob heard the shots and left his viewing position between the twin junipers to run over to his friend. He saw Hollis standing in a state of what looked like terror-stricken shock, rambling the same question repeatedly.

"Did I hit it? Did I hit it?"

"Jesus hell, Hollis!" Billy-Bob shouted as he pushed his friend's pointing rifle downwards. "What in hell did you shoot at?"

"It--it was big and kinda gray, and it was big... and gray..."

Billy-Bob grabbed his smaller friend in his beefy arms and shook him like a leaf.

"Get yer shit together, guy! You said it was gray, so it musta been a coyote! See, I done told you they was here in these woods! But I can't believe it that yer so scared shitless of a cy-ote! You probly missed hitting the damn thing!"

"No... I don't think I did, Billy-Bob. But... I don't think that was no coyote either."

"Say what? You said it was gray, right? That means it couldn't've been no mountain lion or bobcat. So, are you sure what you saw was actually gray? As in, gray like a cloud or cigar smoke?"

"It was gray! And... it was fuckin' huge, Billy-Bob. And it had, it had a mouth like, like this..."

Hollis dropped his rifle and positioned his extended hands to indicate a width of a few feet across.

"Oh, what the shit, man! A grizzly might be huge, but they ain't gray, and there ain't supposed to be no bears in these here woods anymore. And c'mon now, even a bear don't got a mouth *that* big! You got scared out of your wits, totally mis-saw what you really saw or sumthin', and you got the damn nerve to say *my* friends don't know what they're seein' when they get hammered!"

"Billy-Bob..." Hollis paused and began shivering as if the season was the middle of winter instead of a pleasant Nevada day in the spring.

"Yeah? Spit it out, guy!"

"That was no bear I saw. It wasn't no coyote either. But it was huge like a bear, but it wasn't a bear. It wasn't like nothin' I ever saw before."

"Are you tryin' to say you saw Bigfoot or some shit like that?"

"No. I mean, I--I dunno. I just… don't know what it was. But I swear I saw it really clear, 'cause it stuck its head out of the brush, and when it did, I… I saw it real good."

"Look, guy, maybe it was a big old mule deer or somethin', but you need to get your shit together, okay? 'Cause when I investigated what I heard over there, I noticed we have some company less'n a quarter mile past the creek. Company of the people kind, that is, and I don't think they hail from McGill like we do."

All Hollis was able to do was nod his head in acknowledgement of what Billy-Bob said. The expression of shocked horror remained on his face, however, and he knew it was urgent for him to convince his friend that they needed to vacate the woods promptly.

21

On the other side of the creek, a war game was commencing. One that was being fought with high-powered rifles. And paintballs.

Kenna Suzuki was the skilled leader of her two-person team, and she took these games far more seriously than anyone probably should. Her pretty face, festooned with the distinctive almond eye structure of a person of Japanese descent, was highlighted by long, lustrous ebony hair pulled back into a pony tail. A light gray visor was strapped around her eyes to protect them from the paint-filled spherical projectiles fired from their air rifles, and she had on a thick protective blue vest with the Japanese characters ラストガール emblazoned on it.

At her side was her sole teammate and significant other, Lynn Watson, whose shoulder-length, chestnut brown hair was likewise pulled back into a pony tail, albeit a shorter non-flowing version. Her attire was otherwise the same for someone playing paintball tag, but sans any distinctive logo on her vest. She stood a full two inches taller than her leader and paramour and was every bit as competitive in the sport. However, she had had learned a while back to defer to the tactical know-how of her girlfriend when it came to important strategical decisions during this game.

"Where do you think they're hiding?" Lynn asked with a determined grin on her face.

"Where do you think?" Kenna replied in a sarcastic tone that seemed to contradict her soft appearance. "Jackie knows she can't count on Melvin keeping quiet and concealed if approaching us from the front, so she'll be in one of the thickets lining the north, since that's behind us. She'll be hard to spot, so keep a good eye and ear out.

"As usual, Melvin will try to sneak up behind us, but we both know he doesn't give a shit if he wins or loses; he's only in the game to spend some quality time with Jackie. Otherwise, he'd hardly get to see her during the game weeks. He should be easy enough to flag out, so when you detect him, let him have it. Jackie's ass is mine!"

Lynn grinned again. "Ya'll better not be meaning that in the literal sense." She then turned around, bent over, and slapped herself on the buttocks. "*This* is the only ass that's yours, amirite?"

Kenna couldn't help but snort out a quick laugh. "You know it, girl of mine. But keep your mind on the game, and no distracting me like that 'till afterwards, okay?"

Lynn let out a mock exasperated sigh. "Yeah, I know, I know. Your proving yourself a better paintball combatant than Jackie comes before the *really* good things in life. Begging my pardon, hun." She then snorted herself.

"Sorry, but you know me and Jackelyn. We've been at this ever since we started college. She may be my friend, but her arrogance demands she be knocked off her pedestal as often as possible. I'm as good for her humility as anti-oxidants are for her physical health…"

Kenna almost didn't get to complete the sentence. She suddenly grabbed Lynn by her shoulder cuff and pulled her away from a nearby pine tree she was standing in front of. It was a fortuitous move, since it prevented her from being nailed by a paintball that splattered in all its purple glory on the wide wooden frame of the tree.

"Shit, hun!" Lynn screamed. "Did you have to pull me like that? You yanked my bra halfway off my tits!"

"We need to talk less and pay attention more!" Kenna stated as she dropped to one knee, aimed, and fired in the direction behind her.

She heard her paintball hit something much less dense than a tree, along with seeing a quick spurt of orange paint in the distant brush.

At the same time, she and Lynn both heard what they easily recognized as Melvin's voice yelling, "Ow! Shit! I hate these fucking things!"

"Ha!" Lynn snickered aloud. "Serves your wannabe sneaky ass right, Mel!"

"*Maldito*, this paint smells!"

Kenna was well aware of what was about to happen next, so she immediately swiveled until she faced the opposite direction. The paintball soldier managed to just barely spot a quick flicker of bluish-green, and she took three shots in that direction. Jackie was quick on her feet, though, and leapt behind a large aspen tree. Two of the paintballs splattered their orange fury on its trunk; the third whizzed on past it to hit what may have been another tree many yards further behind.

Kenna grinned as she heard Jackie's voice shout, "Fuck!" in full echoing fashion. She couldn't grin too much, though, since her target was still in the game.

Lynn ran up behind her, with her air rifle at the ready. "Did you get her?"

"No, unfortunately. She came close to getting *me* this time, though."

"But she didn't! And now her partner is out of the game, so it's the two of us against just her. Usually she nails me by now, but this game is gonna be over in minutes."

"We'll see, but don't get overly confident." Kenna made sure she carefully maintained her rifle's crosshairs in the direction of the thick canopy of foliage that she knew Jackie was hiding within. "She has a lot of coverage in there, and you need to keep your concentration up if you actually want us to get her before she takes you out of the game."

"Yeah, I know, I know, we get more points if we're both still in when you take her out. So, then, if I get taken out and cost you the points, you're gonna make me sleep on the couch tonight or something?"

Kenna kept her right eye glued to the scope on the top of her rifle without being distracted for a micro-second while replying. "No, but you can bet I'll only go down on you tonight for three minutes instead of my usual ten."

"Oh, you cruel, cruel bitch you!" Lynn said with obviously fake indignation. "I had best make sure we're *both* still standing at the end of this one then. Let's go get her! I am totally going to earn those extra tongue lashes tonight!"

Several yards away, Jackie Cortland kept herself stealthily concealed in the thickets a few yards away from her two friendly opponents. Standing alongside her was her was Melvin, who was now sulking beside a tree while anxiously waiting for the faux combat to end. His girlfriend held her paint-loaded rifle in one hand as she leaned against an aspen tree in full concealment. Jackie's face displayed an extremely cross expression while she aimed.

Just once, you'd think he would take these maneuvers just slightly seriously! But noooooo, he can't even hit Lynn when she's doing her usual thing! Of course, he doesn't care about these combat games, he only cares about me. I really should get another combat partner, and leave Melvin to what he does best, which is being my romantic partner.

But... well, would I really want to spend that much time away from him? But I'm sick and tired of always losing to Kenna because he doesn't know what the fuck he's doing, and he doesn't pay much attention when I try to give him pointers or instructions!

Jackie was knocked out of her vent-filled ruminations by another volley of paintballs hitting the other side of the tree. That was followed by the sound of both Kenna and Lynn reloading and their footsteps moving closer through the brush.

Jackie next heard Melvin's Spanish-accented voice yelling, "Watch out, babe! They're coming for you!"

This was followed by Lynn's voice yelling, "Hush your ass up, Mel! You know that's totally cheating!"

"It is?" he rejoined.

"Damn straight!" Lynn hollered in reply. "'Out of the game' means you're totally out of it!"

"Shit..." Jackie whispered to herself as she realized she had to leave her position and move further out. *The two of them are on my ass, and I'm completely on the defensive. If I can get Kenna first, then Lynn shouldn't be much trouble on her own. And even if Lynn got me after I got Kenna, it would still be a* huge *fucking score for me! Just to see the look on her face!*

Things were about to take a most chilling and atypical turn, however, as Jackie ran further into the woods and through another canopy of foliage.

As the pseudo-soldier made her way through a blanket of thickets, doing her best to be as quiet as possible and not get any burrs stuck to her socks, she suddenly bumped into what first seemed like an odd, white-colored metallic-feeling object. Jackie turned to see that the "object" in question was not only human-shaped, but actually *was* a human being wearing some advanced type of flexible body armor. The young woman also noticed that the armor's thorax region was discolored with the orange spatter of Kenna's paintball from the initial volley she fired at her good-friend-cum-opponent.

The statuesque, somewhat chubby young woman with shoulder-length, honey blonde hair then looked up and found herself staring into the silvery visor of the helmeted figure wearing the armor. This actual soldier was a full foot taller than she was. Jackie further noticed that he was holding a very advanced looking rifle, clearly heavy-duty military issue, in one of his arms.

"Was this your paintball that hit me?" the man asked her in a gruff voice that was somewhat distorted from being modulated through the helmet's speaker.

"Um… no," Jackie choked out, hardly able to wrap her mind around what she was now looking at. "My team's paintballs are, um, purple. Not orange."

"Good," the strange armored soldier replied. "Then the dickhead on the other team who hit me can be the one to apologize. As in, right now. Because your game is over.

"There is something extremely dangerous in these woods, and I'm not talking about myself. My unit and I are here to dispatch it, and your little party constitutes a civilian complication that makes our job a lot more difficult. Because that means we have to worry about protecting you in addition to wiping out our target. That is, before it wipes *you* out, and before it wipes out anyone else after it gets done digesting the remains of your group."

Jackie could only nod her head, not knowing what other reaction to have, considering she was still so startled at the bizarre interruption of their mock combat game. Not to mention everything she was just told by an imposing figure of authority.

"But keep in mind," he continued, "that my unit, and the mission, comes first. We're authorized to eliminate any errant civilians in addition to the target if I deem it necessary, so you and your friends had best follow my orders to the letter and not get on my bad side in *any* conceivable way."

Shit... was all Jackie could say to herself again, only this time she made a point to do it silently. *Does this at least mean Kenna will agree to call this maneuver a draw?*

22

"Some people are puttin' on a paintball war out there!" Billy-Bob told his BFF, who was still in a fear-induced stupor. "Can you believe that shit? They treat hunting like it's some kinda game. Just figures three of 'em are chicks, huh?"

"We... we need to tell them," Hollis jabbered.

"Tell 'em what? To fuck off 'cause these woods belong to *real* hunters who're hunting *real* game?"

"Billy-Bob... we gotta tell 'em to get outta these woods."

"Fuckin' *ay*, man!" Billy-Bob punctuated that exclamation with a thumb's up gesture.

"No... you don't get it. I mean, we gotta tell 'em that we *all* gotta get outta here. Right now. Before it gets us."

"Sweet Jesus, are you on that shit again?" Billy-Bob shoved his friend, who seemed strangely impassive, as if his mind was on something else entirely. "You just stay here an' shit your pants over the coyote or bobcat, or whatever you saw in the brush. I'm gonna go tell those city slickers to get lost. Then I'm comin' back to get that coyote you saw, and I hope you shit your pants *again* when I bring its carcass to you!"

"Billy-Bob... don't leave me here. And don't go off alone."

"Shut up, you big bottle of pussy! I'm gonna go deal with those phony ass soldier wannabes, then meet you back here!"

Billy-Bob turned around and began marching towards the area on the other side of the creek where he knew the paintball combatants were situated. He had walked a few feet when he suddenly heard Hollis make what sounded to him like a tortured gagging noise.

The large-bodied man with the bristling beard turned to see that his meeker friend was being held by a tall, athletically built Native American dressed in traditional Goshute garb, his face adorned with war paint and a feathered strap around his forehead. He was grasping Hollis tightly with his muscular left arm, while holding a stone blade to his throat with his other hand.

"What the holy fuck...?" Billy-Bob uttered as he readied his shotgun.

"Don't be stupid, white man," Greymountain said. "I may only use the traditional weaponry of my ancestors, but I know modern weapons quite well. That is a shotgun, not a long-range rifle, and you cannot hit me with that clunky ammo without blowing a hole in your friend also."

"What the fuck ya want, injun? We didn't do nuthin' to you!"

Hollis continued shaking and staring blankly ahead without saying a word as the Goshute warrior responded to Billy-Bob.

"First of all, you can stop referring to me as 'injun'... *pale face*. Second, it would take me hours I do not have to spare if I told you all the things your people have done to mine, from the time you first intruded on our land centuries ago right up to the present by forcing us to live in those humiliating, government-sanctioned reservations.

"Third, and finally, you can tell me what you know about two other members of the Goshute tribe from the reservation who disappeared in these woods not two weeks ago."

"I don't know shit about that!" Billy-Bob insisted. "Now you let Hollis go! He may be a pussy, but he's still my best friend, kinda like a lil bro, and I'll kill you if you hurt him!"

"Not if I kill you first. Which I definitely will if I find out you had anything to do with the murder of my cousin, who was like a brother to *me!*"

"I told you we had nuthin' to do with anythin' like that! We were just hunting coyote here, not people, not even inj—I mean, *your* people! Shit, I shoulda' known it was you that Hollis saw in the brush that scared the holy shit outta him, and not some animal like a coyote!"

"It wasn't him, Billy-Bob," Hollis suddenly spoke out.

"What you say, bro?" the bigger redneck asked his friend.

"I said... it wasn't this man," Hollis stammered. "It wasn't a man I saw at all." He then turned his head to partially look Greymountain in the face, the latter of whom could tell the smaller white man was literally trembling of fear... not of him. "What's your name, Mister?"

The tall Native American decided to grant the terrified white man's polite request. "I am Greymountain."

"I'm--I'm Hollis. Mr. Greymountain, sir. I think I know what killed that cousin of yours. It wasn't one of us. It wasn't nuthin' human at all."

For some reason, Greymountain could sense the sincerity flowing out of this man's horror-ridden mouth. All the warrior's instincts told him that the pale-skinned man caught helplessly in his grip wasn't merely lying in a desperate bid to save his own life.

"What do you believe killed my cousin, Hollis?" the Goshute warrior demanded to know. "Speak now!"

"I... don't know what it was I saw," Hollis said through increasingly shaky lips. "But it... was horrible. Just *horrible*. Please help us get out of here. Before we all end up like your cousin."

Just then, as if on uncanny cue, a soft flurry of barely audible movement caught Greymountain's ear. He cocked his head slightly, doing his best to make full use of his well-honed hearing, and his lifelong rapport with the rhythms of the Goshute Canyon Wilderness.

"Hollis, do you seriously think you saw sumthin' other than this guy here sneakin' up on us in the brush?" Billy-Bob asked his friend.

"Be silent for a minute!" Greymountain ordered. "I hear something approaching us from behind."

"Are you shittin' us there, red man?"

"No. I am not, *pale man*."

"Yeah, I heard how you said that, and I'll have you know I'm goddamned proud to be white!"

"And I am damned well proud *not* to be! Now, be silent and listen carefully."

Billy-Bob did as requested, while the strange man in their midst appeared quite serious, not just fishing for a distraction. The small-town but large-framed man with the natty beard then found himself unable to deny that he did hear a rustling noise in the surrounding foliage, moving quickly but surreptitiously through the thick verdant cover.

"Hey, sumthin' is movin' out there…"

"Behind you!" Greymountain yelled as he casually tossed Hollis several feet to his side.

The Goshute warrior then sheathed his knife, pulled his compound bow from around his shoulder, and drew an arrow secured in his back-mounted buckskin quiver as quickly as he possibly could.

It was a well-practiced move that occurred with astounding speed. But it was barely completed before the monstrous source of the furtive sound that concerned the trio made its first strike.

Billy-Bob jumped forward at Greymountain's shouted warning while the huge, grayish-white furred creature seen earlier by Hollis charged out of the nearby thickets like the proverbial denizen out of Hell itself.

The furry abomination moved with terrifying speed for a creature its size. It ran on all fours with its hind limbs resembling the hyper-muscular arms of a gorilla rather than those of a four-legged animal.

The appearance of its full form revealed a physique that was quite simian-like save for its enormous maw and long, dangling fingers that displayed bird-like talons in place of fingernails. It was, however, larger and bulkier than a typical male silverback gorilla, and the entirety of its body, save for its face and fingers, were covered in a thick greyish-white coat of fur. Its chasm-like mouth was open wide, exposing a tremendous bite radius that looked to be enough to sever a grown human being in two with a single crunch.

"Jesus shit!" Billy-Bob exclaimed as he attempted to aim his shotgun in time.

The tough-as-nails hunter wasn't as fast as his furry attacker, however, and it swatted the weapon from his hand as casually as a man might slap a rattle out of an infant's grip. It then struck him in the front of his chest and knocked him to the muddy ground as it moved in for the kill.

The beast was stopped short as a hardwood arrow with a sharpened stone head struck it on its right shoulder blade. A second arrow followed a moment later, this one embedding itself in the monstrosity's forehead. The creature moved back and snarled in pain, but amazingly, did not seem to have been delivered a mortal or even truly debilitating injury. Instead, it just pulled the embedded arrows from the bleeding wounds and resumed its attack.

Billy-Bob did his best to take full advantage of this reprieve by pulling himself forward on the ground towards his shotgun, with the frantic hope of recovering it and blasting the creature at point blank range.

However, he couldn't crawl fast enough before the beast fully recovered from the pain and force of the arrows. Upon doing so it grabbed Billy-Bob's right leg in the steel-strong grip of its left "hand." The large man screamed in agony as his fingers fell short of grabbing his weapon by mere inches.

The sight of all this broke Hollis out of his terror-stricken fugue. He took no more than a few seconds as this went on to recover his Ruger, run several feet closer to the monster, and aim the weapon. The lanky man could not allow any inkling of self-preservation or cowardice, whichever one may prefer to call it, to prevent him from doing all he could to save Billy-Bob Tyler. A man who, despite his often less than pleasant behavior, was the only person in the world who cared to be Hollis Clemens's friend.

"You let Billy-Bob go!" Hollis shouted as he depressed the trigger.

The fired lead projectiles all struck their target, and the impact on its thick hide drove the beast back and also forced it to release its grip on Billy-Bob's leg. However, the bullets from that rifle were not of sufficient caliber to penetrate far into the creature's skin; they only caused it enough pain to turn its attention from one intended quarry to another. That is what Hollis hoped for, but it would cost him severely. He knew this and found himself unable to care due to his determined bid to save his only friend.

The furry monster snarled in rage and rushed towards Hollis. He fired the final two bullets in his magazine at the advancing menace, and Greymountain shot two more arrows into its right hind limb in an attempt to add to its injury.

Neither type of projectile could halt the unholy creature's rampage, not even when they struck in unison, and the beast reached Hollis in what appeared to be a blur of motion. It wrapped one of its enormous hands around his neck and effortlessly pulled him towards its gaping jaws. It then swiftly bit the top half of the man's head off with a single clomp of its mouth.

Hollis's body was quivering in its death throes as blood gushed from his bifurcated skull like a crimson fountain, the force of the spurts hurling chunks of moist brain matter into the air along with it.

"You fuckin' sonnuva bitch!" Billy-Bob screamed at the horrific sight of his good friend's slaughter.

Hollis's sacrifice was not in vain, however, as it did give Billy-Bob time to recover his shotgun and jump back to his feet. The grief-stricken but enraged man ran as close as he dared to the monster and blasted it with a double ought 3-inch mag shell from just a few feet away. The monster was unable to shrug that one off, and a sizable wound appeared on its torso. But remarkably, still not a fatal one.

Greymountain moved closer and did his best to augment the wound with two more well-placed arrows. One of them struck the center of the hand-sized hole blown into its torso by Billy-Bob, as if hitting a bloody bullseye; and the second one struck the creature dead in the center of its thick throat.

The injured monster howled in agony and grabbed the arrow shafts, pulling both the wooden sticks and their flint heads from the two perforated spots on its anatomy. This it did in a double but simultaneous wave of motion, not seeming to be bothered by the small chunks of fur-covered flesh that came out of the wounds along with the shafts.

The creature fully understood it could not take much more of this, so it turned and retreated towards a field of heavy thickets. Billy-Bob fired another round, but to his astonishment, the beast ran in a zig-zag fashion, much as a rational thinking being like a human would do to minimize its chances of being hit. Because of that intelligent choice of movement, another of Greymountain's arrows also failed to hit its target, instead implanting itself into a nearby tree.

The monster vanished into the greenery of the thickets several yards north. After that, all seemed silent in the field.

That hush was hardly accompanied by peace, however, as Billy-Bob lowered his shotgun to see the blood-soaked, unmoving body of his lifelong friend laying in the grass. This was the same comrade whom he often belittled as not being enough of a man yet had overcome the greatest fear he ever experienced to sacrifice his life in order to save that of his only friend in the world.

Suddenly, it was Billy-Bob who felt unworthy, and he ran over to Hollis's gore-covered corpse. He held the leaking cadaver it his arms and didn't hesitate to burst out crying despite the presence of the Native American warrior in front of him.

Despite having already grown to dislike Billy-Bob for his racist and abrasive ways, Greymountain nevertheless turned and walked several feet distant while facing another direction, this to respect a grieving process that he now shared and understood all too well.

The brave anachronistic Goshute warrior that was Tim Greymountain also could not help shedding a tear as he then knew the terrible fate that had befallen his cousin, a man he too loved like a brother, as well as Marcus, another member of his tribe. The traditional warrior wasn't even confident he would ever be able to find any of their remains, since he had no way of knowing how much of its prey the deadly mystery beast tended to devour if its ghastly feast wasn't interrupted. And any remains left behind would soon be stripped clean by the forest's normal carrion eaters.

After allowing Billy-Bob several minutes of private mourning, he turned and walked back to him, his bow and arrow still in hand.

"I was obviously wrong when I blamed you and yours for the death of my cousin and his companion," Greymountain said, believing it was the honorable thing to say despite how he felt about this white man, and so many others like him.

"Yeah, I was wrong 'bout some things too," the tear-soaked macho redneck admitted with great difficulty.

"Then you know I share your sorrow. And doubtlessly, your desire to rid the woods of that beast, whatever it is. I suspect it is less a natural part of this world than either your people or mine, or any of the peoples spawned by nature. There was something… alien about it."

Billy-Bob looked up, exposing his reddened face and watery eyes. "I'm gonna bury my friend first. I'm not gonna let that fucker come back and eat his body, or leave him to the birds, if we don't get it before it gets us. But God help me, I'm *gonna* get that hairy cocksucker. With or without you."

"You can 'get' the creature *with* me, as I have no intention of leaving these woods until that disruption of nature is dead. Or, until I am. And we must both admit we will have a better chance if we again put aside our prejudices and work together. Because unlike us, this beast does not discriminate between tribes of people."

"Yeah, whatever. I know." Billy-Bob wiped his eyes and nasal passages before getting to his feet and making note of something important. "Listen, there's sumthin' else. There's more people here. Down that way, past the creek. They're playing paintball, or some shit."

Greymountain turned his head and, for the first time, became cognizant of human activity going on in that direction himself. "We must get to them quickly. Before that beast does."

23

Private Brandon Grumby used the electronic zoom lens built into the helmet of his combat armor to scan the vicinity of the woods around the Goshute Caves and the craggy cliff sides of the Cherry Creek Mountains. The visual enhancer fed all the telemetry it picked up from its surroundings into a detailed holographic image displayed to him on the interior of his visor. That was made possible via the HUD system built into his helmet's miniaturized but highly effective computer hardware.

He held an M251 light machine gun that was locked and loaded, ready to fire a 5.70 millimeter round in fully automatic mode at a moment's notice. Magnetically adhered to the left calf of the armor was a .50 caliber Desert Eagle firearm as an easily accessible back-up weapon.

Both the combat armor and the SAW rifle were upgrades from the ones normally issued to the security personnel and field task force agents of the nefarious Area 51 classified military base located roughly 300 miles southwest at the Groom Lake airfield. He was in the company of Sergeant Terrance "Tee-Bone" Morrison, who stood leaning against a nearby cairn while scanning the opposite perimeter.

"Do you really think it got all the way here from Area 51, Sarge?" Grumby queried his superior officer.

"That would be affirmative, as our tracking equipment doesn't lie," Tee-Bone replied. "Keep in mind that each of those creatures created by Project Hydra were intended to be used as bio-weapons for military applications by the Armed Forces. They were spliced together by Dr. Brice's team with the hybrid DNA of numerous species of predatory animals. Their ability to hunt, use natural stealth and cunning, and relocate quickly from one region to another is off the scale. Then consider that a few of the genome sequences used to create them were extracted out of an alien life form recovered from a crashed derelict spacecraft of unknown extraterrestrial origin in Antarctica."

"Yeah, which means those things seem to have capabilities the big wigs at Project Hydra couldn't anticipate, including a really trippy level of intelligence and that weird ass ability to camouflage themselves. And they looked more fucked up and dangerous than anything I could imagine even during the days I did acid."

"Not only that, Grumby, but those bastards proved smart enough to divert our resources and lengthen their escape time by each moving in a different direction, and to a different locale, after they broke out of the facility."

"Yeah, yeah, sir, but isn't it better that each of our dispatched field units only have to deal with one of those fuckers in each location? I come close to losing my lunch when I think of what all of those things together did to Captain Snyder and his team when they tried to stop them from getting loose from the facility. Not to mention the tech staff and Dr. Brice himself!"

"Poetic justice, I say. But you're under direct orders not to tell anyone back at the base I said that."

"Whose orders, sir?"

"*Mine*, that's who. And don't get cocky and overconfident just because we're only dealing with one of their number here, grunt. These woods provide all the shelter and cover it may need to stalk and catch its prey, including the human variety.

"We may be armed to the chin, and these suits of armor and rifles are a slight upgrade from the ones at the facility, but Captain Snyder and his unit were still top notch. And they got wiped out in *minutes*. In a *laboratory*, where it was far more difficult for these creatures to hide than a big wilderness area like this. We aren't only the hunters in this mission; we're also the *game*."

"And the one we're dealing with is…? Give me a sec to pull up the dossier from the file on my HUD."

"You were supposed to have read that and know exactly which one of the Experiment subjects we're up against while en route to this location. And you knew that, soldier!"

"Sorry, Sarge, but it's just too easy to pull up porn videos from the Internet on this system. And watching that action in 3-

D holographic format is like having the whole thing right in my face. Like, literally!"

"Consider yourself on report, Grumby. *If* you make it back alive that is, considering your squirrelling around like you did on the way here instead of studying the mission files like you were supposed to."

"Aw, Sarge, I'm sorry about that. I just needed to scratch a certain little itch on the way here…"

"Stow it, soldier, and pull up that file and read it! Quickly! I'll cover your ass for the few minutes that will take, since this area appears to be quiet. Captain Jacobi and Private Cooper may be having more luck on their side of the area. If you can really call running into one of these things 'luck.'"

Grumby read the text of the file as it appeared on the interior of his visor. The photo and stats of the quarry his unit was sent to terminate displayed, "Subject #2 of Project Hydra: The Experiment. Nicknamed: 'Fluffy.'"

"Whoa!" he said. "This is one scary looking mother fuck, Sarge! Sort of looks like a stuffed animal my sister had when she was little. Still, I'm glad the cocksucker we're up against here isn't the one with the lizard skin and tentacles. Tentacles really give me the creeps, especially considering I used to have a roommate who was into that hentai shit."

"I told you not to get cocky and underestimate what we're facing. Believe it or not, there are even worse fates than pissing me off. But that's still a horrible enough fate to contemplate, so if you keep up the horseplay, I'll consign you to a month of cleaning Captain Jacobi's private head."

"And you're right, sir, as I sure as hell wouldn't want to have to blow the captain more than I already do."

"If you think I'm kidding, wise ass, make another comment out of turn like that and I'll not only consign you to cleaning the captain's private toilet for six months, but I'll make sure you get assigned extra hours there every Wednesday. Which is, for your info, the one day of the week the mess hall serves those hot burritos he loves, but which sure as hell don't love him back. If you catch my meaning."

Geez, grow a sense of humor along with a personality, Sarge, Grumby thought to himself as he completed reading the file. He then exited out of the virtual dossier and watched the grotesque image of Experiment #2, a.k.a., "Fluffy," fade off his visor's HUD screen.

"Sir, I finished reading the whole file," Grumby said aloud to his superior officer. "As you ordered, sir."

"Good for you, however belated. While you were busy catching up on your homework, I spent the entire time scanning the vicinity for heat signatures, ultra-violet urine trails, foot prints, you name it, and it seems it's clear for at least a mile all around us. This means the creature is likely stalking out Captain Jacobi and Private Cooper over in their designated search area. Neither of them sent us a back-up request yet, but I should still check in with them."

"I'll watch your back while you do, sir."

"Appreciated, Private Grumby, but feel free to stand at ease for now." Tee-Bone put his right index finger on the ear section of his helmet, thus activating his communicator and opening a direct line to Jacobi and Cooper.

"Is everything okay on your end, sir?" he asked. "Nothing on this end, which is why... wait, did you say you have civilians under your watch?"

Wow, sucks to be us today, Grumby thought to himself while he surreptitiously shook his head. He then decided to take his few moments of recess to enjoy the natural scenic beauty surrounding him. The young soldier had his helmet set to 'standard vision,' and he admired the verdant foliage of the area, as well as the pleasant sound of the water cascading down a nearby creek.

Grumby smiled as he caught sight of a few chirping kestrels jumping from branch to branch on a towering pine tree which stood to his left. The aesthetic pleasure of that sighting was soon eclipsed by another view, one which he noticed over a hundred feet above him. There he saw a falcon soaring around in the blue skies above him, majestically flaunting its enviable ability of flight. The bird looked absolutely beautiful as the sunlight highlighted its reddish-brown plumage.

The armored soldier then turned to see a large male mule deer standing just within the creek with its mouth dipped in the water to drink.

"Hey, I never saw a mule deer drinking this close to me before," he said to himself as he stepped towards the animal.

"All right, Captain," Tee-Bone said to his superior officer via helmet communicator as their report came to an end. "Grumby and I will be there to help you deal with those paintball-flinging soldier imitators in a few minutes. With them to look after, I agree that the whole four-man unit should be there. Morrison over and out."

After hearing the 'click' of the communicator disconnecting the "call," Tee-Bone immediately turned to see Grumby staring intently at the large animal in the creek.

"Grumby, what in Hell's name are you looking at?"

"It's really cool, Sarge! A big mule deer buck is standing there drinking, and it's not afraid of us. Must be extra thirsty."

"It's rather odd that it hasn't taken off," Tee-Bone noted as he walked up behind Grumby. "These animals tend to be really skittish around people, but there it is drinking like a cat from its water dish even with two of us standing here and invading its privacy."

"Ha ha! Yeah, really cool, sir. He'll probably drink up the whole creek by the time he's done…"

It was just that moment when Grumby noticed something: None of the distinctive small wakes that typically accompanied an animal lapping its tongue to drink seemed to be emanating from where the deer's mouth met the water. He then noticed that its eyes weren't blinking and seemed to have something like a "glassy" appearance.

"Huh? Is he even actually drinking…?"

Then he noticed the red discoloration of the water gradually accumulating underneath where the deer stood with its mouth in the stream.

Not a nanosecond after that detail caught his attention, the heavy animal's body suddenly flew out of the water sideways and slammed into Grumby. Its terrific weight pinned the soldier to the ground as it landed on top of him. The force of being struck by this very unexpected move caused Grumby to drop his SAW rifle. His body armor just barely prevented his ribs from cracking under the animal's considerable heft.

"Ugh! Sarge!" were all the sounds he could utter as he struggled to push the deer off him.

"What the hell?" was all Tee-Bone could utter in return before he ran towards the creek to aid his subordinate officer.

As Grumby struggled to push the mule deer off him, he noticed that it was completely unmoving, with the glassy sheen of its unblinking eyes being due to the fact that it was dead. The blood and viscera that lay spattered between the carcass of the animal and his upper body armor made it clear that it had died by being slaughtered. But how, then, could it have appeared to be standing in the creek with its head positioned downwards into the stream as if it were drinking?

That disturbing question was answered just a split second later when the deadly monstrosity nicknamed "Fluffy" by its creators suddenly de-cloaked its chameleon-like camouflage ability to reveal it had been standing quietly and partially immersed in the creek all along. It had done this without even making breathing sounds to give its presence away.

The beast's truly remarkable intelligence and cunning enabled it to lure the soldier over by positioning a deer it had silently killed to look as if the animal was standing and drinking, somehow realizing that such a sight might pique a human's curiosity. Whether or not the creature could be credited with anything akin to logical reason seemed beside the point, as its ruse certainly did work in this particular case.

Grumby's adrenalin-fueled muscles enabled him to finally push the gore-drenched deer off him, only to hear an incessant splashing in the stream which signaled that the monster was bearing down upon him with an uncanny speed that was barely slowed by the water.

The soldier realized he would be unable to recover his rifle in time, so he quickly sat up to reach for the Desert Eagle handgun magnetically attached to the armor on his right leg's calf. He wasn't fast enough, however, and no sooner was he up in a sitting position reaching for his piece than he saw the beast's horrifically large mouth open wide with its rows of sharpened teeth bared. And that just mere inches from his face.

The creature jumped on Grumby, its weight pushing him down and proving greater than that of the deer. Reacting with his instinctive fight training, the armored solider quickly punched the creature in the right side of its face as hard as he could. Even with his knuckles backed up by the gauntlet of his combat armor, however, the blow barely slowed the beast's attack and seemed to just enrage it more.

Through the visual screen of his visor the terrified young combatant noticed two things that stuck in his mind: the creature's bright yellow eyes, and the roundish wound present on the skin of its forehead that was, unbeknownst to him, inflicted upon it earlier by Greymountain's arrow. Had he known that, he would have likewise noticed that the seemingly severe injury was already over seventy percent healed.

The infuriated monster used its bulky forearms to lift Grumby up as easily as a child may lift a doll. This presented a major problem for Tee-Bone, who had just arrived near the edge of the creek to witness the nightmarish spectacle before him.

"Grumby, block its bite with your arm and try to get out of the way! I can't get a clear shot at it without hitting you!"

As the beast's jaws lunged at him, Grumby's reflexes proved true to the task. He responded to the orders of the sergeant by placing his armored forearm in front of him to take the beast's powerful bite in place of his face. He quickly said a silent prayer to God that the slightly upgraded class of armor would be enough to keep its teeth from sinking into him until Tee-Bone could get a shot.

Grumby fell backwards as the monster's cavernous jaws closed on the limb he sacrificed to keep his face and throat from being bitten. And to allow Tee-Bone to take his shot.

As the sergeant aimed his SAW rifle, its scope interfaced with the HUD system in his helmet to enhance his natural shooting skill's ability to lock onto its intended target. He then fired a few rounds, with at least two of the bullets striking the beast's forehead and knocking it off Grumby. The creature then fell backwards into the water with a terrific splash.

"Hold up, Grumby, I'm coming!" the tall, athletic African-American officer yelled as he ran up to his fallen subordinate with his rifle at the ready.

Upon reaching Grumby's position and looking over the creek he realized, to his profound consternation, that the huge grayish-white furred corpse he hoped to see laying sprawled on its back in the water was nowhere in sight. The stream was filled with blood and what appeared to be particles of floating gore. Upon noticing the gutted body of the deer laying a few feet to the side, Tee-Bone had to accept that this could have come from the slain animal and not the monster.

After his HUD sensors detected no movement whatsoever besides the flowing waters of the brook and the heat images of a few trout swimming beneath its surface, he reached out his arm to help Grumby to his feet. The sergeant made certain to keep a cautious attention on the creek in front of him as he did so.

"Grumby, are you okay? Can you move?"

"Sarge... help me..."

It was then that Tee-Bone took the liberty of turning his head and looking down at his subordinate comrade. That was when he noticed, to his horror, that Grumby was missing his right arm. The creature's teeth succeeded in penetrating the armor within seconds, and it had torn the soldier's limb off when it was knocked back into the water by the force of Tee-Bone's salvo of bullets.

"Oh, dear Freya! Grumby, hold on! I'm going to call for help!"

"Sarge… don't bother. I'm… gonna bleed out. Get that fucker… for me…"

Grumby then fully succumbed to the shock and his body began trembling as fountains of blood gushed out of the ripped flesh where his arm had been ripped off just below his right elbow. Upon looking at the rapid evacuation of blood from the man's severed stump, Tee-Bone knew that the soldier's assessment of his own condition was accurate. Grumby would be dead within moments.

"Rest well, grunt. And you can bet I'll get that son of a bitch for you."

Tee-Bone solemnly chose to stay at Grumby's side for the few minutes it took for him to expire, so that he did not have to die alone. The sergeant realized that someone who disliked the dying person would be no replacement for family and friends, but he fancied it was still better than spending one's final moments alone.

After Grumby passed from the mortal coil, Tee-Bone pushed the secret deactivation button on the armor to crunch all the accumulated data in its hardware system.

He then dismantled the firing mechanisms of the dangerous firearms left behind by the fallen young man, so they could never be used by any random party who may have stumbled on to them. All of this in case the body and its hardware could not be retrieved.

After saying a quiet prayer to Thor and Freya for his lost comrade, Tee-Bone activated his helmet communicator to report the situation to Captain Jacobi.

24

Many minutes earlier on the other side of the creek -- far enough away that small-caliber gunfire wouldn't necessarily be heard from there -- Captain Jacobi stood giving Kenna's crew a typical

authoritarian spiel. This one brusquely explained who was in charge of things in their newly combined group of government-sanctioned secret ops soldiers and a quartet of paintball-wielding "cosplaying soldiers," as Jacobi put it.

The obvious party in charge included the captain himself and his right-hand woman, Private Leann Cooper. She wore a version of Area 51's combat armor especially contoured to accommodate the figure of a woman. Distinct from the other three in her unit, however, she was the team's official "bunker buster," as instead of a SAW rifle

she carried a truly formidable M141 anti-fortification rocket launcher.

"As I told your friend Ms. Cortland here," Jacobi lectured, "I am Captain David Jacobi, and I'm in charge of the full unit operating in this wilderness area. Another half of my people are on the other side of the woods searching for the creature there. Do not give me any trouble, and you may all make it out of this alive. Or, at least some of you will. I obviously cannot guarantee such a positive outcome."

"I think that armor of yours is really cool, man," Melvin said. "It makes you look just like this action figure I had as a kid."

Jacobi walked over to Melvin and bent over until his helmet's visor was almost eye to eye with the young curly-haired man. "Cut the clowning, Mr. Garcia. This is no child's game, fought with action figures or paintballs. I'm no action figure, but a real 'action' *combatant*, holding a rifle with *real* flesh-piercing bullets, hunting down a *real*, highly dangerous bio-weapon that is likewise hunting both my unit and your pathetic little group as we speak. My task force is all that stands between you and that thing's appetite for blood. Do you understand me clearly, Mr. Garcia?"

Melvin was doing his best not to shake or perspire in front of his girlfriend Jackie. But it was extremely difficult for an easygoing person like him not to be intimidated by Captain Jacobi in his full combat armor regalia and military officer personality mode.

"Yeah, I get you, *tipo*. Totally."

"Good, Mr. Garcia. See that you keep 'getting' me until this ordeal is over."

Kenna pushed her flowing ponytail behind her head and walked up to Jacobi.

"Listen, Captain. I understand the seriousness of the situation you explained to us and that you're in charge bladie bladie blah, but we had no idea what was going on here. This forest is a resort area open to public use."

"And allow me to inform you that public use isn't supposed to include paintball maneuvers, Ms. Suzuki. That paint can be hazardous to the flora and fauna of these woods for all we know, and the ruckus you kick up with your games can stress out the wildlife. Just like how you're now stressing *me*, which I remind you isn't wise."

"Okay, maybe, we weren't supposed to be doing this here," Kenna continued. "But I can assure you that we do care about the wilderness. The paint we use for our maneuvers is entirely non-toxic to the environment. And allow me to remind *you* that we've been doing this for over a year now, and the wildlife seems just fine."

Jacobi stepped another inch towards Kenna. "You have a lot of sass in your ass, Ms. Suzuki. And I don't like it."

Kenna folded her arms and gave the officer a stare down. "Here's the thing that miffs me off about this whole mess, Captain Jacobi. The government agency you work for has endangered us and every other person who might come to the woods, which includes families who routinely camp and hike here, by creating this thing you're talking about and then allowing it to get loose. I'm sure it isn't doing the wildlife you're so concerned about any favors either. I'm sure its presence disrupts the natural ecosystem on more levels than either of us can count."

"You *are* a sassy little tool, aren't you?" Cooper said as she walked up to Kenna with her finger pointed.

"At ease, Private," Jacobi ordered with a raising of his hand. "Ms. Suzuki does have a big mouth that needs to be shut more often, but she does have a point. And courage for expressing it, I might add. And whether we like it or not, and whether we like *her* or not, I do respect that."

The captain then turned back to Kenna and looked down at her. She kept her position looking upwards into his shiny visor, refusing to show signs of fear despite how outclassed she knew that her group was by Jacobi and his soldiers.

"Ms. Suzuki, I know none of this is your fault. And yeah, I'll fully accede that the... problem caused by my agency dwarfs that of your problematic paintballing in a government-regulated wilderness area.

"But you still need to dispense with running off your mouth and defying me every chance you get just to look 'tough' in front of your group. The position I am in right now, and what we're all facing here, will not permit me to keep tolerating it with impunity. If you force us to work against each other, you and your group are going to end up the losers of that fracas. So, let's be fair to each other and work together on this, okay?"

Kenna folded her arms again and put her face in a half-grin for a moment, as if pretending to be in a position to consider the matter. It was just for show, of course.

"Alright, Captain. You talked some sense here. What do you need us to do to get through this intact?"

"Smart girl," Jacobi replied. "I need you and your group to stay between me and my people at all times. I'm going to call the other two members of my task force, which includes my second-in-command, Sgt. Terrance Morrison -- 'Tee-Bone', as we call him -- to help us keep you secure while we send for an extraction copter to fly in here and get all of you out. You will have to make a stopover at a government facility to be debriefed on this matter before you're free to return to your civilian lives, however."

Kenna rolled her attractive almond-shaped eyes and sighed. "Of course, we will. Can't have this shitstorm of yours getting out to the public now, can we? Saving lives at the expense of exposing government fuck-ups is just *too much* of an expense for the government's limited budget."

"Watch yourself, girl!" Cooper said, as she moved forward with her hand raised. "You said you would work with us, and we expect you to follow through with that honorably. Unless you want your pretty little face to meet and greet the backside of my hand!"

Finally, Jackie had taken enough of standing on the sidelines in admitted intimidation from these well-armed figures of authority. *I should have been the one to step up and defend Melvin, not Kenna, because he's* my *significant other,* not *hers! I'm not going to let her prove herself better at standing up for myself and the people I care about in addition to combat maneuvers… and just about everything else that takes some serious ovaries to do.*

Steeling herself against the fear, Jackie ran and intercepted Cooper before anyone else could react to her threat to Kenna.

"No, you're not going to show her the backside of anything other than your ass, soldier woman! She's my friend, and you and your government goons have done enough to intimidate us already. Now back off, or I'll kick your sweet ass right out of that funky armored suit of yours!"

Cooper glowered beneath her helmet and tossed her missile launcher to the ground before raising her fists. "Let's do this, you disrespectful little bitch! I'll take the armor off if you want, I don't need it to put you in line! You don't know the stakes here and what we're risking for you!"

"You mean, what we're at risk *of* because of your bosses!" Jackie snapped back with her own fists raised.

Melvin stepped forward. "Easy, babe. It's not worth it."

"You and the girls are totally worth it, Mel!" Jackie disagreed vehemently.

Kenna then rushed in front of the enraged young woman and held her by the shoulders. "It's okay, Mel, I've got this." She then looked the taller and heavier lady in the eyes while holding her from moving forward and engaging with what she was certain would be a superior opponent.

"Jackie, you just proved yourself, okay? This is not the time to jump out of the shell, though. I do have a tendency to run my mouth off, justified or not, and you sure as hell know that. We need to work with Captain Jacobi like we agreed."

"You mean like *you* agreed! Who died and left you leader of our group?"

Kenna tilted her head and gave Jackie that look she always hated. "Jackelyn, please. This is so not the time to settle our rivalries. I don't want any of us to have to die *at all* before *anyone* is elected leader of this group, okay, hun?"

Melvin walked over and wrapped his arms around Jackie's shoulders affectionately. "What Kenna just said, babe." He then kissed her on her cheek. "*Mis agradecimientos* for standing up for me like that, by the way. You rock, girl."

Jacobi sauntered into the boiling pot percolating before him and grabbed Cooper by her wrist. "Stand down, Private! Now! And how dare you throw a dangerous weapon like that to the ground, where one of these civilians could have picked it up and attempted to blow us away with it! We do not know them well enough to fully assess their character or mental stability yet, nor do we yet know what knowledge they may have with using real military weaponry."

"I was… standing up for your authority, sir," Cooper said in barely controlled frustration.

"Yes, I know, but it was still a bad call. And I had told you to be at ease about this before. And it's bad enough I have to deal with these civilians violating my orders. My people should know better, however. Consider yourself on report. And go pick up that missile launcher, for God's sake! Then get back to your position scanning for any signs of Experiment #2's presence!"

"Sir, yes... sir," Cooper said with thinly veiled reticence as she recovered her weapon and returned to her assigned position.

Just then, both groups were given a start by the unexpected appearance of Greymountain and Billy-Bob as the very unlikely duo rushed out of nearby thickets. Both Jacobi and Cooper instantly pointed their respective weapons at the two interlopers.

25

"Wait don't shoot Jesus fuck!" Billy-Bob shouted. "We, um, come in peace, and shit!"

Greymountain kept his bow lowered and looked Captain Jacobi directly in his eyes, despite their obfuscation by his helmet's visor. The two men were of equal height, and both seemed instinctively able to recognize a fellow combatant on sight. They instantly began sizing each other up as two warriors often do when they first meet.

"Holy shit!" Melvin exclaimed. "Check out that awesome-looking Indian, man! He looks like *another* action figure I once had!"

"And who the holy fuck are these people in the weird outfits, or whatever that clothing is?" Billy-Bob queried. "I didn't see them there before! Are those outfits some new kinda' gear so paintball players don't get paint all over their regular clothes or sumthin' like that?"

"Let me do the talking, Billy-Bob," Greymountain said with steely calm before turning to directly address Jacobi. "I have never seen the likes of that body armor you are wearing, but I do believe the firearms you each have are advanced military issue. So, you are soldiers, am I correct?"

"We are," Jacobi said, exhibiting signs of going at ease but nevertheless keeping his rifle firmly pointed at the formidable-looking, traditionally garbed Native American. "I am Captain David Jacobi, and beside me is a member of my unit, Private Leann Cooper. We're a government task force sent here to pacify something in these woods. And you are…?"

"I am Tim Greymountain. Of the Goshute tribe."

"From that reservation?" Jacobi asked.

"Yes," Greymountain affirmed. "But I am a warrior from a traditionalist faction of the tribe. And would the 'something' you have come here to pacify happen to be a large, gray-furred beast that kills people and resembles nothing that has ever naturally evolved on this planet?"

"You've seen it?" Jacobi queried with a start.

"Damn fuckin' straight we done seen that cocksucker!" Billy-Bob chimed in. "It killed my best friend! It killed Greymountain's cousin before that! And now, we're gonna fuckin' kill *it!* So, we'll all work together for that, right?"

"Hold up, you!" Jacobi ordered. "Mr. Greymountain, you say that you and this… gentleman ran into that creature, and both of you survived?"

"Clearly," Greymountain replied. "Is your agency responsible for that monstrosity?"

Jacobi hesitated for only a few seconds before responding. "Yes, I'm afraid. But my unit has been sent to deal with the mistake, before any more lives are lost. That's all the additional info you're going to get."

Greymountain glared at Jacobi more intensely but retained his cool demeanor. "That was all I needed to hear anyway, Captain Jacobi. I can easily figure out the rest. Thank you for explaining all of this.

"Now it's my turn to explain something. You now know that this monstrous animal created by your employing agency killed my cousin, along with another of my tribe who had family. It also killed Billy-Bob's best friend, who was a good man, as I had the honor of becoming acquainted with him during his final hour in this world. That beast doubtlessly killed many other innocents on its way to these woods after escaping from whatever facility you foolishly thought would hold it, I'll wager.

"I am no fool myself, though, and I will not let emotion get in the way of common sense. I know we need to work together to have any hope of destroying that creature. But once this goal is accomplished, if both of us have survived in the end, then you and I will have some words. And I'll also have some words with your employer."

Jacobi gritted his teeth under his helmet but likewise kept his cool. "Fair enough, Mr. Greymountain. I'll grant you that conversation once this is over. At least on my end of the command chain, as I will not and cannot speak for my employer. Now, you need to listen to me…"

The captain was suddenly distracted by a communique request sent to him from his second-in-command. The flashing red light on his HUD display marked it as urgent status.

"Hold up, I need to take this communique I just received."

"Does that helmet of his have a cell phone or walkie-talkie in it or some shit like that?" Billy-Bob pondered aloud.

"Quiet!" Jacobi yelled.

"I don't like that tone of yours none, military man."

Greymountain put his index finger to his pursed lips and then shook his head, indicating to Billy-Bob to show respectful quiet, and that this wasn't the time to provoke Jacobi and his other soldier. Billy-Bob honored the silent request with a right-hand gesture that indicated, "yeah, whatever."

Now free of interruption, Jacobi clicked the appropriate spot on his helmet and heard the very bleak news about had just concluded on the other side of the creek by this point.

"My God..." was all he said.

"Well, that can't be good," Melvin said nervously.

"Turn on your HUD's GPS and get your ass here now, Tee-Bone!" Jacobi commanded. "This situation just became a red alert, and we need to get these civilians the hell out of here!"

He then ended the communique and placed his hand over his visor in a gesture of frustration.

"What happened, Captain?" Kenna asked while taking her girlfriend Lynn's hand.

"One of my unit was killed by the beast about fifteen minutes ago!" he answered. "Sgt. Tee-Bone is alright, and he shot the creature, but he has reason to suspect it survived without serious injury and is headed here now!"

"Shit..." Lynn said while tightening her grip on Kenna's hand.

"Oh man..." Melvin muttered and began to shake.

Cooper reacted strongly to that news. "Grumby is dead, Captain?"

"He is, Cooper. I'm sorry. But we will mourn him later. You need to keep your watch on the perimeter!"

"I've been doing that, sir," she replied, "but the thermal scans and zoom lens aren't picking up anything. The vicinity is clear for now."

"You need to listen, Private!" Jacobi shouted. "Tee-Bone reported that this creature has the same camouflaging capacity that one of the other Experiment Subjects displayed according to a report from the base. It can evade even these upgraded HUD scanners while cloaked like that!"

"Oh, fuck…" Cooper said.

"Did you just say… this thing can make itself invisible or something?" Melvin asked.

"Yes, Mr. Garcia," Jacobi replied, "that is basically it. Cooper, pull yourself together and be prepared for anything! Including things your eyes and scanning tech can't see."

"Oh, c'mon, *gente,*" Melvin uttered while shaking his head incredulously. "I know this thing is supposed to be dangerous and all, but what you just said is totally whack…"

Melvin never got to finish the statement, as his chest suddenly exploded outward in a shower of gore. His heart, pieces of his rib cage, and what appeared to a section of lung spattered out on the muddy ground at his feet. The only noise he made was a quick coughing sound accompanied by an oral expulsion of blood. At the same time, his eyes opened wide and within a second they settled into a perpetual stare.

A second after that, the Fluffy beast de-cloaked directly behind its victim, with one of its large hands extended clear through the hole it made in the young man's chest. It then rushed into a nearby canopy of thickets at remarkable speed, despite its prey's entire body (sans a few organs) still being connected to the hind limb that skewered it.

26

"Melvin!" Kenna and Jackie screamed simultaneously.

"Jesus!" Cooper yelled as she fired an .83 millimeter rocket from her bunker buster directly at the thick growth of foliage into which the monster had just retreated with its prey in tow.

Her aim was true despite how startled she was, and the thickets exploded in a spray of shredded greenery and liquid crimson.

"Holy Jesus fuck!" Billy-Bob exclaimed as he jumped to the ground for cover. "Was that some kinda fuckin' rocket launcher that chick has? Do they sell that kinda shit at Shop-Smart?"

Jacobi likewise released a few rounds of suppressive fire towards the area where the beast retreated, while two arrows simultaneously followed from Greymountain's bow.

"Melvin! No!" Jackie screamed as loud as she could as a fit of hysteria overcame her.

Kenna and Lynn were unable to hold back their tears either, but they did their best to provide succor to their grief-stricken friend by holding her tightly. All three women fell to their knees at the sight of a young man dear to their hearts being so horribly and unexpectedly butchered right before their eyes. Of the three, Jackie loved Melvin Garcia to the deepest level of the human heart, and she remained on her knees in an inconsolable state of self-recrimination.

"It's my fucking fault!" Jackie screamed as she pounded on her own legs. "He never liked the games! He only came here for me. And I was so fucking mean to him about how bad he was at it! He only came here for me! Just to be with me! Even when he knew all I cared about was winning that stupid game!"

"Jackie, stop it now," Lynn said through her own tears as she again held her friend tightly. "It wasn't your fault. Melvin wouldn't want you to think that."

"It was my fault!"

"Jackie, stop doing this to yourself," Kenna said while wrapping her arms around her neck to provide support. "We can't foresee things like this. If you really cared about the games more than Melvin, you wouldn't have let him continue to play despite how bad he was at it, and you wouldn't be grieving so much now. You *did* really love him back, so stop hating and blaming yourself!"

Kenna and Lynn then noticed the tall figure of Greymountain standing imposingly above them.

"My condolences," he said. "I too suffered such a loss. Not in front of my very eyes, though. But Billy-Bob did. Maybe you could talk and console each other later."

"Thank you…" Kenna said as she returned to embracing her friends so none of the trio had to deal with the grief alone.

Jacobi and Cooper ignored the emotional situation going on a few feet away as they ran towards the blasted remnants of the foliage to look for whatever remains they could find.

"I think I got it!" Cooper said, despite loading another rocket onto her weapon just in case.

"We can't be certain of that, Private," her commanding officer said. "We need to find remains, or we have to assume it's still out there."

"But sir, look at all the blood lying around," she pointed out. "And I think that's part of a bowel laying on that pile of leaves over there."

"That portion of bowel looks human to me, Cooper. I've seen human viscera before, so I think that belongs to the young man the creature killed. And this blood could all be his as well."

"Fuck damn…" Billy-Bob whispered as he walked over to inspect the scene, his own shotgun locked and loaded in front of him.

"Captain!" a deep, familiar, and welcome voice echoed from behind Jacobi and Cooper.

They looked around to see that Tee-Bone had just emerged from the bushes several yards behind them, finally arriving on the scene.

"Thank God you're here, Tee-Bone!" Cooper said. "I'm glad you made it. I'm… sorry that Grumby didn't."

"I'm sorry for that too, Cooper," Tee-Bone replied. "What's the sit rep, Captain? It seems you saw some action here too."

"Experiment #2 appeared in a camouflaged state, like you warned," Jacobi reported. "It took us by surprise and killed one of the civilians under my watch."

"I'm sorry, sir," Tee-Bone said. "For what it may be worth, I lost Grumby right in front of me, while he was under my watch. These things happen under circumstances like this. But what's the story with that war painted Indian and that redneck-looking guy with the unkempt beard and checkered jacket?"

"That would be Greymountain and Billy-Bob. I am certain you can guess which name applies to which just by looking at the two. They're armed civilians, and they're here to help. We may as well make use of them in this situation, as long as they follow our orders."

"I'm guessing those three women are crying over the loss of the other civilian, sir?"

"That is affirmative. The young man was the boyfriend of one of them, and a friend of the other two, I believe. I understand their grief, but they need to get back on their feet and follow our lead."

"Sir, I really do think I got it when I fired the bunker buster at it," Cooper reiterated. "I mean, look at the damage radius here. It couldn't have found sufficient cover in time."

"We shouldn't assume anything until we've confirmed all that blood I see splattered around belonged to our target," Tee-Bone advised.

As if on cue, the beast known as Experiment #2, a.k.a., "Fluffy," suddenly burst out from under a pile of leaves it curled into a fetal position under to avoid the full brunt of the rocket's explosive force. Its skin bore several open wounds to indicate it hadn't completely evaded the blast wave, but it didn't appear to be seriously injured. The scar from the gaping wound left on its sternum from the earlier shotgun blast was almost fully healed and barely visible by this point.

And these signs of the unnatural beast's resilience horrified the group of humans now facing its fury.

27

"Fuck!" Billy-Bob yelled as he aimed the shotgun responsible for wounding the creature earlier in the day.

Greymountain jumped in front of the three women, who were still sitting on the ground distracted by their sorrow. He took a defensive position in front of them and armed his bow, ready to shoot off an arrow in an instant.

Cooper, however, was mere inches from the creature, and was taken completely by surprise. She still managed to point her rifle, but the monster swatted it from her hand with ease while grabbing her by the throat in its other hand. As if making an intelligent choice, it pulled her in front of it for use as a living shield from the weapons of the three men attacking it.

Tee-Bone pushed Billy-Bob's shotgun upwards, where it blew off a round in the air.

"You spoiled my fuckin' shot, you asshole!" the large bearded man hollered at the armored legionnaire in front of him.

"You would have hit Cooper!" he rejoined.

"Not my fault she done got herself in the way!"

As that went on, Jacobi fired a few rounds, only for each bullet to hit Cooper's armored back. The integrity of the armor held, and no bullets punctured her skin. Nevertheless, he knew the multiple projectile impacts still had to have caused her a lot of pain, possibly even inflicting cracks on her vertebrae.

"Shit!" Jacobi yelled as he chambered another round into his STANAG 150 round drum magazine.

Cooper yelped in agony upon being hit with the friendly fire, but she refused to let the pain debilitate her. She was a soldier to the core, and she quickly detached her Desert Eagle handgun from its place on her leg and shot the creature at close range in its neck region. The bullet penetrated far enough to send a spurt of gooey blood from the monster's throat, and it hissed in a rage at the painful wound.

Before Cooper could shoot again, however, Subject Two slapped the gun out of her hand and viciously smashed her three times against a nearby pine tree. The hapless soldier's visor shattered, and her helmet cracked in several places before the creature dropped her limp body and rushed off into a nearby cluster of juniper trees.

During that retreat, it couldn't avoid being hit several times on its shoulders and posterior region by the rounds fired at it in tandem by Jacobi and Tee-Bone. This time they knew for a fact that the blood they saw spurting out originated from the beast's own circulatory system.

Nevertheless, despite the obvious injuries inflicted on it, the creature still didn't seem fatally wounded, and it succeeded in disappearing into the distant brush without slowing.

"I know I hit it several times, Captain!" Tee-Bone said as he chambered a new round.

"I can confirm that!" Jacobi said. "But we still didn't take it down for the count."

He then turned and saw Cooper laying flaccidly against the tree that the fluffy fury slammed her into several times before its latest retreat.

"Tee-Bone! We need to see to Cooper!"

"Ya'll shoulda let me get a shot in!" Billy-Bob decreed. "My shotgun is wicked powerful, and it hurt the fucker before! And I'm gonna hurt it worse again for what it went and done to Hollis!"

The burly man quieted down when Greymountain put his hand on his shoulder from behind. "Your shotgun is indeed quite powerful, but it lacks range. Their weapons provide that, however. We need the help of these soldiers, and what we do not need is to antagonize them, let alone accidentally hit one of them with our 'friendly fire.'"

Billy-Bob rolled his eyes but again conceded to his new friend's wisdom. "Yeah. Whatever."

Tee-Bone quickly joined his commanding officer as he turned Cooper's body over. Both saw that her face, now exposed through the broken helmet, had been caved inwards by the three hard blows against the tree's thick bark. Moreover, shards from her smashed visor had perforated both her eyes, and crimson milky tears flowed down her face from each of the violated orbs. Three of her teeth were missing, and a trickle of blood flowed continuously from her lips.

"Captain…"

"Yes, I know, Sergeant. She's dead. And that son of a bitching thing *isn't.*"

The quiet mourning of the two combatants was broken as Kenna suddenly stood up and began shouting in a rage.

"All right, I'm off the sidelines! I may not be armed with anything more than a stupid fucking paintball rifle, but I'm not going to just sit here and do nothing! I'm going to help you get that thing! I saw what it can do, and I'm going to help you stop it before it kills anyone else!"

Lynn reached up to her paramour. "Babe, calm down."

"No!" Kenna retorted. "We need to do something! We need to help!"

The irate young woman suddenly stopped talking, as she was certain she had just heard a faint rustling noise behind her. The paintball-wielding para-soldier turned to see odd movement in the leaves scattered on the ground, which seemed to be moving in a circular motion as if to close in on them.

"I see it! It's over there!" she shouted.

28

"Where is it?" Billy-Bob said as took up his shotgun while Greymountain put a shaft to his bow in similar preparation.

"There!" Kenna said as she pointed in the general direction. "Watch the leaves!"

The four men behind her did exactly that.

"Captain, she's right!" Tee-Bone yelled.

"Open fire wherever you see the leaves move!" Jacobi commanded.

The two armored soldiers released a series of shots in the direction where they saw the leaves being disturbed but were unable to tell if the still camouflaged creature was being hit or not. Greymountain aimed his arrow with care but chose not to fire unless he was certain he would hit the difficult to see target. He had to be ever mindful of the fact that the supply of shaft projectiles in his quiver was limited; needless to say, he preferred not to have to rely on his stone blade alone any sooner than would be necessary.

Billy-Bob, who realized that the creature he couldn't see was out of range of his shotgun, began giving into his frustration and looked at the discarded rocket launcher that once belonged to Cooper.

"My gun don't got the range, but that bad ass cocksucker shore does!"

As the vengeful bearded redneck began to move towards the discarded weapon, Greymountain grabbed his arm in a powerful grip that halted the hunter in his tracks.

"I wouldn't, Billy-Bob. You are not familiar with such a weapon, and you may cause more harm to us and the surrounding wilderness than the beast itself. Especially considering you cannot properly see it. That is not a weapon to be fired blindly."

"I ain't gonna just stand here waitin' for that cock-smoker to get close enough!"

"That is exactly what you must do. That is exactly what I am doing. I want a piece of that beast as much as you do, my

122

friend. But we must bide our time. Your weapon's ammo is powerful, but you must conserve it for when it can hit the target."

As Kenna watched the spectacle erupting before her, she was determined to make good on her promise to be useful. Especially since she knew the fusillade that the soldiers were unleashing on the creature may not suffice to keep it from tearing into her and her remaining friends for long. She also knew the warriors' ammo supply would not last forever. So, she decided now was the time to act.

With a lithe, fluidic movement reminiscent of a ballet dancer, Kenna scooped up her paintball rifle and tugged on her girlfriend's vest.

"Babe, grab your rifle and get to your feet! Hurry!"

Lynn did as she was asked but remained baffled. "Hun, these stupid paintballs aren't gonna hurt that thing! Look how well it's been taking *real* bullets and arrows!"

"I know we can't stop it with the paintballs, but we *can* use them to fuck up its invisibility!"

"Do you mean…?"

"Hell yeah that's what I mean! Aim your rifle at the grass over there. Watch the leaves closely, look through the scope… and when you can tell where it likely is, let the fucker have it!"

Kenna and Lynn did just that, and a volley of paintballs were unleashed in the general direction they carefully scrutinized. As hoped for, several of the spheres found their target, and the beast suddenly found itself stripped of its biggest tactical advantage when its fur was stained with several splotches of bright orange paint.

The angry and puzzled beast shed its cloak, only to find its grayish-white coat had numerous large spots of orange added to it. Not only did that compromise its power of camouflage, but the bright carroty splotches were high visibility colors, thus making it much easier to spot when trying to hide in the foliage or at a distance.

"Good work, you two!" Jacobi decreed.

"Well done," Greymountain concurred.

After that complimentary statement, the Goshute warrior released his arrow, which embedded directly in Subject Two's left eye. The monster howled in agony but still wasn't taken down. It began rushing about its intended quarry in a very quick, zig-zagging pattern that made it difficult to hit.

"Greymountain managed to really hurt it, I think!" Tee-Bone hollered. "Open up on it now!"

Jacobi and Tee-Bone fired a few short, controlled bursts at their now clearly visible target, and a few punctured the creature's hirsute legs. That only seemed to slow its incredible speed a single notch, however.

Despite its obvious intelligence, the creature was driven by a relentless rage to hunt and kill the beings before it, as if its synthetically hard-wired DNA left it no other options for behavior. It was created to be a living weapon on the battlefield, and that was exactly the function it was performing to an exemplary degree. Against unintended targets, however.

With its best tactical trick rendered useless by human ingenuity, Experiment #2 now seemed to realize that going for a more direct attack was its best option. It now had to rely on the other advantages it had over its prey, such as its fearsome speed, strength, and resilience.

The beast's uncanny mental acuity then seemed to instinctively identify Jacobi as the leader of its quarry's resistance. Hence, the creature singled him out from the others and began rushing towards him.

"Die, you son of a bitch!" Jacobi bellowed while he shot at the hellish monstrosity as it charged him directly.

The captain's bullets struck as intended several times until its magazine was empty. The fluffy fury was more than willing to weather that hail of bullets, as it had by now surmised that the pain-inflicting sticks used by its prey had a limited output. It was confident that its thick hide bolstered by a similarly thick coat of fur could resist what projectiles were left in Jacobi's rifle, and this proved to be a well-founded presumption.

"Captain, watch out!" Tee-Bone screamed as the monster barreled into his commanding officer, causing him to drop his spent rifle in the process.

The extremely tough soldier beat at the monster's face furiously. This actually managed to give the monster pause for a moment, which provided the tough soldier with the second he required to shove his index and middle finger into the still not fully healed eye that was punctured by Greymountain's arrow. Subject Two howled in pain and several spurts of its blood shot out of its re-pierced eye socket.

Jacobi hoped to drive his armor-covered fingers all the way into the creature's brain. Before he could manage that, however, the furry abomination had clawed through the armor covering his torso and ripped into the fragile flesh beneath it… and then into the even more fragile internal organs beneath that. Not to be outdone, Jacobi managed to get hold of his handgun and get off a shot towards the beast's face. Due to the close range of its target, the bullet flew into the mouth of the genetically engineered horror and out the side of its face.

Greymountain fired more arrows into it, but soon found his quiver empty. Tee-Bone likewise fired several more rounds, only to have his last magazine run out of ammo. Most of those remaining bullets struck their target, but even that caliber of lead projectile couldn't penetrate deep enough into the creature's body to fatally damage whatever vital organs its bulky form contained.

The Native American's final arrows perforated spots that would have been lethal points on all large animals he knew, but they still didn't prove fatal to the monster they were fighting. The products of Project Hydra's Experiment were unlike any other creature on Earth, and the Goshute warrior was not familiar with the intricacies of its physiology. Not even an arrow in the eye could take the beast down, and he wasn't certain that it couldn't regenerate the lost organ and recover its vision in full if given time.

At the sight of the melee, Billy-Bob finally saw his chance.

"I got you now, fucker!" he shouted as he ran towards the monster.

Jacobi managed to hold onto life and keep his bestial adversary distracted just long enough for the intrepid redneck to get within two feet of it. He aimed his shot gun at the side of its hairy abdomen and let off a shot. A blistering hole was torn into the lateral portion of the monster's rib cage, and the redneck combatant saw small chunks of fur and flesh blown from the wounded region. He could also swear he heard its ribs cracking.

Billy-Bob managed to deliver another serious wound to the living slaughter machine, but still not a fatal one. The creature howled and scampered off Jacobi's mutilated body to charge in the direction of the large man who had again managed to inflict a painful wound upon it with that loud stick of his.

Billy-Bob knew he wouldn't be able to reload in time, but it turned out he didn't have to. Tee-Bone rushed up to the creature and shot it twice in the side of its head with his Desert Eagle. One bullet punctured partly into the side of its cheekbone, while the other managed to enter the canal of its left ear and pierce the eardrum. This caused Subject Two the worst pain it had yet to experience in its short life, and it turned to slash at its attacker with incredible speed and ferocity.

Tee-Bone tried to move back as fast as he could, but despite well-honed reflexes built up from hours of training he didn't quite make it. The monster's nails cut into the soldier's stomach area, and his body armor just barely saved him from evisceration. The fighting man fell to his knees and put his hands over his stomach due to the intense pain.

The sergeant looked down and saw streams of blood flowing out of the four serious dermal tears on his abs. Nevertheless, he said a silent prayer to the war god Tyr that his bowels were still inside of him and not spattered into a pile on the ground.

I always wanted my abs to be ripped, but not in this manner... he unhappily joked to himself as he struggled to hold in the blood and stay conscious.

Billy-Bob then rushed forward and slammed the hard, wooden butt of his shotgun into the side of the creature's face. He actually succeeded in cracking both its right cheekbone and send a tooth flying from its mouth. The monster swung its front limb and backhanded the man off his feet in retaliation. The shotgun flew from his grip, and he lay on the ground about fifteen feet away with the wind knocked out of him.

Subject Two looked from one direction to another, the sharp pain and vertigo brought on by its punctured eardrum leaving it in a state of utter confusion as it struggled to decide which felled target to charge and finish off first, Billy-Bob or Tee-Bone.

That decision was taken out of its taloned hands as Greymountain leapt on its back. He managed to get a firm grip by wrapping his powerful left arm around the monster's throat while simultaneously squeezing on its larynx and windpipe with as much force as he could muster. In his free right hand was his self-made stone dagger, and he began thrusting its business end into the side of the creature's neck repeatedly.

"Die, beast! Never again will you lay a tooth or claw on one of my tribe! Nor anyone else!"

The beast resisted this attack and jumped about furiously, trying to throw the man inflicting that constant flurry of pain off it in the manner of a mechanical bucking bull turned up to full throttle. Greymountain held fast, however, while his orange-flecked adversary likewise refused to fall despite the amount of its blood now staining the flint of his blade and the surrounding grass.

The creature soon changed tactics, however. It began rolling about the ground in a manner akin to a person trying to snuff out burning clothing, hoping to use its weight to deliver a crushing injury to the man attached to it. Greymountain felt his bones and muscles rapidly taking severe punishment, but he refused to yield even as the creature made the same stubborn refusal. Both hunters were determined to snuff the life out of the other first, in a savage duel to the death that would have impressed even the gods.

But before the outcome of that battle could be decided, a quite unexpected event was to occur.

29

Jackie suddenly broke out of her impassioned grief and went into a berserk rage. It seemed that was triggered by the sight of the creature at last being injured just enough that it finally began to *really* feel it. That sight also seemed to cause her pent-up anger over her boyfriend's death to come to the surface at full force.

"You killed Melvin!" Jackie screamed as she jumped to her feet and picked up her paintball rifle. "I'll kill you now!"

"Jackie, stop!" Lynn yelled as she ran after her friend.

"Oh my God!" Kenna said as she followed her paramour.

Jackie stopped a mere two feet from the struggling monstrosity and began bashing it over the side of its head with the butt of her paintball rifle. The spheres it projected may have been near-useless against the creature as a weapon, but after seeing Billy-Bob make his move, she was determined to follow suit.

Jackie made sure to aim each blow of the rifle butt against the creature's most obvious wounds. This included both the arrow shaft stuck in its left eye and its bleeding punctured ear just to the side of the first injury.

Subject Two's injuries were successfully worsened by Jackie's assault, and so was its level of pain. In a surpassingly strong flex of its muscles born of an extreme adrenal burst, the beast finally managed to throw the clinging Greymountain from its grotesque form. The Goshute warrior landed hard on the dirt several feet to the right, and he gritted his teeth tightly when his attempts to get back on his feet were met with spasms of agony that traveled across the breadth of his battered anatomy.

The monster then turned to Jackie and howled at her, opening its mouth to its full extent to make it clear what it intended to do next. Determined to give as much as she got, the heavy-set woman lashed out and struck her monstrous opponent in the side of its face with her rifle. She managed to hit the beast's already fractured clavicle, hurting it further.

While Subject Two winced in pain, Jackie screamed in a grief-fueled fury and leapt on top of her furry opponent, battering it relentlessly with her weapon. But how much longer could she hold out like that on her own?

It was a concern she needn't have had, since Lynn and Kenna arrived moments later and followed Jackie on the offensive attack she initiated.

The creature found itself under a relentless assault from the trio of enraged women as they battered its hirsute form relentlessly with a combination of their hard rifle butts and their steel-toed simulation combat boots. This pig pile ended when, with one mighty heave, the Fluffy Fury pushed upwards with such force that all three of its attackers were knocked clear from it at the same time. Kenna and Lynn landed hard on the ground behind it, while the third lady landed on her back several feet in front of the creature.

Jackie was stunned by the force of the landing. When the haze from her vision cleared a moment later, she saw the beast's demonic-looking, slavering gullet opened directly above her.

That was, unfortunately, the last sight her eyes were ever to behold on this world, as the creature lifted her effortlessly and sunk its teeth directly into her torso. Its frighteningly powerful jaws easily tore through her protective vest and into the flesh and bone beneath. As it bit down its razor-like teeth punctured clear through both of her breasts and crushed the bones of her sternum like hollow plastic crumpled in a person's fist.

Jackie Cortland let out one final gasp of air and expired with her mouth and eyes remaining wide open. Thankfully, her life ended mercifully quick.

The horrific Experiment #2 then turned its pain-wracked head towards the other two women lying on the ground several feet in the other direction. The monstrous abomination released what sounded like a hiss of delight in anticipation of finishing them off in similar fashion.

Before it could move more than a few feet, however, its severely wounded body trembled under the impact of Greymountain jumping upon it again. He ignored the pain coursing through his own physique like a constantly generated electrical shock as he thrust his dagger into the soft flesh under the monster's jawbone.

"Now, where were we, beast?" he said through a bleeding mouth.

Would his second attack be enough to finish the monster before it finished him, though? That question was almost irrelevant to Greymountain, however, as all that really mattered to the Goshute warrior was striving to carry out the attempt to his last breath. The obligation to put his all on the line to avenge the life of his cousin demanded nothing less.

Meanwhile, Kenna pushed herself back to her feet, only to fall back down again when a feeling not unlike a dagger being shoved into the back of her shoulder blade tore through her. Obviously, some bone in her upper back had been broken, and she was in a world of pain. Nevertheless, after the sacrifices she had seen others make on her behalf, the woman who fancied herself a soldier was still resolute in honoring her commitment to do all she could to aid them in taking the monster down for good.

The attractive Japanese-American thus limped over to where Lynn had fallen. Kenna had to get her paramour to stand up and join her, as she decided to recover Cooper's discarded rocket launcher and attempt to use it herself. She knew the weapon was quite heavy, and she wasn't sure she could lift and aim it properly with her broken shoulder bone. The intrepid young woman required some help, and she needed her beloved significant other to provide it for her.

"Babe, you need to get up! I know you're hurting, but we have to get that rocket launcher, and I can't do it alone. I dunno how long Greymountain is gonna last over there."

Kenna's eyes then widened in horror as she realized that Lynn would not be getting up to help her. Ever again.

When the young woman was thrown from the beast and hit the ground, her head slammed against a large rock imbedded in the mud. The impact shoved it clear thru the side of her skull and into the brain. She lay completely still with her mouth wide open, and blood flowing from her eyes, nostrils, and mouth.

"No... no..."

Kenna, don't you dare lose it, girl! Not even after this! Greymountain needs your help, or he's gonna die too! And then no one will be left to avenge everyone that creature killed. Including Lynn. Dear God, Lynn... and... and Jackie...Melvin...

Kenna forced herself to summon greater reserves of strength than she ever had before and succeeded in putting her intense grief on pause. The young woman's unrelenting will fueled the movement required to get her over to where she remembered the rocket launcher had fallen after Cooper was killed. Kenna found the weapon laying exactly where she recalled it would be, and she groaned in agony while lifting the heavy weapon despite the pain that shot through her broken shoulder blade.

Kenna quickly scampered close to the continuing battle, now fought by Greymountain alone. The number of bruises and cuts visible across the length of his body made it clear he wouldn't last for much longer, but he continued chocking and stabbing the struggling creature in every soft spot of flesh he could find as it continued its own intensive attempts to throw him off again. He knew he had to hold onto its neck exactly as he had been doing, for if one of its hands was able to grasp or slash him, it would be all over in seconds. And the same would occur if it knocked him off-position just enough to put him in range of its cavernous jaws.

"Look at me, asshole!" Kenna shouted at the creature as she forced herself to lift and point the rocket launcher at it.

The beast's attention was caught despite its struggle with the human warrior latched onto its throat. The grayish-white and now orange-spotted monstrosity growled with the intention of charging at her before she could unleash the projectile it knew could be fired from that stick in her hands. Greymountain forestalled that attempt by striking the monster as hard as he could in the side of its injured head with the thick wooden hilt of his blade.

"Fire the weapon!" he yelled to her.

"I am!" she yelled back. "Just hold your fucking horses, willya?" *God, please let me know what I'm doing…*

Kenna groaned in pain again as she struggled to hold the weapon and aim it properly… only to receive a literal helping pair of hands from behind. The injured Tee-Bone had managed to get back to his feet and help her use the weapon.

"Hey, remember me?" he said.

"Thank God…" she murmured.

"I'm thanking *all* the gods who ever resided in the golden realm of Asgard," Tee-Bone replied. "Now, listen. Both of us are hurt too bad to do this alone, so we have to work together. But we gotta do it fast, because the Indian has a minute left at most. Hold it up the way my hand is moving, aim it like so, and we need to hold it in place here till we get a clear shot. And we need to aim it just right."

Tee-Bone guided her every movement in accordance with his verbal instructions, all of which she carefully followed to the letter.

"Okay," Kenna said as she struggled to keep aiming the bunker buster. "But what about Greymountain?"

"We just have to hope he can get clear in time. This is our last chance. We can't fail to do this. No time to be sentimental here."

Kenna shed a tear from each eye and silently cursed herself before facing reality. "Yeah, I know…"

Upon seeing what his two allies were doing as he continued his own struggle, the warrior called Greymountain decided to make a final bold move. He summoned the last of his rapidly fading strength to reach in front of the creature with both hands, grab the top and bottom of its huge jaws, and pull them open as hard as he could. At the same time, he twisted its head so its gaping chasm of a mouth was facing forward, directly in front of Kenna and Tee-Bone's line of fire.

"Do it now!" Greymountain shouted at the top of his lung power.

"Now, Kenna!" Tee-Bone exclaimed in affirmation as both aimed the weapon and pulled the trigger.

The pre-loaded rocket whooshed out of the front of its mobile launcher at fantastic speed towards its target. Greymountain managed to hold Subject Two's mouth open until the .83 millimeter projectile entered its gullet and lodged in the creature's throat. At that precise moment, the warrior released his grip on the choking monstrosity and fell directly underneath its huge form.

The rocket exploded barely over a second later, and the monster's hideous head was blown to pieces. Its body hit the ground with a loud thump. What was left of its brain matter seeped out of the remaining lower portion of the skull to discolor the earth beneath and behind it.

"Yes!" Kenna screamed. "Tee-Bone, I think we *really* got it this time! Please tell me we really got it! *Please!*"

"Kenna, we really, truly got it this time!" the sergeant assured her.

"Please don't let it still be alive! Please, God!"

Tee-Bone dropped the rocket launcher and pulled Kenna to face him. "It's not alive. We got it. We really got it. You did good."

The stream of tears flowing from her eyes then intensified. "Lynn is dead! She's dead, Tee-Bone!"

"I'm sorry," the soldier said in the gentlest tone he could manage as he gave her a much needed embrace.

Because Tee-Bone admittedly needed the embrace as much as she did after the ordeal they shared, he ignored the stinging pain in his torn lower ab muscles to conduct the gesture.

"Jackie is dead too!" Kenna then screamed as the consequences of the ordeal hit her like a freight train. "And Melvin! Oh my God!"

"I know, I know," Tee-Bone replied. "Let it out, it's okay. But we have to see to Greymountain. Okay? You're a real soldier now, Kenna. You earned it. So... on your feet, soldier!"

"Yes, sir," she said through tear-soaked eyes as she followed him towards the carcass of the beast.

Kenna never thought she could feel so relieved at seeing a bloody carcass rotting under the sun before. Tee-Bone moved his hands against the side of the creature's body, willing to take all the pain required to spare Kenna from having to put pressure on her injured shoulder. He moaned in great discomfort as he pushed with all his athletically-honed might. Despite the limits imposed on Tee-Bone's strength by his lower abdominal injuries, the beast's huge form slid aside just enough to reveal the bloodied body of Greymountain laying beneath it.

"Hey, Greymountain…" Tee-Bone choked out. "Are you… are you still with us, man?"

The Goshute warrior remained still.

"Greymountain!" Kenna screamed.

His eyes then popped open.

"Thank the Great Spirit," the muscular Native American said to himself quietly. "Shaun, you and Marcus have been avenged. And… I have lived to tell the tribe what happened to you both."

"Oh, thank God!" Kenna hollered as she jumped down and hugged him.

Tee-Bone and Kenna helped Greymountain to his feet, and despite his own injuries, he too was able to stand. Thankfully, and exactly as he intended, the robust warrior fell behind the creature's massive body just as its head was blown off, so its dense form would take the brunt of the explosive force and prevent any shrapnel from hitting him.

The three then turned to see another form straggling towards them from the west, having likewise just recovered from having the hell smashed out of him. Billy-Bob Tyler held his left arm, which suffered a fracture of the ulna when he hit the ground.

"What the fuckin' holy hell happened…?" the pain-wearied redneck inquired. "Did you get that cocksucker?"

"The cocksucker is gotten," Tee-Bone confirmed.

"See for yourself here," Greymountain added as he pointed to the beast's headless carcass. "Shaun and Marcus are avenged, and so is your friend Hollis."

"Hollis..." Billy-Bob turned his head and closed his eyes in anguish. "I wish I was the one who done blown the mother fucker away."

"You helped deliver your share of damage to it," Greymountain assured the disconsolate man. "The most important thing is that the creature has been taken down."

Billy-Bob then slumped to his knees, still holding his broken arm. "Hollis... oh, Jesus. I was such a rotten friend. Now you're dead, and it's all 'cause I dragged you out here to prove you were a man. Well, you did prove it, you little cocker. But... why did you have to go and die while provin' it?"

The usually tough man of over six feet in height buried his face in the torn sleeve of his one good arm. Greymountain walked up to what he figured was, however unlikely, his newest friend and put his hand on the crotchety redneck's shoulder to offer both sympathy and empathy.

"Just as I feel I wasn't the best cousin I could have been to Shaun. I am thinking I could have spent more time with him, and I could have chosen to go on the scouting trip into the woods that cost him his life when he asked me. But I did not, because... allow me to confess. I wanted to binge watch a new TV series on Netflix that weekend. You are not alone in your feelings of shame and sorrow, Billy-Bob."

Several feet away, Tee-Bone finished wrapping an emergency bandage stored in the back of his armor around his sliced abdomen. That helped to staunch the bleeding until he could see a medic and get the wounds properly stitched up. He then sent a communique through his helmet back to Area 51 for an extraction team to come and pick up him, three civilian survivors, the remains of his fellow soldiers, the remains of several other civilians... and the remains of an artificially created monstrosity that he fully agreed his agency never should have created in the first place.

The soldier sat beside the grieving Kenna, whose inner strength kept her sane.

"I summoned help," he told her. "Good thing the communicator in my helmet wasn't broken during our tussle with Experiment #2. I'll get us all medical aid and the government will pay for it... and I promise the later debriefing will go smoothly. The remains of the creature will be disposed of, leaving no proof it ever existed. That will be good enough for the agency."

"Wonderful," Kenna said with a curt tone. "Glad I don't work for them. Doing that is on *your* conscience. Let's pray the next batch they make won't escape again. Or the fucking laboratory that made them gets shut down or blows up or something before it can make any more in the first place."

"I hear you," Tee-Bone said. "By the way, I know this is not a good time to satisfy my curiosity, but, maybe it is better to talk rather than sulk over what we just lost, and... well, I'll just come out and ask it. Those Japanese characters on your vest. What do they say?"

"They spell out the word *'Rasutogāru.'* In English it means... 'Last Girl.'"

"By that, does it mean...?"

"Yeah. It does. I'm a fan of slasher films. And a friend gave me that nickname not only because I'm such a big fan of the genre, but also because... well, I was usually always the last person in either team to be left whenever we had paintball war maneuvers."

"Um... wow," was all Tee-Bone could say as both he and Kenna began brooding over the sadly tragic irony of her nickname.

TRUCK STOP BLUES

Dustin Dreyling

30

Sherman's Alamo Truck Stop
Alamo, Nevada

The night was just beginning to submit fully to the assertive advances of the dawn in Alamo, Nevada. Sherman's Alamo Truck Stop was the kind of place people flocked to before they went to bed, or after they had just woken up. It consisted of three businesses in one, an all-night restaurant and bar; a convenience store and gas station; and an auto repair shop, specializing in fixing the big rigs that were the main clientele of the place.

On this particular morning, a few hours after the end of the late-night party that commenced every Saturday night in Sherman's Bump House Restaurant and Bar, the place was near deserted. The customers were comprised of only a few trucks and their trailers in the lot for the evening, plus a smattering of locals and passers-through. A few cars sat in the parking lot for the restaurant; their owners no doubt there for the town's best breakfast, were all parked well away from each other.

Attached to the Bump House was Sherm's Convenience, the twenty-four-hour gas station slash mini-mart. They carried a little bit of everything you'd expect at that sort of store. This primarily consisted of a nice arrangement of hot items, such as paper-wrapped burgers and burritos, and a full coffee and soda bar, all self-serve. The pumps outside catered to all vehicles, the large metal canopy that looked over the fuel dispensers boasting six regular fuel pumps, while four diesel pumps sat apart. Each of these had their own individual canopies over the pump area itself, and each one was spaced far enough apart to allow a truck to pull up in between each pump and fuel, while the driver stayed dry in the off chance it actually rained.

Finally, on the back end of the place was Rickler's Vehicle Maintenance Shop. Trent Rickler was a friend of Sherman's, and his resident mechanic. He had a crack group of guys in his employ, as well as his daughter Anita. She was a regular chip off the old block, and Trent's only reminder of his deceased wife, Imala.

They could easily fix just about anything wrong with a rig, and usually had the part in stock in an underground warehouse beneath the small but adequate garage. If they didn't, Rickler knew a guy in Vegas that could deliver right quick at the drop of a hat. For a price, of course, but that was business.

Rickler's Vehicle Maintenance didn't unlock the doors until 8 a.m., but Rickler's daughter Anita was lurking around the place already, prepping to open.

A short distance away from Sherman's Truck Stop, it grew closer. Tearing across the landscape, the thing galloped -- if one could call its odd-legged run a gallop -- at approximately twenty-five miles an hour at best, making good time from its former residence. It was hungry and could smell the food moving about the buildings a short distance away. The part alien lifeform was ready to burst, the hunger in its rumbling belly seemingly insatiable, but it knew it was being followed by humans from its escaped prison. It was not worried about this fact; however, it had enough time to prepare for them. It spotted the buildings and chose a place behind some large transport vehicles to hide and wait.

At the same time, a little further south, a black SUV sped up Highway 93 with six persons inside. Each one was wearing black armor fatigues, including masked headgear, and armed with some form of firearm or two. They did not speak, but simply stared out the window expectantly. A small screen set into the dash of the vehicle had a radar-like display tracking a red blip that was just ahead of their position. It was marked only with the number "three."

Inside the Bump House, Aubrey Miller topped off coffee for the old man at the end of the front counter before she walked back behind the bar. The truck stop's clientele was so varied in their needs that going back and forth between the traditional wake-up/breakfast items the more professional ordered, and the alcoholic, "let's-keep-our-buzz-going" mentality of the other demographic that visited her domain maintained, it was a wonder she kept her sanity from evening to evening.

The gaudy restaurant, designed with the intention of being a hopping dance club, yet remaining a 24/7 diner, was internally hideous in the daylight. Some of the older patrons looked horribly out of place there, like the old man at the end. The gaudiness paid off, however, when the sun went down, and all the colored lighting came out to play.

As a club, it was actually well put together, and people came from all around to get trashed on a Saturday night. Local music, mostly disc jockeys but sometimes bands, would play. The Alamo P.D. usually had their hands full on that night of the week, thus warranting the unusual number of officers that made up their small-town precinct.

Alamo was a small town, but on a Saturday night, the Alamo Truck Stop was hopping. Fortunately, and finally for Aubrey, it was early Sunday morning, which amounted to a strange collection of late-night misfits and early morning risers. Bought out by a slickster asshole from Houston, the truck stop had been renovated and reconditioned by the rich bastard before he turned it into a prolific, if presumptuous, pit stop on the popular Area 51 tour route.

This is why Aaron Salas and Johnny Kaufenberg were visiting the recently renewed truck stop and diner. Aaron was a single dad trying to make a little cash at the end of an off-custody weekend; and Johnny was a baby-faced, pain-in-the-ass who loved his girlfriends more than himself. The two cousins, related by the hitching of their first cousins, were always together. Johnny and Aaron had shared a small two bedroom with Aaron's girlfriend, and had put in time together at a local fire extinguisher manufacturing company. They were out in the middle of nowhere on their way to Vegas for some fun following some side work for a guy they both knew near Alamo.

The cousins rolled into the parking lot in a Honda Civic from the turn of the century. It belched some indiscriminate fumes before dying as Aaron killed the engine. The two men got out, stowing their smoking apparatus as they did so.

"Dude. Did you play *Bioshock* yet?" Johnny smacked his cousin as he asked his question about a decade old video game.

"Johnny, you know she won't let me play games," Aaron implored of his cousin.

The two were good friends, having mutually used each other to survive family reunions for literally decades. Neither had a sibling they felt such camaraderie with, so their loose but technical relation was treasured in a time of ridiculous values. Aaron and Johnny were, for all intents and purposes, like brothers.

"They're like competition to her or some shit like that," the slightly younger man exclaimed about Johnny's favorite game.

The cousins sauntered into the restaurant, glancing around at the remodel with raised eyebrows even though neither of them had ever been there before the renovations. Johnny pointed at the "please seat yourself" sign, and Aaron walked to a booth near the back of the place. This section had a good view of the pumps outside through giant, wall length picture windows at the front.

Aubrey arrived at the men's table, poured them both a coffee, and inquired as to their intentions at her table.

"Y'all want anything?" She didn't like asking people she thought were only investing in wake-up juice, but you never knew.

"Actually, Aubrey, I'd like the Twelver, please," Johnny said. He pointed at the menu as if the woman had no idea what was on the menu, but she nodded just the same.

"Bacon, sausage, or ham?"

"Ham, please."

"Toast, English Muffin, or Bagel?"

"Wheat toast, please, Hot Stuff."

"W-what?" Aubrey looked Johnny dead in the eyes and saw only sincerity in them. She floundered, off-put by the younger man's leering stare, before laughing. "Thank you." Then she sauntered off, her obviously inflated ego showing with every step. Aubrey was *not* used to flirtation in her dead-end section of life.

"Johnny, we don't have time for that," Aaron said sternly, his face dark and serious. "We gotta meet Lyle and his pack of dogs in an hour or so. Those guys are pricks, and I don't want to be late. If we fuck this up, they *will* kill us."

Johnny stared at him for twenty seconds, the humor gone from his face. He shook his head slowly back and forth, a *tsk tsk* noise issuing from his mouth. "I can't believe you got us mixed up in this, or that you had to say what you just said to me."

"What the fuck ever, man. I don't want to die. Why is that so unreasonable?"

Johnny leaned in close to Aaron over the table and whispered. "That's why you don't make deals with crazy, redneck survivalists, man."

"I'm out of options. I needed more cash to pay for my daughter's day care, her health insurance, her everything else. This job will be cake if we just follow the plan.

We meet up with Lyle at the address he texted me with, pick up the package, and drive our asses to Vegas. There we meet up with one of his friends." Aaron sighed before continuing. "Then, we pick up our money from Lyle and go home!"

Johnny leaned back in the booth, looking around at the smattering of people in the restaurant. He didn't *think* they had been talking too loudly.

Shit. Too late now. He felt like a fool, letting Aaron discuss their *entire plan*, most likely an illegal one.

"We should shut up about it, right now," Johnny said, making a show of glancing around nervously.

"Pfft! Are you shitting me right now?" Aaron had a look of incredulity on his face. "These people don't care what we're talking about over here! Dodgson! We've got Dodgson!"

"I don't care. Shut it."

Aubrey the waitress came back with the Twelver for Johnny minutes later, shooting him a fantastic smile that he returned without hesitation. She set down the main plate of food, then the serving of pancakes, and finally the holder of different syrups. The square of butter atop the stack of pancakes ran down the surface as she set the plate down, leaving a glistening trail of golden goodness in its path.

"Thank you, Aubrey," Johnny said, eyeing up the name tag on her left breast once more.

"Anything else?" The waitress looked back and forth between the men, inquisitively.

"No, that'll do it... unless I could get your digits and maybe call you sometime?" Johnny enquired. "I'm not from around here, but I get out this way quite a bit these days."

Johnny's eyes glanced at Aaron for the slightest of instants before locking back on the buxom blonde obviously submitting to his charms. She smiled so big he thought her head might crack open. Then she just turned and walked away, moving on to the next occupied table.

Aaron laughed uproariously at his cousin. "Ahhhhh! Ha! Ha! Ha, you jackass!" His guffaws turned to giggles before he ceased altogether. Johnny's face was beet red, as being snubbed was not commonplace for him.

Johnny noticed the rest of the place once again as he dug into his meal. The horrible combination of sports bar and dance club in the decor made him shake his head once again as he chowed down. Aaron had his face buried in his smart phone, scrolling with his index finger almost absentmindedly.

There were three old guys at one end of the bar, and a lone geezer falling asleep at the other. A group of four twentysomethings occupied a booth by the front window, while a couple sat in a booth across from them and two down. In the middle of the place sat three rows of tables running parallel to the window row of booths at the front. Seven people were spread out among these, their aloneness painfully apparent.

"Geez, this place is kinda depressing this early in the morning," Johnny said. He had torn through the pancakes and toast and was digging into the default scrambled eggs and cheese that came with the Twelver. As he happened to glance out the front window once again, everything went absolutely insane.

A giant black SUV roared up to the lines of gas pumps under a tall metal canopy with "Alamo Truck Stop" in cursive LED lights on its sides, where it came screeching to a halt. Immediately, six people who could only be described as soldiers dressed all in black disembarked from the vehicle. Two of these people ran to the back tailgate, while the other four took point at each corner of the canopy. Each of the latter foursome carried either an MP5 or combat shotgun, two of each weapon being represented by the quartet. They appeared to be looking out for something yet unseen beyond their positions.

While Aaron and Johnny both looked on, the two men that ran to the back split, the shorter one continuing to the fuel door while the other seemed to take stock of something they couldn't see from where they sat inside the restaurant. With no apparent issues, the shorter soldier began to fill up the gas tank.

Johnny wondered about the clerks working the gas station, and how cooperative they had been dispensing fuel to armed men who pulled up in an unmarked SUV with no questions asked.

"Guess they've got an inside man," he mumbled to himself, while his cousin kept staring out the window. "I wonder who they're looking for."

"Hope it's not Lyle," Aaron said.

The man at the pump finished up and hastily returned the still dripping gas nozzle to its holster, nodded to the man at the rear, and jumped in the driver's seat to start the vehicle up. The guy at the back stepped away as the SUV tore out from under the canopy and floored up to the restaurant's entryway, blocking the doors when it finally came to a stop.

People began to murmur about the place at a rising volume. Aaron and Johnny both stood up, each uttering different profane inquisitives about the situation outside.

They joined the throng of customers beginning to line up at the front windows to see what the hell was going on. The driver jumped out once more and ran to the still open hatch, pulling out what looked like a folding tripod for a pipe cutting machine and standing it up. The other man had followed the truck to the front doors and helped the first man pull out the remaining item from the back, which they attached it to the apex of the three-legged trivet.

It was a machine gun. *Like Blain from* Predator, *only bigger. XM214, I believe,* Aaron thought. He had a love of guns, something Johnny wasn't as crazy about, but he still accompanied his cousin to the range quite often at home. It was something to do, at least as far as Johnny was concerned.

"Are they being hunted by *Predator?"* Johnny's verbalizing of Aaron's thought made the taller cousin look down.

"Shit, I hope not, man," Aaron said in a slightly high-pitched, anxious voice.

The soldiers under the canopy all turned suddenly towards the building, the act barely registering to the onlookers inside before some huge *shape* plowed into the parked SUV like a wrecking ball. The vehicle lurched forward from the impact, crashing through the doors and windows to either side.

People fled from their vantage points as glass exploded everywhere, diners scattering in different directions like a scared herd of buffalo. The soldiers outside shouted in disbelief at the thing rising up from the mangled wreck as their teammates ran towards them from the canopy, weapons raised but silent.

A thick mass of ropy, cephalopod-like arms shot out, whipping at the two men by the machine gun, barely missing their targets as the creature stomped towards them. They abandoned the machine gun, running to the other four men heading in their direction. That's when Johnny got his first glimpse of It from where they hit the deck when the windows had exploded.

Standing roughly ten feet tall at the shoulder, atop three clawed hooves, the abomination seemed to have been made haphazardly by its creator. A tapering, pear-shaped body covered in armored plating that resembled sharpened exhaust fan louvres jiggled as the thing approached the soldiers, who stopped in their tracks as the men driving the SUV reached them.

The monster's tentacles thrashed about, the eight-foot lengths seeming anthropomorphically pissed off at the lack of prey within their reach. This was evident from the way they flexed and clenched at the regrouped team of soldiers. Two muscular, but slightly stubby arms waggled around in the air from where they stuck out in the front of its rotund belly.

Then there was the ugly creature's head. It looked like some kind of nightmare hand puppet the way its wide, toothy jaws came and snapped together on a neck laden with rolls of fat. Strange, hair like protuberances waved atop its head as if they each had their own gravity, almost seeming to blow in the wind from several different directions at once. It had beady eyes, pupil-less and glowing with an odd pink hue across a honeycomb pattern, and they seemed to be looking everywhere and nowhere at the same time.

Black drool coursed out of its mouth like the monster was slowly, constantly regurgitating; the vile saliva splattered on the driveway as its horrific source stalked towards the armed soldiers. It was waving its little arms at them, comically.

Just for a split second, Johnny could have sworn he saw the number "three" tattooed on the thing's neck before its slobber covered it up.

Without warning, the soldiers opened fire, 9mm bullets and solid slugs tearing into the beast, the mangled SUV, the remaining windows of the restaurant, and several people inside who jumped up to run away from the scene outside. One of the trio of old guys that had been sitting at the bar went down in a pool of blood as he tried to flee from the vantage point he and his buddies had taken up when the SUV first arrived. The other two dove to the tiled floor, eating the chunks of glass scattered about the place like jagged marbles.

Aubrey ran towards the bar with the couple that had been seated by them when they had first gotten there. Aaron looked back as a man behind him cried out in agony. A ragged bloody hole had appeared on the unfortunate soul's back shoulder, sending him crashing into the side of the bar before he could get behind it.

Johnny smacked Aaron's arm and pointed towards the bar, indicating where he was going. Then he began crawling in his prone position in that direction, where Aubrey and the injured man's female companion tried to help the wounded guy get behind the bar through the server entrance. Aaron followed, scraping himself up good on the broken glass as he dragged himself after his cousin, too frightened to look outside at the confrontation between man and the mutated science experiment gone rotten.

The soldiers flanked the creature, MP5s distracting it as shotgunners came around the sides until they surrounded it. The two unarmed soldiers at the vehicle took advantage of the monster's distraction, making their way back to the tripod mounted machine gun as it tried to focus on the men surrounding it. Under the metal barrage, the creature made a noise reminiscent of a wounded frog. Dark purple blood with darker spots resembling flecks of black gold poured from dozens of holes in its flesh.

Just as the two men got back to their abandoned XM214, the thing charged the soldiers peppering it with 9mm gunfire. The speed with which Subject Three closed the distance caught everyone by surprise, and the two men were torn to literal shreds in a flurry of movement. Stubby arms gripped and restrained them as a tentacled fury tore strip after strip of armored flesh from bone.

Dual screams of pure agony were easily heard over the booming retorts of the .12-gauge shotguns as the men behind the murderous thing finally opened fire, albeit too late to save their fellow soldiers. Midnight purple lifeblood sprayed everything as each shotgun blast tore craters into the monster's flesh and shattered its back plates as if they were made of ceramic.

As the monster spun on the men blasting it, the creature's cephalopod arms launched the gory remains at them. This distracted both shotgunners with a bloody mess of human entrails, along with bits and pieces of muscle tissue and bone. Then it was upon them.

The XM214 whirred for not even a second before a fusillade of ammunition spat out from the black weapon's spinning barrel. More of the monster's back plates fell away as the .223 caliber bullets tore into it. Within seconds, the seemingly cosmetic armor was destroyed, and the purple fluid-covered beast rushed the two men and their gun. Before either could pull their sidearms or even try to flee, the unnatural creation had swept up both men in its squid-like arms and clapped them together like a pair of muddy shoes. The hapless soldiers' necks instantly snapped as their helmeted heads collided.

31

"Aubrey, how bad is it?"

Aubrey looked up through mascara streaked, tear-stained eyes, full of uncertainty, at the customer who had flirted with her right before the monster ruined the last hour of her shift. His young face, with a few scattered chin hairs, actually calmed her a bit as she tore her gaze away from the bloody hole in her other customer's shoulder.

"My name is Johnny, this is my cousin, Aaron. Let me see his shoulder, please."

Johnny winced as the crying young woman next to Aubrey wailed her man's name inaudibly and repeatedly, which was absolutely useless in the chaos. His involuntary facial gesture caused Aubrey to notice the tear-stricken girl once more. She grabbed the girl and pulled her close, muffling the poor, wailing thing and moving back further from the downed man. She looked pleadingly at him as she buried her face in the hysterical young woman's dark hair and began trying to soothe her with shushing sounds and empty lies of positivity in their fates.

Aaron looked at the husband first. The unconscious, face down man's shoulder was bloody and raw looking where the bullet had entered and shredded his flesh.

"Not your average 9 mil, that's for sure. I know those were MP5's, I've played enough *Call of Duty* and read enough Chess Team books to know what one looks like," he said.

The sound of rapid fire sub-machine guns, heard alongside the excruciating sounds of people being ripped to pieces, abruptly ended. The audible voids were then quickly filled with booming blasts from the combat shotguns.

Johnny glared at Aaron. "Really? Pop culture references? Grab that first aid kit under the counter behind you."

The shorter cousin pointed at a small, red and white plastic case on a shelf behind his head, which stood next to stacks of disposable napkin loads for the dispensers. Aaron snagged it and handed it to Johnny. Outside, the shotguns were silenced, replaced by gurgling screams.

Johnny tore the case open and pulled out antibiotics, gauze, and a roll of wrap. He instructed his cousin to hold the man down and keep his arm pinned while he wrapped the bleeding shoulder as tight as he could. Unsure about the antibiotics, he just clamped the gauze down as Aaron held the man, who was beginning to struggle and cry out in pain.

"Hold him, Aaron!"

"I'm trying, he's covered in blood, you know."

"What the fuck are you doing to me? G'yahh! That shit hurts, motherf—!"Aaron's fist connected with the back of the screaming man's head, knocking him out again.

"Dude, what the actual fuck?"

"Quit staring at me, pretty boy. Wrap this guy's shoulder before he wakes up again!"

Aubrey and the man's wife just stared at Aaron. The former was shooting him daggers from her eyes.

"Don't look at *me* like that. If he'd have kept struggling like he was, it would've gotten worse. Then he'd have bled *more*. Do you assholes think that would have helped?"

Aaron crawled away from them towards the server entrance, shaking his head. He then risked a peek over the counter. Outside, the sun was awake and working its way into the sky from the dawn position under slightly overcast skies. The destroyed SUV took up a good percentage of the view.

The soldiers themselves were everywhere. Covering everything. It was like they were attacked by a wood chipper in desperate need of sharpening. The ragged chunks laying strewn about seemed not torn but *pulled* apart. Aaron promptly hurled all over the countertop. The flood of mostly coffee vomit cascaded across the shiny surface, flowing over the other side in a putrid waterfall.

There was no monster in sight. Nor any of the other people save for three poor souls cut down by the gunfire, with two of the center table loners meeting the same end as the old guy from the counter. Aaron looked back at his cousin's progress. Using self-adherent wrap from the first aid kit, Johnny had wrapped the man's gunshot shoulder up nice and tight, and even went around a couple times with medical tape to secure it. The women were trying to help him reposition the man against the shelves under the counter on the far end.

"I don't see the thing anywhere, you guys," he said in a controlled volume just above a whisper. "Just dead people all over the place."

"What? What is that, some kind of joke?" The man's wife -- she was indeed wearing a fat rock on her left hand -- stared at Aaron with burning eyes. "People are dead and there's an ungodly thing running around outside, and you're cracking jokes!" It was not a question.

"Well, I mean—"

"No! You're an asshole! What the hell is wrong with you?"

The married girl was furious at Aaron. Aubrey scooted back towards the front counter, giving the angry brown-haired lady room, and placing them on either side of the... *moving man?*

Sure enough, the guy was coming out of unconsciousness once more, already grimacing in pain and making noises indicating as much. His wife was all over him, kissing and consoling her injured husband like he was a sick little kid, not an adult with a bullet in their shoulder.

The man's agonized grunts became louder, as did his wife's comforting noises. It was as if she didn't know what had happened outside considering the way she fussed and fawned over him.

Aaron and Johnny looked at each other, concern and annoyance apparent on both of their faces. Aaron then looked back outside. The sun had broken through the clouds and shone down on the grisly massacre outside in a way the seemed like someone was trying to show it off with a spotlight.

Still no monster.

Then the screaming started.

32

Christian Merriweather was a trucker out of Illinois that had stopped at the Alamo to refuel his little bottles of go juice that advertised five hours. He also needed to stock up on jerky and gas up the truck, just as he did at every stop. At 6'5" and 300 pounds, Christian was a big dude.

He'd only ever had one-night stands in his life and most of those were on the road. Between listening to audiobooks and rocking out to whatever good song he could find on satellite radio, Christian was comfortable in his lonely lifestyle. He had a cat that lived in his truck with him, an orange tabby named Sigourney, or "Sigo." She was a well-behaved feline, and he even took her for walks from time to time. It was Sigo that was the reason he was even still in the convenience store, as he had been looking at the three kinds of cat food they sold there. Dry, wet, or good question. He ultimately grabbed the can of wet *Friskies*.

A loud crashing noise spun him around to see a torrent of some dark green goo pour from the air conditioning vent, with chunks of something *squirming* in the liquid as it gushed all over the rack of chips and onto the floor. An employee mopping by the refrigerated cases of soda was drenched in the backwash, knocking him off his feet. He began to scream, and Christian noticed he was covered in snapping, clawed *things*.

Little round balls of goo with half a dozen crab claws jutting out in every direction, the horde of things crawled up the poor bastard in a frenzy, ripping and tearing at his body and face with their razor-sharp appendages. Blood quickly pooled up around the man as he slapped and clawed in vain at the swarm covering him head to toe. Throughout the attack the creatures emitted a chittering noise that Christian would have thought cute on a *Pokémon* or some crap like that, but not so much coming from tiny little monsters as they ripped a man apart.

"Holy shit!" Christian backed away from the doomed man, and ran to the front door of the place, where the girl behind the counter pointed behind him and screamed.

Two people ran out the door as the trucker turned around at the pony-tailed clerk's finger gesture. He wished he hadn't. They had finished the poor guy mopping the floor and were already upon him. His window of opportunity had closed. As the mob of little beasts smothered and devoured the trucker, the biggest meal they had ever encountered in their short existence, Christian screamed himself hoarse trying to beat them off.

They seemed to be tearing his flesh apart and then the slimy part absorbed him through the open wounds. It burned like fire whenever the nasty things crawled along his body. His legs were quickly reduced to useless stumps by the tearing, dissolving attackers, so he pulled himself along the floor, glaring at the girl who had made him pause in his attempt to flee. She was booking it out the door like she had done it on purpose, looking back with a *sorry, buddy* expression on her face. He shouted several useless expletives about her nether region and her mother at her.

Christian reached in his pocket and thumbed the door lock button on his rig. As he finally succumbed to the devouring clawed goo balls in one last screaming wail, his last thought was the hope that someone would take care of Sigo.

33

Molly Barnes ran into the daylight like the devil was on her ass. She didn't know what the hell those things covering Dan the custodian were, but they ate him alive. They probably would have eaten her too, had that big, dumb trucker not paused when he did, her pointing finger making him look like a monkey who always does. *Monkeys always look! Better him than me, I've got things to do with my life besides working at a shitty truck stop for $10.50 an hour,* she thought maliciously to herself as she ran towards her Buick Skylark from the late nineties. The ugly brown sedan was being stubborn as of late, but she hoped it wouldn't be when she needed it to start more than ever before.

Please, please, please, became her internal mantra as she got to the driver's side door, unlocking it with the key.

Molly slid into the seat like a pro and slammed the door shut. About twenty of the little gooey crab abominations slapped into the closed window on the door. Stuck fast with their disgusting bodies, dozens of snapping crustacean claws clicked against the window in a feeble attempt to break the glass. She could hear them croaking like toads in mating season through the window as they kept trying to smash it.

"Haha, you little shits! You can't break that glass with those tiny things!"

Molly began to giggle hysterically at her realization. *I am safe in here. They can't break through that glass. No way!*

Then they proved her wrong, and Molly wished she hadn't been such an evil bitch to the trucker.

34

Ryan Kettleman was outside when he saw the cute girl from the gas station running out of the store with a panicked expression on her face. He was sitting in his truck, watching a messed-up sci-fi cartoon with twisted homages of Doc and Marty from *Back to the Future* as the main characters, before he went inside for breakfast. She ran to an ugly Buick and got in quickly. Ryan's eyes widened in disbelief as a wave of nasty things followed right behind her, some leaping at the window, where they began to hack at it with their tiny claws until the glass finally broke and caved in on the poor girl. Her screams echoed off the buildings as the torrent of living horrors filled the car.

Ryan rolled up his windows, hit the lock button on his door, and prayed like a horrible person that the things would be satiated from devouring the skinny blond girl. He gulped hard, realizing he'd be lucky if she weighed 110 pounds. Then he debated his options as the nasty creatures ate everything that had been Molly Barnes not even two minutes prior. Within seconds, he began to sweat, the truck heating up quick in the rising temperature of the new day. Soon the trucker was drenched and realized he was a fool. He hit the Air Conditioner switch and cranked it up to high.

The plastic vent covers blew off inside his cab as dozens of the vile creatures invaded his space to escape the cool air assaulting their tender, gooey flesh. The last two of them shriveled up as soon as they exited behind the others, dying on the carpeted floor of the truck, something neither noticed by Ryan nor useful to any of the survivors still inside the truck stop. The revelation, as well as five more of the goo claws, died along with Ryan, as the climate control system continued to pour the chilling air into the already cooled vehicle.

35

Anita Rickler hid in the third stall of the ladies' restroom inside the gas station, biting her quivering lip to keep it still. A large African-American guy hid in the stall next to her, probably a trucker by the looks of his garb: a ripped, sleeveless flannel shirt and a… well, a truckers' hat. The half Paiute, half Caucasian woman didn't care that the big man was hiding with her, just that she wished he wasn't such a mouth breather. It seemed loud as hell in the confines of the restroom, sloppy and ragged. By the smell of him, she attributed the ragged part to smoking.

His name was Mason, and he originally hailed out of Minnesota, something about a cloud. *Saint Cloud?* Whatever. She didn't know squat about Minnesota except for their sports teams and that Minneapolis was the major city. He didn't have much of an accent beyond "ya know?" And he didn't even say that much.

The two of them were hiding from the horrible things they had seen chase down Molly ten minutes before. She tore ass out of the gas station only to be overwhelmed at her car when they smashed right through the girl's window to get at her. From the bathroom window, they had seen the things move on to some unfortunate schmuck sitting in his truck watching something. *Probably porno,* she thought, then felt guilty for thinking that of the dead.

"A-Anita?"

"Yes, Mason?"

"How long have you worked here?"

"Not a good time, Mason. You can hit on me later, when we aren't hiding in the women's restroom."

As the truck stop's resident grease monkey, Anita had been fixing rigs with her father all her life, until he was stolen from her by a massively fatal heart attack not even three months ago.

"Don't take it personally. I'm just not going there with you while those damn things are out there. I know rifle fire and shotgun blasts when I hear 'em, too." She paused, thoughtfully. "Those weren't hunters shooting," she added with absolute certainty.

"Uh, right, okay then. But I'm gonna ask you later, because I think you're right fine, girl."

Mason's attempts at swooning Anita through the stall wall made her actually giggle in its ridiculousness and because she actually hoped they could talk later, provided they didn't die, of course. For some strange reason, she liked the scrubby trucker in the stall next door, repulsive though he was.

"Okay, Mason. It's a date. Just take me somewhere the hell away from here. Deal?"

Mason guffawed quietly next to her.

"Deal. I'm gonna look around for those fuckers, okay?"

Anita freaked for a second, almost screaming "no" at him, but realized it had been quiet for at least fifteen minutes since they had hidden in the restroom. She nodded unseen in the stall before realizing the futility of what she was doing and replied, "Okay, but I'm coming with you, and don't give me any of that macho sexist bullshit."

Mason was quiet for a few seconds, which annoyed her a little bit, but then responded.

"Okay, but stay behind me and watch my back, deal?"

"Deal," she smiled to herself, and stepped down off the porcelain toilet to the floor.

They exited the women's room and warily inched down the tiny hallway to the back-storage area and manager's office. Mason was about to carefully open the door to the storage room -- and back door -- when a moist, slithering noise pulled their attention to the front of the store.

The gooey claws were covering the main window adorned with a neon sign hanging by the door proclaiming, "I assure you, we are open!". The little creatures wriggled and squirmed in their slimy juices mixed with red liquid that had to be blood. The fluid had begun to run down the window from so many of the nasties. There had to have been at least fifty of them, probably more.

A barely audible "yipe!" escaped Anita's mouth before she clamped her hand down hard over her mouth. Mason just glanced back at her, an expression of concern on his face, before looking back at the little monsters covering the glass.

A deep, low bellow slowly filled their ears, rising in pitch until they could discern the direction it was coming from.

"What the hell is on the roof?" Mason looked quizzically back at her, knowing full well she had no clue.

The slithering sound returned and went away again so fast that when they looked back at the window, only slick, gory puddles and slimy trails leading up to the glass remained. The nasties were gone.

"Let's get the fuck outta here," Anita said, meeting Mason's eyes before finishing with, "pardon my French."

36

Aaron ran towards the Honda Civic with Johnny right behind him. They were making an attempt to get the car, pull it up to the front doors -- now crushed by the crashed SUV -- and to *somehow* load up the other three people and get the hell out. Just as they jumped in, Aaron behind the wheel, sirens and flashing lights roared into the parking lot as three squad cars labeled "Alamo Police Department" came to a screeching halt in front of the obviously blood-stained driveway where the remains of the soldiers *had* been. Now there was nothing but blood stains. *What the hell happened to all the gore?* Johnny seemed to have been thinking likewise and looked at Aaron worriedly.

They were noticed right away when the closest officer stepped out of his vehicle. The man's revolver was suddenly out and pointing at the two sitting in the running Honda.

"Freeze! Kill that engine now and show me your hands!" The mustached, dark haired cop tightened his grip on his .45.

Soon, four of the six cops were aiming their pistols at Johnny and Aaron, who had obeyed by shutting off the car and raising their hands up clearly in the dominating daylight that had officially taken over. The other two were scanning the perimeter of the gas station and restaurant lot. They paused at nearly every reddish-brown patch of pavement, noses wrinkled in disgust at the rancid smell in the air. It was the putrescence of something dead and rotting in the slimy black water of a remote swamp, mixed with something else. Something wholly unnatural.

Based upon the expressions on every one of the cops' faces, even with their service pieces continually pointed at Johnny and Aaron's squinting mugs, they could tell that nobody really thought the two of them were guilty of anything. Not the way their eyes looked everywhere but at them.

"We don't see anyone inside, sir," Gutierrez called out near the SUV blocking the entrance before the two men resumed looking through the windows, their guns drawn.

"Sarge, what the hell is that *stink*?" A short cop with crew cut red hair and a slightly darker beard lowered his weapon and covered his nose, looking back at Sanderson and Gutierrez, the two officers walking the perimeter and checking the scene.

"I don't know, but someone yank those assholes out of that car," the sergeant, a blond-haired man with two days' worth of stubble, said to the short cop. The petite officer nodded behind him to the next squad car, and the officers standing beside it.

The larger of the two, a mountain of a woman with her golden colored hair pulled back in a bun, ripped open the Civic's driver's side door and pulled Aaron out.

"C'mon, swizzle stick," she said. Next, the mountainous lawwoman barked at a second officer, another mustached, cookie cutter cop stereotype. "Get the other one outta there, Simon, and bring him over here."

Both men were cooperatively wrangled from the vehicle and walked towards the squad cars. Johnny, silent until now, suddenly pulled out of the stereotype's grasp and pointed behind the cops gathered at the vehicles.

"Lookout!" Then he was tackled to the ground, as Aaron yelled out in surprise from Mountain bun's grip.

Gutierrez, the only Hispanic on the force in Alamo, was lifted in the air by something unseen, his body convulsing simultaneously as a dark, ragged hole split his sternum. Bright red blood gushed out around the invisible thing sticking out of his chest. Because that was the only explanation that made sense. Something freaking *invisible* was jutting out from his body, lifting him off the ground.

"It's... it's a goddamn *Predator*, like the Arnold flick," the red-haired cop said. "It has to be, right, Sarge?"

"I don't know, Wilson, but *open fire!*"

The barrage of weapons fire split the unusually empty parking lot. Whatever had killed Gutierrez quickly flung his bloodied corpse at the sergeant, the dead man's skull connecting almost too perfectly with his commanding officer's head. Sarge's body went instantly limp as his skull caved in and his neck shattered from the collision of both craniums at such a speed.

Then the thing materialized out of thin air where Gutierrez has been skewered alive, bellowing loud and raspy at them. Its bulbous stomach had shrunk. A vertical scar, still raw looking with congealing gore coating the sides, stretched from what appeared to be its chest down to the nether regions beneath its stomach and triple-legged abdomen. The creature appeared more streamlined, more... *capable.*

Its legs were not that of a herd animal any longer. Now the reverse elbows of a canine or feline stuck out from behind each leg, a thorny protuberance pronouncing each joint. It stood up high on those same legs, raising the crimson stained appendage that ended Gutierrez. It was a praying mantis-like arm -- an arm that had not been there when it had first appeared -- but the business end was more like three thick needles bound together than an actual hook or blade. Each third of the spearing cone was covered in sharp scales, and each point stuck apart from its sibling by inches, making the weapon almost more of a prong than a needle. Blood ran quickly off it and down Subject Three's arm. The monster's head-wide mouth opened to the cloudy sky, and it roared.

The ear-splitting cry dropped everyone. The redheaded officer hit the dirt, clawing at his head. Aaron and Johnny screamed on the ground nearby, flanked by the giant female officer and the mustached stereotype, both flailing in vain against the horrible noise. Sanderson, Gutierrez's partner, was prone on the pavement just behind the creature, incapacitated before following through with his attempt to sneak up on it, a shotgun lying useless on the ground next to him. He grabbed at his head like a brood of alien leeches was wriggling around inside his brain. The officer's throaty scream was raw and hoarse, cutting through the creature's audible assault.

Suddenly, a shadow over Sanderson caught his attention, just as the roar ceased. The officer looked up just in time to see a clawed hoof slam into his face, ending his existence. The thing tattooed with the number "three" on its neck shook its leg rapidly in an effort to expel the dead man's head from its foot. This provided the downed humans with a minuscule chance to recover.

Johnny grabbed at Aaron and pulled him to his feet as the monster descended on the red-haired cop. To his credit, three reports issued from his pistol as the legion of tentacles flowing out of its body grabbed Sanderson and shoved him into its gaping jaws. The dual rows of death began to chomp spastically, almost cartoonishly so, as bodily fluids gushed forth and the poor man's form disappeared unnaturally fast down the beast's gullet, bones and all. It resembled a wood chipper with a pair of serrated, wind-up teeth for the feed tray and no exhaust chute... so far. The cousins looked at each other with shocked faces and made for the car again.

As Subject Three moved on to deal with the other officers, Aaron started up the Honda and floored it, tearing around the side of the building and stopping at the back door for the restaurant. The vehicle skidded a bit in the gravel-covered back area that was the smoking section for all the employees of the truck stop's three businesses.

Aubrey came out of the door, saw them in the Honda, and yelled back inside before holding the door for Lena and Aiden, the couple from the restaurant. They had finally learned their names before making for the car. The three ran up to the Civic and got in, running an optimistic word for the injured, hobbling Aiden. It was only pulled off thanks to Lena's major assistance, but nobody would hold that against the bloodied man.

"Go! Go! Go!" Aubrey screamed at Aaron like he *didn't* realize they were in the car, but he gunned it just the same, merely rolling his eyes in annoyance. They drove out of the lot, where Aaron turned to the right sharply and tore back around behind the building, ending up on a suburban street.

A few houses whizzed by as he broke fifty-five going down the side street, nearly running down a man walking his dog (who cursed "those damn kids" with a raised middle finger) and someone's cat before they narrowly avoided ramming into a house at the end of the block. Aaron cranked the wheel and veered left back onto what looked like the city's main drive, zipping passed a diner full of bewildered locals. Suddenly the world brightened as the sun broke through the overcast gloom.

"Dude, what is that?" Johnny pointed at the dark shapes coming closer to them through the quicksilver dancing across the uneven road ahead.

"Fuck. Trucks," Aaron nearly mumbled.

"Trucks? Like the Army?"

Aubrey leaned forward over Aaron's right shoulder, barely doing so in the cramped Civic. Aiden was in the middle, draped across Lena in the tiny back passenger's side seat.

"Maybe, except they aren't camouflaged or green," Aaron gulped before continuing. "They're pitch black."

As the obviously military trucks bore down on them, Aaron went poultry. He turned sharply once more, hitting the gas and racing down a northbound road. As they sped past a credit union, Johnny spoke.

"They shot past us, man! We're good!"

"Aaron, slow down!" Aubrey's voice warbled with fear as the panicked driver took his foot off the accelerator and applied the brakes.

He pulled into someone's driveway and parked the car. Aiden groaned loudly in the backseat, his wife shushing him softly.

"Well, we're here!" Johnny's quip was not received well.

Three of the four other passengers told him what he could do in differing levels of extremity, ranging from visiting Hell, to lewd acts with sheep, and even self-mutilation of the genital variety.

Aubrey just said two words. "Get out."

Johnny and Aaron both got out in a nearly synchronized fashion, immediately turning to push the front seats forward and set their traveling companions free from the back seat's claustrophobic clutches. Aubrey disembarked first, she herself turning to help Aiden out, right as the two men both heard the sound of revving engines growing louder as the vehicles they belonged to came closer. They looked up to see the black trucks returning, and fast. The sun flashed for a second, then the world exploded.

A massive force crashed down on top of the Honda, crushing the two people inside, along with the top half of Aubrey, who was leaning into the vehicle when the monster landed on Aaron's car. The poor waitress's bottom half was torn raggedly from the rest of her as the Honda's frame closed together on her torso. Her severed half flopped down onto the pavement as if it were made of rubber, and the internal contents dripped out from the impact to spill on the ground in a pile.

Johnny and Aaron looked up at the nasty beast towering above them on the ruins of their ride. Dumbfounded and slipping into shock like it was going out of style, they waited for their likely painful fates without taking their eyes off the strange creature. Its tentacular arms danced like nightcrawlers on a hot griddle as it seemed to gloat over its impending victory.

Subject Three pulled its new mantis arm back, its two original arms waving in excitement like Barney the dinosaur and struck. A spinning object connected with the appendage, slicing clean through it like a hot knife through room temperature butter. The severed limb fell harmlessly on top of Johnny, with a particularly bony joint smacking him in the head and making him see stars. The grotesque limb felt like it weighed a couple hundred pounds, but he pushed it off and scrambled away. Aaron got the hell away as well, despite having issues gaining traction on the gore-covered road before running towards the house they had pulled up to.

Johnny looked back at the scene behind him as automatic rifle fire and shouts caught his attention. The men who had poured from the now parked trucks wore silver-visored helmets and futuristic looking tactical armor. They brandished weapons that looked more like power tools than guns.

The monster was pissed. All its appendages, including the mantis arm stump, moved erratically while gushing purple blood with flecks of black as it stomped up and down on its newer legs. The front soldier raised a skill saw-looking device and pulled some sort of trigger. A clear, rippling disc shot out from it, sinking deep into the monster's chest, dropping three severed tentacles to the ground. There they writhed impotently for a few seconds before lying still. Subject Three took a deep breath and paused, with its mouth agape and a look of surprise stretching across its face.

A pained, pitiful wail broke free from the thing's throat, as the clear disc's entry wound into Three's chest began gushing more of the dual-colored blood. Its cries grew louder and more high-pitched. Then a second disc streaked through the air, this one horizontal instead of vertical like its predecessor, and embedded itself into the monster's tattooed throat. Its keening wail was silenced with a soggy squelch, and more of the purple ichor spewed from the new tear in its flesh.

Four more clear discs cut into the beast, one slicing through its back leg as the other three buried themselves in its main mass. Johnny, still transfixed from the spot he had scooted to, just under a tree in the house's front yard, noticed the clear disc that had severed its leg lay melting on the sidewalk to the left of the driveway. *They're shooting saw blades made of ice?* His brain tried to eat itself yet again as his gray matter slowly processed the new information.

The monster fell on its backside after awkwardly wobbling for several seconds on the two remaining front legs. The scabbed torso and abdomen split open, and dozens of clawed gooey balls gushed from their strange captor's body.

"Control squad step up!" One of the soldiers yelled.

Johnny watched three men with what looked like futuristic flame throwers take the front line and open fire on the goo horde. Three blasts of what seemed to be some kind of electrical flames puked from the weapons and tore into the goo balls. Almost appearing like liquid sparks, the prototype weapons erased the attacking innards of Subject Three. The downed main part of the monster cried out in anguish where it lay, deflated, on the pavement.

The control squad ceased firing and stepped back to let the acrid smoke clear. The balls of goo had been reduced to crusty charred crumbles where they had met the electrical weapons of the armored soldiers.

"Executioner squad, move up," the same unseen speaker in a mob of armored troops barked, and four new soldiers took the control squad's place.

Their boots made noise as they stepped into the expanding lake of body fluids pouring from the monster's torn open belly and numerous wounds from the ice discs. They each carried a weapon that looked like a military grade Nerf gun; the dart attached to the end of the barrel was bright yellow with four red wings protruding from the base. The three men and one well-endowed woman took aim.

"Fire!"

Four rockets streaked from their launching apparatus and slammed into the monster's fallen form. It screamed once more before evaporating in a blinding white flash, followed by a strangely muted boom that was more like a cork popping than an explosive blast. Johnny's eyes took ten seconds to readjust, and when he could see again, he scrambled backwards a little bit more.

The thing's fat, decapitated head had landed near him, its honeycomb looking eyes staring at him. Blood-covered jaws rested askew on each other, as the angle which the large, beach ball-sized head had come to a rest at allowed gravity to pull them into a weird grimace. Johnny started screaming, his mind finally breaking from the morning's events. Even Aaron calling his name as soldiers surrounded him with guns pointing at his face did not end his childlike cry.

A bitch slap with a rifle butt from the nearest armor-clad trooper, courtesy of the well-endowed female from the execution squad, shut Johnny up and turned his world black. But not before the soldier who had hit him made a comment.

"Little baby."

37

Mason and Anita waited until the black military trucks had rolled out of the parking lot before they had gotten out of the truck's cab. The long semi-trailer, proclaiming a popular department store franchise's super deals as being the top in the country, stretched back about fifty feet behind the sleeper cab of the tractor truck's business end. They had run past it in their attempt to flee the deathtrap, when Mason heard a cat meowing. Finding the doors surprisingly unlocked, and with both of them having compassion when it came to animals stuck in vehicles in the hot sun, the two made a move to at least free the animal.

Then Anita had seen a giant, hulking thing hop down off the backside of the gas station section of the Sherman's Truck Stop, and with an escaped whimper of an almost silent quality, she jumped back into the truck with the rescued feline. After a hand beckoning from Anita, Mason followed without even seeing the creature. After he shut the door quietly, the trucker turned and looked just in time to see the ugly ass thing seem to disappear. His mind came to the same cinematic comparison as everyone else who had witnessed this ability of the creature, but he elected to keep it to himself.

Next to him, Anita keep repeating the profane word for defecation under her breath. The thing was still there, as they could see it in the morning light, overcast or not. The monster rippled like water, and then even that seemed to disappear. Only when the light hit it just right did they spot it once more before it was gone.

The gunfire and screams began seconds later. Subject Three roared suddenly, the deafening noise hurting their heads even in the rapidly heating truck's cab. Then it stopped, and a Honda went tearing around the parking lot they couldn't see. The vehicle appeared at the back of the restaurant, where a waitress and two other people got into the car, with the male member of this trio obviously injured. Then the car peeled out of the lot, circling back around near where Anita and Mason sat in the parked truck, and took off down the first street behind the truck stop.

"We should do the same as them," Anita said and began to rummage through the cab with one hand, with the other cradling the young tabby, who meowed at her.

Mason took the cat from Anita when she discovered a spare key taped to the side of the old school external cassette player, likely circa 1990s. She inserted the key into the ignition and looked at her companion with uncertainty.

"Do you even know how to drive this thing?" Mason asked her.

The woman shook her head. "No, and I'm pretty sure we should just sit tight for a bit until that thing goes away," Anita said.

She turned the key to accessory and rolled down the driver's side window, which was facing the trees in someone's back yard adjacent to the truck stop. The warm air outside blowing in was a relief compared to what was in the cab. Not to mention that she and Mason weren't smelling all that great. Her anti-perspirant had quit working while she was hiding in the bathroom. And Mason's man stank was normal for him, as far as she knew, ashe had been fragrant from the first time she had interacted with him.

Anita also discovered that the trucker had messed up one of his wheel frames on the highway, thanks to a mean chunk of rock he had run over. Between the stale ashtray smell and his lack of personal hygiene, she usually tried to stay upwind of him if possible. In this task, at this moment in time, she was very unsuccessful.

"Mason, can I ask you something?" There was a little bit of honey in her voice, laced with sarcasm.

"What's that, Anita?" His eyes never left the building, constantly scanning the view before them.

"Do you ever shower?" She met his surprised look with a dead serious stare. "You fucking stink, my friend!"

Mason's bottom lip quivered for the slightest of seconds before his inner male asserted its dominance and his face hardened to stone.

"Not... not as often as I'd like, no," he said with obvious shame.

The trucker's big head hung down until his unkempt beard touched his chest. Anita instantly felt horrible but did not regret asking. *The fucker* stinks, she justified to herself before responding.

"I'm sorry, man, but it's hard to breathe in here, and I know it ain't all me," Anita said while giving him an apologetic glance.

Mason looked up from his shame at her, the sliver of warmth she let her eyes show doing the job almost instantly. His face softened, although the shame was still there.

"I'm sorry, Anita, I promise I'll take a shower first chance I get," he said with confidence, and offered his hand to her for a shake. She accepted it.

"Deal! I won't bring it up again," she said.

Then a dark object caught both of their attentions, as well as that of the year-old kitten, as it shot up through the air at an angle. Strange legs, tentacles, and a thick body registered in their vision, but was moving up into the air so fast they didn't have enough time to really see what they were seeing. Before they had finished interrogating each other on what they had each seen, three black military trucks roared into the lot, likely stopping where the bulk of the carnage had taken place with the local cops out front. Anita and Mason had seen soldiers with crazy helmets and strange guns checking the perimeter, and they had hidden in the sleeper cab of the truck, hoping beyond hope that they wouldn't be discovered. Area 51 was too close, and neither of them believed the government wanted them to know what they knew from the day's events. Not if they remained alive, anyway.

Before they knew it, the trucks were tearing past the large vehicle they hid in, much to the cat's vocal dismay. The dark convoy followed the route from which they had originally come, which was the same direction the little Honda had driven towards. After being sure the coast was clear, they climbed out of the vehicle. Mason stood in front of Anita in a fashion that made her think he was trying to shield her. She smiled a little inside, until a fresh whiff of the smelly man erased it.

Suddenly, the woman realized they were likely now expendable due to their observance of the morning's events. A mental list of places they could run to scrolled through her head like a vertical stock ticker. She was stuck with Mason, and vice versa, at this point. Her cousin, Dimitri, always told her conspiracy stories about the government when it came to covering things up, from JFK's assassination to 9/11 being an inside job, as well as UFOs and cryptozoology. Anita thought he was half crazy, and she partly believed every word he said. Then she smacked her forehead with her hand. Mason looked back at her inquiringly.

"What's up, little lady?"

"I know where we can go. Let's get that trailer off the rig and get out of here."

"Okay, but we need some supplies first. I don't know about you, but I'm dying of thirst."

Mason eyed Anita up and down, and for once she didn't really mind.

Ugh. What's wrong with me? Am I actually thinking about Captain Stinky here? Her chastising thoughts didn't change the unexplained need to stick with the large, dark-skinned trucker.

"Yeah, I suppose we should, but keep an eye out for more of those things." She thought for a second and added to her warning. "Or those military assholes. I'm pretty sure they'd shoot us on sight, given what we saw."

Mason nodded enthusiastically. "Yup. I agree with that, one hundred percent."

He made his way towards the back entrance for the gas station, Anita close behind.

38

As soon as Anita and Mason opened the back door, they regretted it. The offal stink of gutted animals hit them so hard, they both hurled all over the back walkway. Anita expressed some colorful sentiments as Mason wiped his mouth on his shirt sleeve.

"Dear God, that's horrible," he said.

"You're damn skippy," Anita nodded. "I think... we should check those dead cops for weapons."

The fear in his eyes, although not full blown, was very apparent. "What? Are you crazy? You want to go out front?"

"That thing is gone, and so are the soldiers. Also, I don't know if you've noticed," she paused with a concerned look in her eye, "but where the hell did everyone else go? There were like a dozen cars and a few trucks in the parking lot when I got here this morning, and that was maybe a half hour before that thing and its nasty spawn showed up."

Mason looked deep in thought, with a furrowed brow. *God bless him,* she thought, *but I can almost hear the hamster wheels squeaking.* He pressed his lips together in dismay before he finally responded.

"Either that monster got 'em, or the government did," was all he said.

Then he went inside the building. *So much for weapons,* she thought. Anita took a last look around outside before she followed him into the place that smelled worse than they did. The pair stepped quietly down the hallway, past the back office and restrooms.

The cat had begun to fight Mason's grasp of it, making mewling noises until he let it down. The kitty ran off ahead towards the store. It stopped dead where the back hallway opened into the main area. The cat's head flicked to the left, its eyes locking on something, and it hissed. The look on the little thing's face was that of abject animal fear. Then it bolted back to the door they had come in through and pissed all over the floor. Like a warning alarm, the little kitten with the long legs began to caterwaul, hurting their ears. That's when the stench hit their noses.

"What. The. Fuck?" Anita covered her face with her t-shirt collar in a mostly futile attempt to block the extremely organic musk that overpowered the smell of death and shit that had hit them when they had first opened the back door.

"I don't like this, Anita. We need to get out of here," Mason pleaded with his companion, trying to spin her around to go back the way they had come.

"Stop it, asshole. I need to see what the hell that smell is coming from."

She pushed past him and ran into the store, with Mason vainly attempting to stop her.

The woman wasn't prepared for what she saw.

The store was full of slimy, pustulent-looking sacs of what almost looked like... *snot?* They were attached to the ceiling on rigid hunks of the stuff that the spheres seemed to be made of. Her thought, while uncertain, was already convinced that she wasn't far off with her assessment of the nasty, gooey spheres of *whatthefuckever* they were. Or what was probably inside them.

While they didn't have any crustacean claws, they *did* look identical to the tiny, murderous balls of goo they had seen take out Molly earlier. Anita looked down and saw the remnants of the unlucky few who didn't make it out of the store before the things attacked. They would have to be identified by teeth. The thought made her stomach turn horribly in on itself.

There was a muted, muffled crunching noise, coming from the farthest snot ball from where they were situated, and Anita's hair stood on end. *It's waking up.*

"We really need to get out of here, honey," Mason said as he grabbed the woman's arm and tried to gently steer her back in the opposite direction. She stubbornly tugged out of his grasp.

"Don't call me 'honey,'" Anita griped as a second and a third sphere began to move.

The latter... *egg -- it's a fucking egg --* was getting poked at by something on its inside. With a wet tearing sound, an armored

173

pinching claw the size of a large dog broke out into the world, snapping away so fast that it appeared as if it was running out of time to do so. Mason shouted in surprise, making Anita flinch, and waking up two more of the things in the eggs. Soon, all five of them were shaking and tearing, as multiple chitinous claws carved out escape paths for the things inside.

When Mason saw inside the egg whose inhabitant was closest to freedom, he almost lost control of his bladder. The big Minnesota man grabbed his smaller companion, threw her up over his shoulder despite her protests and punches, and ran. The trucker didn't stop running until they got back to the rig. He flung open the passenger side, threw Anita in the seat as gingerly as he could, given the frantic way he was moving, and ran to the driver's side.

As soon as he opened the door, the cat ran out from under the truck, nearly scaring the shit out of him as the feline meowed angrily and jumped up in the cab. Anita was swearing at him from the passenger's' seat but was making no attempt to move from where she sat. In fact, she buckled up and urged him to hurry. Mason got up into the truck and slammed the door shut, silencing the annoying buzzer that had been insistent that he had left the key in the ignition.

"Shit! We never took the trailer off!" Anita shouted in the cramped confines.

Mason laughed. "That's okay, I do this for a living, remember?"

He started up the rig right away, the diesel engine sounding healthy, like a giant purring cat. Mason checked everything, including the mirrors; once he seemed satisfied, he looked over at Anita, the cat already curled up in her lap.

"Okay, here we go!"

The truck and trailer pulled away from the parking spot and up onto Highway 93. He turned right and headed south, towards Vegas. Mason's brother, Nathan, lived in the outskirts of the city and owned almost a hundred acres just north of the City of Lights. They could hole up there and figure out their next move. Anita was all for it, punching it into the GPS while stroking the cat's fur with her free hand.

Before they had left Sherman's, neither of them had noticed the round, snot-like globs stuck to the back of the outside of the cab. As the truck tore down the highway towards Sin City, the globs began to pulse, growing a little larger on every tenth beat or so. Inside, growing things pushed against the round walls of their mucous prisons. Things that were getting hungry.

Inside the cab, ten miles down the road, Anita finally began to let go, to allow herself to feel optimistic. They hadn't even seen another vehicle since leaving Alamo, which set off all sorts of flags in her head, but she ignored them all so desperate was she to escape from the crap they had just been through. If they hadn't been silenced by now, maybe they'd be okay. Maybe the government didn't know about her and Mason. Maybe they'd be fine. Maybe...

The first of the eggs on the back of the truck, now two feet in diameter, began to hatch.

39

Twenty-four hours later, both Johnny and Aaron woke up inside an old automobile, a Crown Victoria from the eighties. They were dressed only in their underwear, with no means of identification or currency of any kind. They had no memory of the day before, nor any clue where they were. After driving east for twenty minutes, they came upon a road sign with a name they recognized:

Las Vegas 112 Miles

"Lost Wages, here we come," a mentally exhausted Johnny yelled with half-assed enthusiasm, causing Aaron to chuckle. "I sure hope Lyle isn't too pissed we stood him up."

"He'll be fine. He told me if we didn't meet him in time, he had some other guys lined up." Aaron paused before continuing. "Although I'm thinking our business arrangements are finished. But, we have more important things to worry about right now."

He gestured to their lack of clothes with a look back and forth between them. "We can stop by my friend Nate's house, just outside of Vegas. He's got a place with a lot of land. He'll hook us up with clothes and stuff. He owes me," Aaron said, confidently. "Everything will be fine, man. You'll see."

THE DEVIL AND THE CORAL QUEEN

Alex Dumitru

40

Eben Yoshida didn't want to do this part. However, he'd been given very little choice in the matter. It wasn't like he was an expert in interrogation. He didn't specialize in the extraction of sensitive material from the unwilling, or even in getting someone to talk to him at parties. Indeed, in his nearly sixty years, he had never particularly excelled at the social niceties in any setting. If he'd had his way, any of this job could have been handed to someone else. But he rarely did. Not anymore.

He adjusted his lab coat as he walked into the chamber. A bank of audio equipment, video monitoring screens, and analytical printouts sat in front of a ballistic glass partition that peered out into darkness. It reminded Eben of an empty aquarium, which sent a repressed shudder through his spindly frame. He nervously ran a hand through longish graying hair. Agent Hayes was already at her station along the bank of equipment and looked at him, arching an eyebrow. *Well?* It seemed to say. *What are we waiting for?*

Eben sat down next to the monitor that displayed a thermal image into the chamber beyond. Based on that reading, the subject appeared to be alright. He sighed.

"Problem, doctor?" Hayes said.

Eben looked up. "I'm just... was just thinking how you guys don't really need me for this part."

"Maybe not," Hayes conceded. "At this stage of the game your input is... well, academic. But they think your insight into Experiment Five will help with the analysis of the testimony we're gathering here."

"They do, huh?" Eben sighed again. Hayes swiveled in her chair, looking more directly at him instead of the sidelong glances. She was intense, like a focused laser had been housed in a slim African-American frame. Eben didn't like the weight of that beam on him one bit. He'd felt it far too often working for this project, from top brass that wanted the results he'd always been able to provide, no matter what.

"They do," Hayes said. "I do." The dual statement hung in the air between them for a moment. Then, Eben nodded.

"Let's get started then…" he said.

Eben leaned forward and flipped a switch next to the silver neck of a microphone. A speaker next to it, an audio feed into the room beyond, hummed with barely audible breathing.

"We're ready to begin," Eben said. For a long second, there was silence. Then…

"…Hello?" The voice came through the speaker in a tinny squeak.

"Please don't be alarmed," Eben said. "We aren't going to hurt you. We just want to get our facts straight, okay?"

"Why can't we turn some lights on in here, huh?"

"Please, let's just start, shall we?" Eben said. *Nice one, Yoshida. There's that charm that made you so good with the ladies.*

"What do you want to know?" the voice said.

"Whatever you can tell me about what happened to you on the Coral Queen…"

CORAL QUEEN INCIDENT REPORT
SURVIVOR TESTIMONY TRANSCRIPT
NAME: LEANN MARSH
AGE: 32
STATUS: PASSENGER
RECORDING COMMENCED 0930 HOURS
LEANN:

I wasn't supposed to end up alone.

Sorry, that probably makes me sound so self-pitying. But it's true. I was never supposed to end up on that boat all by myself. Well, me and a couple hundred other people. But you get what I mean. When you go on a big cruise like that, it's either families or couples. Anyone single is either a creep or a sad-sack like me. But it was supposed to be me and Karen. That bitch.

Sleeps around on me with that cow from her firm, and what does she get as a reward? She gets to dodge the bullet of this nightmare. It isn't fair.

(sighs)

Anyway. Where should I start?

INTERVIEWER:
Wherever you feel appropriate. Where did you depart from?

LEANN:
Miami. Was glad to get out of there and get out on the ocean. I thought it would have been fun to stay in the city for a little while, but by the time the Queen was departing I was done with it. More old people than you'd think. Hot, noisy. And like I said, no one to enjoy it with.

But honestly, I didn't like the ship much better. I won't lie. I'd probably get in more trouble for lying to the FBI if I did, right? Wait? Are you guys FBI? Or like CIA? ...NSA? Homeland Security? Like seriously, who handles this? Monsters? This whole thing, man--

INTERVIEWER:
Please, just stick to the events that occurred on the voyage, uhm... ma'am.

LEANN:
Oh, okay. Sorry. Again. I guess, well... for me the first thing was my stateroom. It was really close to the engine room, or something mechanical, I don't know. Was way down in the guts of things, took me forever to find it. And it was just noisy for a such a little place. All I could hear in there was the rumbling and grumbling of this ship, and it sounded like living next to a giant washing machine that was always running.

But that was where I think I heard it the first time.

I was unwinding, first night. Don't worry, I'll get to the second night, I'm just... just not ready yet, ok? Anyway. I was a little drunk. Well. Pretty drunk. And I'd spent a decent portion of the time in the stateroom in that cramped, stinky little bathroom for one reason or another, y'know? And I was laying on the bed, kinda just feeling equal parts seasick, sorry for myself, and generally like I was going to die, when I heard this sort of... keening noise? I don't really know how to describe it, but there was this sort of wail, coming from inside the wall that made all the damn noise, and it was like nothing else I've ever heard in my whole life, let alone on a cruise ship. Not that I've been on a bunch of them, but still. It was so... sad. Like it was the most lonely thing in the world. Maybe I was projecting, right? But still, it had this quality like a lost puppy or a mourner. And it didn't sound mechanical, so it stood out even more. To me anyway.

      (pause)

My god, do you think that's why it did all this? Because it was lonely? Jesus, get a Facebook account, don't dismember and disfigure a couple hundred people.

INTERVIEWER:

So, you think you heard it, the first night? Was it trying to communicate?

LEANN:

… No. No, I don't think it was trying to communicate. Not in any meaningful way. I mean the first night? It was probably only just getting started on what it was working on down there, the little performance piece it was putting together.

No, you wanna know what I think? I think it was making that noise hoping someone would come looking for it. Y'know how cats meow? They do it to imitate humans, but this article I read says that listening to a cat meow fires off the same trigger in the brain a person has when they hear a baby crying, it makes you want to find them and help them. Explains crazy cat ladies, right? A couple or twelve fur babies to sub in for a bunch of rug rats that either left or never happened in the first place? So, this noise… this sad, sad lonely noise. I mean, I almost got up and went looking. But I was feeling like such warmed over hell I never did. After going and making the bathroom that much more stinky, I'd practically forgotten about the noise. It had stopped anyway, so I didn't really give it another thought. Just passed out.

Now I think about it, it probably got what it was looking for, so why make all that fuss anyway? Listen, you mind if we take a little break before I get into the next part? I just sorta… I need to get myself together.

INTERVIEWER:

Yes, that's alright. We can resume this later. Would you mind, um… could you let one of the others know we'd like to talk to them?

LEANN:

Yeah, I'll try.

RECORDING ENDS

41

Eben cradled his head in his hands. It made a chaotic sort of sense, but he still needed to get some other pieces. He felt the laser beam of Hayes on him again and looked over.

"What?"

"Is Miss Marsh correct? Subject Five? Did it implement that kind of tactic when it hunted?"

"Five had this knack for drawing things out, but not like that. Its hunting and combat capabilities were a secondary thing anyway; we weren't trying to exploit those talents the way some of the other projects were. What we had in mind were the intricacies of how one of the base species used in the gene-splicing communicated."

"Right, so you don't know. Gotcha. Better question: How the hell did it get on a boat? To the Gulf of Mexico even? The subjects escaped in Nevada, so how did it cross the damn desert?"

Eben smiled for the first time since entering the chamber.

"Just because it was primarily an aquatic species doesn't mean it couldn't stand a little heat and dry air. Octopi have been known to make overland journeys for a short time, and of course they are canny problem solvers. Five had a little bit of octopus in him, along with everything else. Along with his abilities to gather information from host creatures, my guess is he hitched a ride on the bottom of a semi trailer once he knew what they did, followed a way to the sea, and started looking for food. And information."

"Which did it like more, you think?" Hayes asked.

Eben smiled wider. "Oh, he loved both."

CORAL QUEEN INCIDENT REPORT
SURVIVOR TESTIMONY TRANSCRIPT
NAME: MIKE ERIKSON
AGE: 27
STATUS: CREW
RECORDING COMMENCED 1022 HOURS

MIKE:

Everyone cheats. That's nothin' new. Believe me, everyone thinks they know how, everyone has a system, but everybody cheats. The real assholes are the ones who act like they frickin' invented it. And man, the later it gets in the casino, the more they start thinking that the fourth martini just gave them the edge they needed to conquer that slot machine; or worse, outsmart a dealer like yours truly.

Honestly, this job sucks. The pay is lousy, the hours are worse, and then there's all the co-workers, if you can call 'em that. More than two thirds of them from countries I can't pronounce and the other third, Americans like me? Hell, you think I sound cynical? I only been on the Queen a year, I'm a sweetheart. Some of em, man, I'm glad to see em go. Get eaten by some sort of sea monster... hey, good riddance. Less time to chap my ass in the gullet of some fuckin' octopus.

(laughs)

INTERVIEWER:

Please stick to the events you were involved with, Mr. Erikson.

MIKE:

Right, whatever. So, the best way to describe working on the Queen is you work hard, you play hard, you work harder, then you play harder, you die a little inside, then you repeat that. Every morning is Monday morning. You gotta find time to unwind somehow, and my preferred method was with the ladies. But of course, that brings me back to my point that everybody cheats.

When the thing happened, I was in my room. More specifically, the shower. Believe me, it wasn't that big a difference, your shower curtain is always trying to get to know your biblically in there. If you try to turn around you could accidentally knock your door open, know what I mean? But it was all mine, which was rare enough, and made me kinda popular in the ways I wanted. I was finally off shift and expecting any second for either Vivica, maybe Stephanie, to come by with a little grass and a desire to party. Getting it on with the other crew members, it's really the only way to stay sane on that fuckin'barge. Relations with the guests is strictly prohibited, and honestly, why bother? Only three types on a cruise anyway: Newlyweds, Over-Feds, and Nearly-Deads.

Anyway, I didn't think nothin' of it, hearing my door open. Knew I was in for a good time hearing someone come in, far as I was concerned. I heard giggling, then my name. Tammi. Nice. She wouldn't be bringing any smoke, but she liked booze and she was, uh… let's say acrobatic.

I told her to give me just a second, and I go reaching for my towel. I hear the door open again. Tammi makes this weird little squeak noise. I finally turn all the way around, and for a second, I don't know what the hell I'm looking at. I think it's the water in my eyes for a second, and I wipe my face off real quick with the towel, but then I can see it's not me. The air around Tammi, it's gone all weird and she's standing there with this look like she don't know what's happening, but the way she's standing it's like she's propped up. And this shimmer around her, like she's out of focus or I'm looking at her through a Coke bottle. It's still there for a second, then it goes away.

And I swear to Christ I wish it hadn't. It wasn't even all in the room I don't think. Just these long arms, like big snakes wrapped up around her, all squeezing down on her. I just… I freeze up, you know? And behind her I can see these eyes, these awful red eyes that are like a foot apart and just staring at me outta the hall. Then she's swept out of there and for a second I think it's running off with her. And here I am with a towel in one hand and my dick in the other… what am I supposed to do, go save her? Fuck that.

But I realize pretty quick it ain't leavin', it's just… repositioning, and then I'm all wrapped up too. I don't remember all that clear what happened next, it was all really fast. But we were in the dark when I came to my senses.

And this big… just this friggin' *maw* is hanging over me and I can't move. I can't move. I'm a big guy and it has me pinned with these suckers like I'm not even there. And that mouth, and all the teeth… it's getting closer and I think this is it, it's gonna eat me, my life is a horror movie, joke's on you, Mike. But turns out it's worse. This… this stuff starts dripping out, and it hits my leg.

I've never felt pain like that before. Just the sheer… it was almost cold, y'know? That's how hot it was. Least it felt hot. Either way, it burned. And I watched it spray this crap down and it just ate through my leg like piss through snow. I try to scream, but all that comes out is this tea-kettle noise and my mouth gets covered by another rope of muscle. All I can do it watch at it moves to the next one.

(long pause, heavy breathing)

I was, uh… I must have been in shock by the time it came up for my arms. And the whole time, as I'm drifting away into this kind of haze, I'm thinking *why*? Why is it doing this? What the hell is the point? Shouldn't it just eat me? Then it flips me over and I'm nose-up to the cold tile and all this weight settles on me, and I think for a second that the joke gets worse and the thing is chopping me up and now we're gonna *party*. But that's when I feel this pressure on the back of my neck, and uh… everything kinda fades out after that.

Then I woke up here. Wild, huh? Like, seriously? Who has a dream like that?

RECORDING ENDS

42

Eben shook his head and flicked off the intercom. Some people and the things they said to themselves to get over something terrible.

Hayes blinked. "Is... is this for real?"

"You ask me like you weren't listening. He believes every word of it; plus, he seems to think we have brought him back from quadruple amputee status."

Hayes got up from her seat and started pacing.

"This thing is totally unlike the others. What the hell did you build it for in the first place?"

Eben laughed, a quick series of sounds his throat seemed to choke off into little bites.

"Because you guys asked me to. It's my job."

"You know what I mean. What were the desired results of Subject Five?"

"Well, primarily we were looking into how he communicated. There was a lot of conflicting, confusing data to be sorted through with initial experiments, especially if you thought of communication in human terms, just talking and writing, all that."

Hayes paused in her tracks. Her eyes moved with an almost audible click to lock on him.

"You mean... telepathy?"

"Nothing so subtle. No, the species that Five originated from had a different, more... direct method. Not linking two minds through space, but instead linking two nervous systems. Directly. Sort of the difference between wi-fi and a dial-up. Poor man's mind reading, but we still spent a couple billion on it, I'm sure."

"How?"

"The same way a spider spins silk, Five can create a strand of biomatter that mimics the function of nerve tissue. Once he weaves that tissue into the nervous system of a host, he can access anything he wants. Quite handy for interrogations, so I'm told."

"You've used it for that?"

"Not personally. I was the head of the team that put him together, synthesized his DNA sequence, crafted him from the ground up. People from your department, whatever that is, handled his application experiments. NDAs all around, and pardons for survivors of the procedure. As I recall, no one has been pardoned thus far."

"Anyone ever tell you lab boys that you are fucked up?"

"Your bosses hired me."

CORAL QUEEN INCIDENT REPORT
SURVIVOR TESTIMONY TRANSCRIPT, CONTINUED
NAME: LEANN MARSH
AGE: 32
STATUS: PASSENGER
RECORDING RECOMMENCED 1100 HOURS

INTERVIEWER:
Miss Marsh? Are you ready to continue?

LEANN:
I think so, yeah. How long are you guys going to have to keep us in here anyway?

INTERVIEWER:
Once your quarantine period is over and we have all the pertinent information about this incident, we'll arrange what to do next. Now please, Miss Marsh. Tell us what happened the second night.

LEANN:
Ok… ok…
I made a conscious decision the second night that I wasn't going to get as drunk. It hadn't done me any favors the night before and I wasn't looking forward to an entire week of being hungover *and* seasick. So, the second night I was just trying to take in some of the other stuff there was to do. I should have

noticed that even on the second night the crowds were… well, let's say thinned out a little bit. But my memory of the night before was a little hazy anyway, so I was really just taking the opportunity to enjoy the night and the ship without the added hassle of a bunch of little kids and old folks in my way.

My god, that must make me sound horrible, right? Considering what most likely happened to all of them. Probably just wishing I'd shut up. Shit or get off the pot, right? Anyway, I'd been trying my luck at the casino, but it wasn't exactly going my way. Gambling was really more Karen's thing either way, and I was getting nowhere with it. And it wasn't helping my resolution to stay more sober than the night before being that close to the bar anyway. So, I decided to head off and find some more valid forms of entertainment. Something to do. Or someone. I would have taken either.

You know, people tell you that cruise ships are like these big floating cities, but you don't realize how true that is until you walk around in one for a while. All that was missing was the homeless people, to be honest. But as I passed a dance club, a few bars, a spa, I realized I could have been in any part of the city on any Saturday night, in a sense. But looking back at it, despite how cramped up together and tightly packed it was… it still felt just as empty as anything on land. All these people, desperate to have a good time because, dammit, that is what they paid for, and not a one of them knew what was coming. What was already there with them. That the Devil crawled and slithered amongst them.

But by 8 o'clock that Saturday, there were a few people aside from me that had started to realize something was wrong. I met one of them not long after giving up on the someone angle and deciding instead to find something. Which had inevitably led me to the back… wait, would that be called the aft? Anyway, near the back they had this little micro movie theater that was always playing something, and you could just wander in and out of it. I didn't even care what the movie was. I just decided to wander in and be part of somebody else's problems for a little while as we made our way out to the islands. I settled in, and just kind of turned my mind off for a bit. It was some kind of action adventure thing at first, then the guy in it started shooting lightning out of his hands and I rolled my eyes. Apparently, it was based on a comic book like every other movie in the world these days, so whoop dee-doo. Bored. I was about to leave when I heard something. A sniffle.

Remember when I was talking 'bout cats and making the brain go want to help a baby? Well, I may have mocked but there was a little girl crying about two rows behind me, all by herself. Now, I may come off like a bitch sometimes, and I won't lie, I was having a shitty week; but at no point was I going to let a little girl sit by herself and cry in a dingy little movie theater on this overpriced cruise line.

She was blonde, one of those big mops of gold waves you see on kids from Minnesota, y'know? It was hanging down in strings around her face though, like she had been sweating too. I went over to her, dug around in my purse, and eventually found what I was looking for.

"Here," I said, handing her a tissue.

She looked up at me like I was from another planet, but eventually she reached out and snuffled her nose into it. I sat down next to her.

"Um, are you okay, sweetie?" I asked.

Another long pause, then a nod. Then another sniffle.

"I'm Leann. What's your name?"

A shorter pause this time. Then, "Mindi… with an 'I.'" Which was goddamn adorable, and it nearly broke my heart on the spot.

It was right about there that somebody shushed us from the front of the little theater. As if we were in a real one. Seriously, the nerve of some people.

I turned to the little girl and whispered to her. "You want to get out of here, Mindi with an I?"

"My mom said to wait for her here, and she'd be back with Max."

"Is Max your brother?"

"Sister." Another sniffle. "It's short for Maxine. She sucks."

"So, Max is why you're crying?"

"She's ruining our whole vacation."

"Aw, don't say the whole thing. It's just getting started."

"Yeah, I guess. But everything so far, anyways."

"Ruined?"

A nod from Mindi.

"Well, how about we at least get out of here for a minute. This movie sucks more than your sister. Which sounds like an achievement."

That one got a smile and a nod at least.So, we got up and walked out, Mindi trailing behind me like the lost little puppy she was.

INTERVIEWER:

At what point did you make visual contact with the subject?

LEANN:

Right, sorry. Fuck me, right? I'm telling you about a little girl lost and you want to hear about the horror show that was going on underneath us. Well, you can just sit there in your dark little room and listen, because this is my story and I'm telling it to you the way it happened to *me*, okay?

INTERVIEWER:

(short pause, cough)
Continue please.

LEANN:

Okay then. If you insist.

So, we talked out in the little lobby of the theater for a while, just chatting, but as time passed it got pretty clear that her mom was not going to be back any time soon. Whatever her sister had gotten up to, it was pretty much a washout for the whole evening. It was starting to get late, and there was a good chance that little Mindi was going to fall asleep out here before Mama showed up looking for her.

"Listen," I asked eventually. "I think maybe we should take you back to your room, let you wait for them there, ok? Do you know where it is?"

Mindi shrugged. "Mom has the keys anyways…"

"Well, maybe we can get you to the information office, see if they can get you a copy or let you in at least. How's that sound? Don't worry, unless she's fallen overboard, your sister will turn up and your mom will find her, okay?"

"…Okay."

And with that, we were off into the floating city again. I didn't know yet that we were looking for what was probably a dead woman. And that Mindi… poor Mindi…

193

Is… is she here? Do you have her here in one of your dark, bare little rooms in this place? Please tell me she's all right…

INTERVIEWER:
Please continue your story, Miss Marsh…

LEANN:
Oh Jesus…
Fine…
So, we got moving, trying to follow the maps that are scattered throughout this place, and eventually among all the buffet lines, the tennis courts, and the bars… *Eureka!* A shabby little office with one middle-aged Cuban woman in it, tucked away where it was probably voted by ten different ship designers as least likely to be found.

"Are you the girl's mother?" she asked.

"No, I just explained that. Her mother is looking for her, and she--"

"Then if you want, you can leave her here. Maybe her mother will come looking for her."

"That wasn't what I was asking. I was asking if you could let her go back to her room to wait for her mother."

"What room?"

"I don't know, but I figured that maybe you could type it into your little computer there and find out? Maybe get her a copy of her key?"

"We don't do that here. That's guest services."

"You fucking kidding me? Where is this, then?"

"This is information."

"And that's literally all you're going to give me?"

"That is what you need to know."

…So, we left.

Turns out Guest Service was a little easier to find, but by then I was just ready to give up. Jump ship. Hell with all of you guys, go ahead and enjoy your damn boat. Mindi was just following along, probably resigned to the fact that her vacation

194

was going to be following some lady around to a bunch of places that she didn't feel like going to for the rest of her life, whether it was with me or her mother.

"You know what? Hell with this," I said, after another ten minutes of walking around the promenade and trying to follow crew directions and wall maps. "I want ice cream. You want ice cream?"

Mindi finally made the last hour worth it by lighting up like a damn Christmas tree. This strange woman had gone from reluctant taxi back to mom to deliverer of free ice cream. At nearly nine thirty, no less.

The ice cream shop they had on the boat was kind of like anything you would find in a mall. I have always thought that pink anything was gaudy, but a five-foot pink plastic ice cream cone that is lit up from the inside just reached this whole new level of nearly perverse and I was just uncomfortable looking at it.

But the banks of coolers behind the counter with their tubs that seemed to go down into the ocean were so deep, all full of different colors, flavors, and toppings under glass were a pretty welcome sight regardless. If only there had been someone there. Mindi was looking at the cone too, with a mild horror I understood. I was getting a weird form of penis envy looking at the thing.

"Hello?" I called out. The little stall was still lit up, and beside the apparatus for making shakes I think was a door into the back.

"Excuse me? Can we get some ice cream?" I said, because hell, I had to say something.

I leaned over the counter a little to see if I could catch a glimpse through the little round port hole window in the door, and that's when I saw it was actually slightly propped open. A pair of black work-shoes, the sensible kind with the ridged soles you get when you work food service, were sticking out. And before I could say anything else, they were sucked into the door, the opening left swinging gently.

Oh, hell no, my entire brain said.

Shouldn't we go check? My conscience said.

And that was when the strange keening noise came back to my memory. How strange it had sounded. I don't know why at the time I thought of it then, but it reminded me there was a little girl with me. I called to her gently.

And when the door opened slowly and some... some *thing* started to slither out inch by inch, I screamed her name and we ran.

RECORDING ENDS

43

"Well, she was just about useless, I think." Hayes said.

Eben shook his head, poring over the readout from the screens in front of him. Something about the fluctuations in body temperature were making him wonder.

"No, no I think we might be onto something here. See, the little girl she mentioned. She's part of the Hansen family. We have a Victoria Hansen, don't we? So perhaps we should move on to her next."

"Yeah, maybe. Seriously though, how many more of these are there?"

"Survivors in this talkative of a state? Or with the ability? Four more."

"Lunch?"

Eben consulted his screens once more, scratched at his grey stubble.

"They're not going anywhere, Doctor," Hayes said. She was trying to stifle a growling stomach and didn't want to have to use force on the small man, but she would if a sandwich were not forthcoming.

"Sure… sure, I guess they aren't. Lunch."

CORAL QUEEN INCIDENT REPORT
SURVIVOR TESTIMONY TRANSCRIPT
NAME: VICTORIA HANSEN
AGE: 43
STATUS: PASSENGER
RECORDING RECOMMENCED 1320 HOURS

INTERVIEWER:
Mrs. Hansen, are you awake?

VICTORIA:
(slurred speech)
I... what? Where am I? I'm sorry, I'm... I'm so tired. What is this place...?

INTERVIEWER:
You're in a safe facility, Mrs. Hansen, where you're receiving treatment after the incident you were involved in. We would... we'd like to ask you some questions, if we may. Do you think you can do that?

VICTORIA:
I... I think so. Where's Max, where's Mindi? Are they here?

INTERVIEWER:
We've taken care of all that, Mrs. Hansen, so no need to worry.

VICTORIA:
(muffled) Trying... can't remember where I... left my phone.

INTERVIEWER:
Don't try to move too much, Mrs. Hansen. You're on some... pretty strong pain meds.

VICTORIA:
I'll say.

INTERVIEWER:
If you like, we could start with your daughters. One of the other witnesses said you were trying to find one of them during the incident?

VICTORIA:

Yeah. Maxine… Max. She didn't want to go on that cruise, wanted to stay home and… I don't know, text or something. That's all she does, far as I can tell. That and sulk. Of course, her father couldn't go, so she wanted to stay home too. All that around my birthday too. That's what this was supposed to be, my birthday present. But then Wayne couldn't go, Max started being a terror, and Mindi started with her usual antics. She's a quiet, sweet thing most of the time, but whenever her sister starts being a bitch, Mindi fires right back one hundred percent.

She started calling her "Maxi-pad" somewhere during the second day out, and that was it for my Max, she just stormed off. Of course, I knew where she was probably going, and I didn't want Mindi to be part of all this.

There was this boy, Casey or Cody or something his name was, I think. He had come up and started talking with her the first night in that big main hall of theirs with all the lights and the Egyptian looking stuff, the one at the back of the ship? Anyway, he and her started hitting it off that night, and even once we'd gone back to the room I could hear her little phone buzzing back and forth with him all night. She was right above me. We had four bunks in our little room, one for each of the girls, then Wayne and I were going to be in the lower ones. Well the one across from me was just extra space to keep our luggage, but that was actually kind of convenient.

Anyway, once she had stormed off I figured she would be meeting him somewhere. So, I left Mindi at the little theater they had so I could look for Max a little faster and maybe, just maybe, if I caught her doing something she shouldn't be my poor Mindi wouldn't have to see that. She wants a phone too, and after seeing her sister change into a little ogre because of one, I'm glad I didn't give in…

I'm sorry, what was I talking about?

INTERVIEWER:

Max had run off?

VICTORIA:

Oh, right, yeah…

So, I tried up and down the promenade, even poked my big ass into the little dance club they had on one of the decks but couldn't find her. Then I remembered that that Casey or whatever had mentioned something about maybe going swimming. I knew that Max wasn't wearing her bathing suit when we had gotten dressed earlier that day, so I figured maybe she had run off to the room to get it and change. I checked the pool first and didn't see her there. So, she was probably on her way down there to get it. And she was going to get it alright. Being willful was one thing, but trying to ruin your mother's birthday? She'd be lucky if I let her out of that cabin the rest of the week…

I remember just groaning when I got to the little elevators that went down to the lower decks. Out of order. Of course, they would be. So, I went to the stairwells. Not exactly the height of luxury in there. More like something out of a parking garage back in Chicago.

And it smelled something awful in there too. That was when I first heard something odd. It was not long after I caught that smell… oh god, it's like I can still smell it…

(inaudible)

I … I remember… at first it was just a blur, I never quite saw it right, not fully. It swept up out of the stairwell, and it just knocked the wind out of me, started dragging me like I was a toy. All of a sudden, the whole place was just streaking past me, all the doors I wasn't supposed to go past, all these halls that I hadn't seen… all of them, *all* of them just…. *slicked* with blood. It was cold and sticky, and this thing that had me was just surging through it.

I could see its humped up back, the long trailing boneless arms, the fins, and when it turned back to look at me those… *eyes*. Those eyes… they were like something from a nightmare, one where you wake up crying for your mother. For… Max used to have the worst nightmares, convinced herself something was outside her window. I told her there wasn't any such thing.

I'm such a bad mother. Mothers shouldn't lie…

Then I was somewhere else… somewhere dark, but there were sounds… I could hear moaning, like after an accident… these weird, sort of wet noises. Then there was a little light… a little screen…

(moaning)

Ohhhhh gaaaaaahhhhhdddd, it was Max's phone! Oh god, I remember! I remember everything!

(fast breathing, weeping)

I saw it! *I saw it all!*

INTERVIEWER:

What did you see?

VICTORIA:

They were hanging theerrre…! So many of them! So many faces! *Bodies! All cut up, their arms were gone, their legs were gone!* Ohhh, oh god, they were all tied together to the wall like meat! Just meat, but they were still… *still…*

(choking sounds)

Screaming! I was screaming!

Then I felt it crawl up over me. The arms were wrapped around mine, around my legs, and I knew it was going to do the same thing to me! *I couldn't stop it! I couldn't stop it!*

(gasping ragged breaths)

It burned me… then it ate the rest. I heard that huge mouth, all those grinning, flashing teeth, just sucked them up… like spaghetti… but crunching all the while. Then I felt something else, something at the back of my skull, my neck… a pressure. Compared to the rest… it was almost like I couldn't feel it…

But then the voices came. I was lifted up by the Devil and placed into the Choir of Hell, the Symphony of Hell… I heard their voices, not just their pain and the screams, but all their thoughts, everything they knew… everything I knew, we were all one.

All one. All suffering. All damned to live like this. The Devil who had done this to us, he had made it so we would stay like this as long as he needed… he wouldn't let us just die…

INTERVIEWER:
Why not, Mrs. Hansen?

VICTORIA:

Because he had looked into us. He had looked into our minds, and our hearts, our souls... at first just to learn, to find safety, to feed... but the more he saw, the more he came to realize...

INTERVIEWER:

What? What did he realize?

VICTORIA:

That we were all so small. So petty. So weak. That all we were good for was to suffer.

And that he wanted us to suffer.

He realized... that he *hated* us...

RECORDING ENDS

44

Eben Yoshida sat back in his chair. His blood felt cold in leaden hands. Hayes looked at him, but for once he didn't seem to notice it. She straightened her jacket, adjusting in her seat.

"Are you really surprised, doctor?" Eben jumped.

"What?"

"Are you really that surprised that that thing decided it hated us?"

"I'm more--"

"Stolen alien DNA, mixed up with a couple other species, to see what would happen. Grown in labs, poked, prodded, experiments all. Then you give it practically bullet-proof skin, the ability to spit acid, and the power to tear your mind apart. Are you really surprised that when six of these things got out they decided to rip us all a new one instead of trying to go back to the stars or something?"

"Actually... no."

Hayes arched an eyebrow.

"I was more surprised... at the sheer size of the bio-neural network it created. Basically, what Mrs. Hansen became a part of was like a... an organic Internet. Minds instead of servers, thoughts instead of information. And it started with the crew, the people who knew all the ins and outs of the ship, the secret places passengers couldn't see, couldn't go... they never knew what was coming until it was too late."

"You sound... proud."

Eben smirked.

"Wouldn't you be?"

CORAL QUEEN INCIDENT REPORT
SURVIVOR TESTIMONY TRANSRIPT
NAME: CODY JACOBS
AGE: 17
STATUS: PASSENGER
RECORDING COMMENCED 1400 HOURS

INTERVIEWER:

Mister Jacobs, could you tell us what your relationship was with the Hansen family?

CODY:

Uhm, I didn't really know them that well, aside from Max. Her mom was a little pushy, I guess. But I only knew her for like a day, y'know?

Max was cute. Funny. We liked the same movies and stuff, we just got along really well. So, I guess we both thought it would be fun to hang out since we were some of the only people we'd run into that were the same age. There were seriously a lot of old people on that boat, man. Like, you don't even know.

So, I was there with my brothers, and my parents. They were having fun, but Kevin and EJ are a lot younger, so they were kind of focused on them, which was cool. I got to roam around myself a lot that first day once we got everything unpacked and settled into our rooms. It was fun. I knew I was gonna get just fat as hell with all the food they had around there, but who cares? It was vacation. Go big or go home, right?

But it was that second day that got really weird. I felt like I was the only one who was noticing it sometimes, but it was not just all in my head. Something was off. I finally figured out what it was when we were all at lunch, actually. EJ and Kevin were being their usual selves, just being eight and nine, y'know? So, I don't think my parents were really looking, but like, something was off.

Then it hit me: Where are all the people who work here? Like, there were still some of them, but they were all kind of running around confused and things were obviously not getting done as fast. And I get that they were kind of trying to be invisible, right? That is, like, part of the deal. You have fun, and if they do it right you never know how hard they worked to make sure you didn't have to do shit. My dad talked about that on the flight to Miami, to be courteous to them because they work really hard. But it's like day two and there is basically this skeleton crew running around, and the other guests are all just kind of ignoring it.

So, later I get a text from Max. Apparently, her mom is being a total bitch and her sister is bullying her, so she wants to meet up somewhere, hang out, basically avoid them as much as possible for the day. Obviously, I'm down for that, so I say yeah. But that was when stuff started to get weird...

PHONE LOG, CODY JACOBS AND MAXINE HANSEN
TEXT MESSAGE LOG TRANSCRIPT

CODY 7:15 pm
Where do u want to meet?

MAX 7:16 pm
We should go to the pool! (smiley emoticon)

CODY 7:16 pm
Srsly?

MAX 7:20 pm
U don't want to see me in a swimsuit, lol? Sad face.

CODY 7:22 pm
No, I do. (winking emoticon) But aren't u trying to avoid people? Like your mom?

MAX 7:22 pm
your mom. (laughing emoticon)

MAX 7:22 pm
Besides, already down here looking for it. Ugh, why does it reek down here? Our bathroom is so gross, for realz

CODY 7:25 pm
So see you at pool?

CODY 7:30 pm
?

MAX 7:35 pm
U should come down here instead

CODY 7:36 pm

What? Like, to your room?

MAX 7:37 pm
Why not? (winking emoticon) My mom is not here.

CODY 7:38 pm
But she will totes be looking for u

MAX 7:40 pm
Ur right. Room is not safe. Meet me down here, we can find somewhere.

SURVIVOR TESTIMONY TRANSCRIPT, CONTD.

INTERVIEWER:
How was that weird?

CODY:
I don't know, she was just like normal "let's hang out" one minute, then just creepy DTF the next? I thought it was weird. Sure, a little hot too. But mostly weird. I think just because the day was getting so weird by that point. I hadn't seen my family in a few hours. I was kind of worried that Max was getting all freaked out by her family issues, so I decided even though she was being weird, it was probably better to talk to her in person.

TEXT MESSAGE LOG TRANSCRIPT, CONTD.

CODY 7:55 pm
Srsly, where r u?

MAX 7:56 pm
Close. (winking emoticon)

CODY 7:57 pm
I can't see u

MAX 8:00 pm
>I can see u…

CODY 8:01 pm
>Har har. Srsly it does smell down here. If we get caught down here, we could get kicked off boat

MAX 8:03 pm
>Just around corner, found a nice private spot (winking emoticon)

CODY 8:03 pm
>Not exactly romantic down here

MAX 8:04 pm
>Open the door, u might change ur mind

SURVIVOR TESTIMONY TRANSCRIPT, CONTD.

I don't know why I kept going down there. I guess there isn't a word for when you're half worried about someone, half horny. But the deeper I got led by those texts, and the less people I saw, the weirder it got. I…we were, I guess…in the parts of the ship we're not supposed to see. Like, the parts that are full of pipes and shit? Below decks, basically. But it was like she knew where I was, 'cause she led me right to that door. And even though that smell was everywhere, and the whole thing felt creepy, I kept on like an idiot…

(shuddering breaths)

That was when I saw it. I opened the door… and… I usually don't notice little details and stuff. My teachers say I lack focus. But Max had this little mole in the crook of her elbow, she'd try to cover it up sometimes when she was self-conscious, I think. I saw that first. But not far above that… her arm just stopped. The light from the hall went past there, but the arm just… didn't. There was just raw meat, and these ropy red strings of something that looked wet and hairy at the same time were trailing off to somewhere I couldn't see. And her phone was in her hand. And her thumb was typing. I saw it hit send just before something moved in the dark. Just before red eyes opened.

My phone buzzed in my hand. Just three words:
HERE I AM

RECORDING ENDS

45

Hayes flipped the switch to the "off" position. Her laser was back at full strength and she pointed it right at Eben.

"Have we had enough yet, Dr. Yoshida?"

Eben shrugged. "You have to admit, it was a pretty novel use of his ability to interface with the human nervous system. He's a pretty smart cookie. Or was, anyway."

"Go die in a fire."

"Just a few more to go, then we can finish up our little evaluation."

Hayes just sighed and slumped back into her chair.

"Fine. Bring on the old guy."

CORAL QUEEN INCIDENT REPORT
SURVIVOR TESTIMONY TRANSCRIPT
NAME: MARSHALL SWICKARD
AGE: 68
STATUS: PASSENGER
RECORDING COMMENCED 1450 HOURS

MARSHALL:

You pricks don't have any right to keep me here, dammit! Now where's my wife?

INTERVIEWER:

Mr. Swickard, there is no reason to be alarmed. The danger has passed. We're just trying to get as clear a picture as possible of what happened and--

MARSHALL:

I'll tell you what happened! All hell broke loose on that damn boat is what happened! So, I guess you want to hear what happened with me though, right? Well, maybe I don't feel like it. I know when my rights are being violated, dammit.

INTERVIEWER:

Mr. Swickard, I can assure you that everything in our power is being done to locate your wife, but things are sort of hazy on this end about how you came to be in... the circumstances we found you in. So, could you please tell us about what happened in the Main Ballroom?

MARSHALL:

(sighs)

Fine. Sure. Not like I have dick else to do in here.

I don't suppose you're married, whoever you are. Or if you were, I doubt you are anymore. If you were, you'd understand that a man has no greater duty in this world than to keep his wife safe. Happy. Cared for. And that was a duty I don't just take seriously, dammit. I cherish it. Which is why that was my first concern when things started to go south. Enid was my only concern. Still is.

I just can't help but feel like I've failed her, sitting here not knowing where she is. But if anything, I can tell you can help in finding her. Well, then... here goes. Hold on to your ass, as they say.

Enid and I had spent most of Saturday night in the casino. That was always where we liked to really let out hair down the second night, usually.

See, we had been on the Coral Queen line pretty much every year at the same time since we retired; it was becoming a real fixture for us. Like-minded people of a similar age -- or old farts if we're not beating around the bush -- are easy enough to come by in Florida, but we enjoyed traveling and meeting new folks as well. And this year wasn't any different in that regard. We had a wonderful first night, I'll tell you that for nothing.

Traveling always bring out the adventure in Enid, if you know what I mean. And the next day was re-acquainting ourselves with the place, seeing what had changed, what was just as nice as last time. And that second day, by the time we left the casino, just felt wrong. The service was terrible and there was just a lot of people getting short with each other because of it, I think. Some people have no grace under pressure, see?

Anyhow, the Main Ballroom was where the captain made his big announcement. And... that was where everything went bad. He stepped up on the bandstand and was tapping the mic to get everyone's attention.

"I want to address some of the concerns you have all been bringing to me," he said.

I could tell he was a little shaken up but wasn't sure what to make of it. I figured it was probably something mechanical that was going on below-decks. And that he was going to announce that we had to turn back towards the mainland, or that we'd be heading back at another port; something like that.

"My staff and I have been getting a lot of service related complaints, and I agree that is unacceptable. Our staff is usually top-notch, but I am sad to report we've been having some... issues with short-staffing as of late. Also, there are some technical problems below-decks that are keeping some of our crewmen more occupied than we would like..."

Just like I figured, and I said as much to Enid too. We were going to be turning back, no way around it. I'd heard about crap like this happening on other boats, other companies, but not (redacted). Anyway, I was hoping we'd get comped a new stay on another liner or at least get our tickets refunded, something like that. But, then someone else in the crowd shouted up to him. Sort of a thick heavyset battleship of a woman, with this little tiny blonde girl stuck to her side like glue, just staring up at her.

"You've got more than just crew missing! There are passengers that aren't turning up anywhere either!" she said.

And that got some people muttering. It was certainly news to me.

"Captain," she went on, "I don't know what's going on here, but there is something wrong on this ship. Something is happening and we need to go back to the mainland!"

This one was met by a whole swath of folks just going ape-shit. Who did this big broad think she was cutting their vacation short?

"Please, please, everyone just stay calm. Now, I know we have some passengers unaccounted for, but our security officers are looking for them now. That is under control. There is no cause for alarm, and we won't be turning back or cutting our voyage short, because there is no need. Now, we also have had some passengers reporting an issue with a strange smell on certain parts of the ship."

He wasn't wrong. I had been catching a whiff of something all day that had gotten my dander up; sort of a slimy bad shrimp smell. In fact, I could smell it a little before what happened next...

"We want to assure you all that our waste treatment facilities are perfectly functional, and no gas leaks have been detected, so you're not in any danger from--"

And that was when his damned head came off. Not like it fell of or something or rolled away. Nothing like that. Just... poof. It was gone. Then there was a stump; then that stump started spraying blood.

For a second, nobody moved. It was like we were watching one of the magicians they'd had on the ship a few years before. There was a gasp, but it was like we were sort of waiting for the next part of the trick or something. I wasn't sure what had just happened. I mean I was, but my brain just hadn't processed it all yet, like it was still trying to come up with an explanation for it.

Then, by god, we got the second part of the trick when his body finally got the message that he was dead and fell over. Something just... appeared. Right there on the stage it just faded into view, like someone flipped a switch and now it was here. And it was enormous. At least ten feet up, supporting itself on these long tentacles like a damn octopus.

Four of them were huge and sinewy; then there were four smaller ones down the trunk of the thing that held up the back half. It had a head the size of a damn Volkswagen almost, with a set of teeth and jaws that dripped this clear stuff that looked like it was smoking when it hit the floor. Along with blood, and quite a bit of that. And then, in defiance of anything else that might have made sense about this thing, on what could only be described as one of the "shoulders" that tapered down into a tentacle was a thick black number: Five.

Once that thing showed up, the crowd broke. The spell was over, and the panic started. They folded in on each other and before I knew it, the mob was on us. I tried to keep my had in Enid's, but she was pulled away from me. And as I was trying to keep track of her, that *thing* dove in.

I heard of kids doing stage-dives at rock concerts and such, but I never thought I would see a sea monster with spikes running down its head do one. There were a few people who got crushed beneath the bulk of the thing as it hit the floor and I could swear it grinned hearing them crunch underneath it. Then, it let loose with those arms, swinging them everywhere. People were getting caught up and hurled like they weighed nothing.

One gal was running away from the thing when it cracked one of its arms like a bullwhip. I swear I almost lost it when she opened up like uh, a ripped trash bag and her insides just spilled out onto the dance floor in this huge fan of red. Just as soon it turned away, already focused on someone else, too busy to enjoy what it had just done apparently.

There was this sort of gap between the teeth at the center of its lower jaw. I saw it start to work that spot together for a few seconds, and then it shot this weird red cord at someone. It stuck in them like a little harpoon at the back of their head and they went glassy-eyed, just flopped over like a doll.

I tried to push against the crowd, but the flow was too strong, there was too much, too many of them. I couldn't find Enid and I couldn't make the choice between the mob and this thing even if I wanted to. Pretty soon I was down, and my head got knocked against the floor...

When I got my wits back, I could barely breathe. I felt this huge pressure on my chest and I thought, *Damn, this is it. After*

215

almost seventy years of eating right, you're having a heart attack because a killer squid stole your wife.

But it wasn't a heart attack. Once I came to all the way I saw it for what it was. Bodies. I was under a stack of people, most of them dead or dying. Blood soaked into my shirt, but none of it was mine. All I could think of was finding Enid, so I pushed up at the weight of it all. I tried to shift the weight on top of me, I screamed Enid's name, tried to get my shoulder up against the wall of meat that had fallen on top of me. Then, as if by some miracle, the weight shifted, and they all started to fall off me.

But it didn't take long to clock that it was no miracle. It was that thing. It had heard me and was digging through to find me, anxious to finish the job, I suppose. I pushed up as hard as I could to get out from under and I guess that surprised him because as soon as I could get to my knees I was scurrying away from that thing as fast as I could. I saw the shadow rise up behind me just as I saw the flutter of Enid's dress pass out the doors. Something slapped into the back of my head, and everything went black…

I'm guessing that was when you all showed up with the cavalry like you did, 'cause the next thing I knew, I was on back in a shitload of pain, and surrounded by a bunch of guys with some *damn* scary looking guns…

And of course, the first thing outta my mouth was, "Have any of you fine fellas seen my wife?"

RECORDING ENDS

46

"My god, they still don't have any idea, do they?" Hayes said.

Eben shook his head, consulting the screens and readouts. "EEG reads as normal, but the patterns are getting erratic. We need to wrap this up, I think."

"I still can't wrap my head around this," Hayes said.

Eben checked a sheaf of printout in his hand.

"Well, the last one on our list here was present at termination, so we might get the best information from her. Worth a shot, I say. Might as well. We're running out of time."

CORAL QUEEN INCIDENT REPORT
SURVIVOR TESTIMONY TRANSCRIPT
NAME: SAMANTHA EATON
AGE: 37
STATUS: CREW, NURSING STAFF
RECORDING COMMENCED 1530 HOURS

SAMANTHA:

That roar is going to stay with me forever, I think. It sounded like a hundred voices, but it came from somewhere inside that creature, whatever the hell it was. I don't think I understand entirely what you hope to get from all this. I certainly wasn't trained to deal with that sort of thing. But I guess I was the best one equipped for the job once Dr. Carruthers was disemboweled. I never heard of a field promotion on a cruise ship, but when your boss has his guts all over the floor, you put up or shut up.

I heard the start of the commotion down the halls from the medical center. We're on the same deck as the lowest level of the ballroom, so we were the first place that survivors started flooding in. I wasn't sure what everyone was going on about at first, but a few seconds later, well… I figured it out once the thing showed up.

We got as many people inside as we could, and then we just started barricading the doors with anything we could find --

beds, tables, anything. There was this woman with a little girl, she had blood on her face and was limping while holding this little blonde girl close to her. Somewhere she had broken an emergency hatch open and had a fire axe in her free hand.

I still don't know her name, but in that moment, she became my new best friend.

The doors heaved as the creature hurled itself against them. I saw wood beginning to splinter from the edge of the frame, so it must have been really massive. Gaps started to form in the sides, and in an instant the arms were slipping through and swinging in swift arcs. That was when we lost Dr. Carruthers. But that woman with the axe put the little one behind her and just started swinging and chopping.

I'm not sure when we started to hear the gunfire, but it was almost as much of a shock as seeing that thing for the first time. You could tell it was distracted, even without seeing it fully, as its focus on the attack just went away. Axe woman just went for it then, hacking with everything she had. There were spurts of blackish blood and they sprayed all over the walls. Now the thing was tearing at the doors and screeching that awful roar again. In a splintering crash the doors were completely ripped out and I saw the whole beast coiled up and snarling at the woman with the axe. It spun on its limbs and snatched at the axe, sending it clattering across the infirmary. I tried to scoop it up, but the motion only served to get me noticed.

I don't know why it decided to grab both of us and leave the others behind, but I think it had something to do with the chattering gunfire I was hearing from somewhere in the distance. It didn't make sense. If the monster was here, who were they shooting at?

I didn't have time to think about that then, though. We were rushing down corridors towards the lower decks, being pulled along in a grip like being wrapped up in a steel boa constrictor. I think maybe a rib might have cracked along the way.

I saw the bodies in the glare of the flashlights in the tunnel. The whole passageway was wall-papered with the maimed. Stripped of limbs and shorn of their clothing, it was like torsos of mannequins in an insane art gallery, but each one moaned and flailed against the glistening red mesh that held them in place and seemed to link them together. They should have been dead, but every pair of eyes I saw was alive and screaming, and soon so was I.

The flashlights were on the end of rifles being brandished by what I assume were your men. They were going from body and to body and putting a bullet in each head, leaving them to jerk spastically, then flop into lifelessness, still suspended by the tendrils pressed into the back of their skulls.

The creature hissed at the men like it was scolding them, and began lashing out in the close quarters, still gripping me and the woman from the infirmary. I'm not sure how many of them it killed, but the gunfire started to become more intermittent. Even in the dark I could see the thing was bleeding too, gouts of black fluid splashing onto the floor. It looked at the world around it, then spun around, pressing its back to its attackers and pressing us to the ground. That was when I felt the piercing, crunching pressure on the back of my skull; something pressing down into my spine, my head then… *oh no… oh God, I remember now.*

No. No, this is impossible.

What have you done to me?

(voice in recording shifts, begins changing)

CODY:
Where Am I? What Have you done with me?

MIKE:
I'll kill all of you, you pathetic creatures!

219

VICTORIA:

I'm the Devil to you! You can't kill the Devil! I'll consume every last one of you! *First your mind, then your body!...* Oh, oooohhhh god, Max? Mindi? My babies, where are you? *Where are you?*

LEANN:

Nooooo! No! I wasn't supposed to end up aloooooooooooo – I wasn't (garbled, unintelligible)

RECORDING ENDS

47

Eben Yoshida backed away from the viewing port that looked into the chamber beyond. Agent Hayes followed in short order with her hand on her gun.

"That stuff is gonna hold, right?" she asked, her eyes flicking from the vibrating glass to the door.

The little man was in her way, but that wouldn't be an issue if it came down to it.

Eben sighed, reached into a pocket, and brought out a pack of cigarettes. He began patting himself for a lighter.

"Yeah," he said. "I think we're good. He's too weak to make his way through, even if he knew what was happening. Which he obviously doesn't... too bad."

Eben found his lighter, brought the cigarette to his lips, and flicked on the tiny flame.

"Hit that switch for me, would you?" he said while gesturing at the console.

"What's it do?" Hayes enquired, hand still on her holster.

Eben smirked. "Turns the lights on in there..."

Hayes reached over and flicked it. The chamber beyond filled with light. There was a screech. Like a roar, but with a hundred voices inside it. The thrashing limbs were pocked with bullet holes, still seeping black fluid as it shrieked and cursed. A mouth that shouldn't have been able to speak howled for a woman named Enid -- who it had probably eaten -- with the voice of a dead blackjack dealer. Red eyes that had glared with hate at the entire human race wept thick, viscous tears for a cheating ex named Karen.

Eben blew out a stream of bluish-gray smoke.

"Poor idiot. Was connected at the end. What with all those minds part of the bio-net it had created, when they started dying they had to go somewhere..." He chuckled. *"That,"* he said, pointing with his cigarette, "is what you call an unforeseen glitch. Hell of a design flaw to overlook."

"A glitch?" Hayes pondered while watching the dying creature flail in its madness.

Eben nodded. "Lucky if I can keep my job, to be honest. Maybe the next one we can figure out how to counter the feedback of a dying host brain. Gonna have to hire a neurologist. Maybe two."

"Next one?"

"Oh yeah. Can't keep this one. What good is an unstoppable alien killing machine that thinks it's a retiree, a Millennial, a house wife, or a middle-aged lesbian depending on the mood it's in?"

Hayes watched, speechless, as Eben walked up to the controls and began punching in a series of codes into one of the keyboards.

PURGE CHAMBER? came up in neon green block letters on a monitor, above a flashing cursor hovering over a Y/N.

Eben punched "Y" and the chamber lit up like a small sun. Hayes covered her face and yelped. Eben simply turned his back to it and took another drag on what was, in his opinion, well-deserved smoke. This wasn't how he had wanted to spend his morning. After a few seconds, the thrashing stopped, the screeching faded, and the light from the radiation scrubbers faded.

"Welp," Eben said, crossing his arms. "Here's to Version 2.0…"

DARK HELIX

Breyden Halverson

48

The beast rose up from the relatively shallow depths of Crystal Springs and snorted out of its nostrils in anticipation and annoyance. Like a hawk searching for prey, its glowing white eyes scanned the area and the landscape beyond, keeping an eye out for anything that might come its way. Whether it be the Area 51 operatives sent to catch it or some known predator infringing upon the area, it was determined no one and nothing would ever catch it exposed in the area; and even if they did, it would be their last sight! And either way, it would not be going back to that place if it had the will or wish to do so.

The genetic experiment let out a breath of satisfaction as it grinned at its continued elusiveness. There was no way the operatives at Area 51 would find it here.

Its developed camouflaging abilities have helped it to blend in seamlessly with the surrounding environment. Even the water, which would normally do no good for regular escapees or animals hiding from their hunters, its camouflage was good enough to become near-translucent in the water.

The beast rose up out of the water, after which it stood on its four hind legs and gazed at the scenery surrounding it. To humans, the beast would be a nightmare in the flesh. Dubbed "Subject Six" by Hudson and the people at Area 51, the creature stood over ten feet tall on four praying mantis-like legs.

These limbs were covered in malformed, black exoskeletal plates rising from the base of its feet up past its hips. Its body was covered in a night-shade colored exoskeleton that was surprisingly light for a creature of its size, with jagged edges going up and down in various areas. Its medium length neck was covered with spike-like points coming up from its head downwards. The creature's two arms were long and covered with the exoskeletal mass, twisted and unsettling to the human eye.

At the end of the arms, however, two mantis-like blades shot out, with a curved claw on each side. From its human-like body, a long tail moved quietly in the water. On it, the malformed exoskeleton stretched upward to multiple moving pincers, as if they were chopped from some centipede-like horror and reattached to Subject Six. At the end of it, two fingered, claw-like stingers were positioned like that of a scorpion's stinger.

But, the head held the most drop-dead, shit-your-pants element of all! Around the head of Subject Six, a serrated, skull-like bone covered most of its face and left to those seeing it, showed just the beginning of its crocodile-like mouth and a pair of glowing white eyes.

On the back of the genetic nightmare, a tattooed "6" all in blood red would have been seen by those in the daylight or in a lighted area, anyway. But Subject Six didn't care about any of that. The tattooed number on the back was invisible to the creature itself, and of no concern to Subject Six. It hated numbers and being numbered; the instant it saw a number, it felt like its existence meant nothing to its creators, they be human or not. Subject Six hated its own number, every number, everything that is and ever has been numbered. But *names* it liked... a lot! It didn't know why it was fascinated with names... but maybe there was more *individuality* in a name.

And it has already given itself a name: *Helix!*

Suddenly, a scent wisped through the air and into its nostrils. Helix stopped and let the smell pass through, allowing it to register in its genetically artificial but superior mind. A hiss of eagerness and twisted curiosity escaped the creature's mouth as it turned its head in the direction of the scent.

A human smell; but it wasn't one of the Area 51 militia sent out to capture it. This one didn't have the smell of special gear, no weaponry, nor the smell of blood it produced while at the base. No, this smell was something different. Helix heard its gut rumble as toxic saliva began to be flow from its gullet in salacious anticipation upon detecting this new arrival. Now thoroughly roused from its slumber, the best quickly camouflaged itself in preparation for this new arrival. It was very curious to see who was there... and if he or she was worthy enough to be killed by it!

49

"And then, you and I went to see the stars outside our house that one time to see if we can spot any UFOs. That is still one of my favourite nights ever," said Bryan Corner as he made his way through the springs, holding onto his equipment while looking at a photograph.

He stopped for a moment to look at the evening scenery around him and sighed heavily. "If only you were here with me at this time. It still beats missing you every day, little bro," Bryan said as he recalled the journey that led him up to this point.

It took him hours to drive into Nevada from his northern Californian home, and infinite amounts of coffee to keep him awake throughout the trip. But, in the end, it was worth it. It was worth waiting since his childhood to come close to Area 51, which was practically the stuff of movies, science fiction novels, horror stories, and so on.

But it wasn't for himself that he came out here at such a time. It was more for someone else's sake; someone whom he loved but couldn't make it in the end. He held up the photograph of a handsome, dark haired and blue-eyed young man ten years younger in a wheelchair and held it amongst the stars. It was his younger brother, Mike Corner.

Mike was diagnosed with an unidentified terminal illness at birth and the doctors told his parents he may only have eighteen years to live, during which his condition would only get worse as he aged. He and his parents secretly worried about the years of struggle that would ensue, along with them dealing with the stigma attached to people with such a disability. Still, Bryan was determined from an early age to give his younger sibling the best life possible and one of the ways he did it was introducing him to the stars.

A faint memory glimmered of him at ten years old holding his baby brother, both of them silent and staring at a particularly starry night. After that, their pastime activity was looking at the heavens together. And that was when Bryan told

Mike about the stories of UFOs, accounts of extraterrestrial life, and the story of Area 51.

The last positive thing he remembered before Mike's condition went to shit was his promise that once his brother turned sixteen, he would take him to the fields just outside of Area 51. That was two years before Mike passed away one September morning.

Bryan felt around his bushy cheeks, feeling weeks of growing out his sideburns, as well his failed attempt to grow a beard. He sat down next to a tree near the abandoned Crystal Springs and sighed as he watched the stars for a while. He felt his heart ache as if sobbing about the loss of Mike. The past five years without his little bro in the house had been hard on him and his family. Despite the difficulty, he decided to go to the legally permitted outskirts of Area 51 and search for proof of alien life from there.

"Well, time to get on it. Isn't that right, good ol' Mike?" Bryan said as he began to unpack his gear to watch the night-sky.

That is until he heard the water move, making a sudden sloshing sound.

Bryan whipped his head around and looked towards Crystal Springs, in almost complete darkness and without retrieving a flashlight. Even in the darkness, the moonlight shone on the springs. The beam managed to illuminate enough of the water for him to see *that something huge was there and was possibly watching him!*

He then saw what looked like large, two-toed claw marks in the mud leading up from the water and into the other side of the river.

"I'm not alone," was all Bryan could muster before the wave of fear came over him.

It was then that he heard the nearby sound of squealing wheels grinding to a halt.

50

Cloaking in the fading daylight, Helix silently moved around while watching the vehicles of Area 51 close in on the otherwise abandoned spot. A convoy of the security team from Area 51 had just pulled onto the side of the road and it could now hear the echoing shouts of the men. Helix narrowed its eyes in disbelief.

Were these humans really that stupid to let their presence be known to it? At least, the guy with the sideburns near the Springs had the smarts to make a half-decent effort to keep himself quiet.

Helix looked left and right, glancing to see if there was a hiding spot nearby for it to hide. Even though it could travel at high speeds, it was only able to do so for a limited period before tiring out. The exoskeletal material on its body was partly to blame; even though its tough hide was lighter than the carapace of most insects, at such a size and weight, it still wasn't feather light. Helix also didn't care for simple slaughtering unless it detected complete anger, anguish, repulse, or any other negative emotions from potential human quarry.

The creature found satisfaction in what would humans called *baiting;* the toying with the victim's mind before he/she/it kissed their ass goodbye. Then, it would make its move and go for the kill.

But it needed somewhere to go to do that. As the armed men were starting to commence their search, Helix looked around. Then it glanced over its shoulder and made the equivalent of a grin. The perfect hiding spot was only a proverbial hop, skip and a jump away. The horrific creature raised a mantis-like pincer and cut into one of its exposed portions of flesh. Helix let out a grunt as a glowing, bright yellow blood split onto the ground.

It next turned towards the place it wanted and "grinned" in satisfaction. If the operatives were stupid enough to follow the trail, they would be heading right into a trap.

Less then fifteen minutes later, Helix found itself gasping in exhaustion at the abandoned cemetery of Hiko, a small, ranch-based community not too far away from Crystal Springs. The graveyard itself was a sad sight to see; it sat on a barren rock ground and was surrounded by a steel fence, probably to keep out intruders. Numerous tombstones of various, forgotten names sat in their places, mere placeholders for remembrance and nothing more. The whole area is not too large, but big enough that it would've supported a respectable amount of people.

The deserted town itself was something else too. Helix passed the ruins of what looked like a cabin-sized house and a brick wall as it stepped off a surprisingly grassy area. Nothing that suggested life remained in the old town; a stark contrast to the other ranches nearby, which had people living an agrarian lifestyle.

Helix took a step towards one of the tombstones, ignoring the vast grassy patches of agricultural land nearby and looked at the name etched onto the otherwise plain surface. The settling sunlight gleamed its last light for the day onto the stone and illuminated the engravings. It read:

JOHN CASTLES JR
AUG. 25, 1873 -- MAY 8, 1939

A minute seemed to last for an eternity before Helix lashed out its mantis-like claws at the tombstone. Repeatedly, with an angered yet pained cry, the genetic engineered monstrosity struck the tombstone over and over, with each strike growing more furious than the last. Finally, the top of the rock with including the etched-on name was smashed off and it fell to the ground with a loud thud.

But the name was still there… it was *still there!* Helix lifted one of its forelegs and stomped the engraving into its version of oblivion. The creature huffed as a vicious mixture of envy, anger, sadness, and longing shook its body as it stared at the broken pieces of the name scattered at its feet. It couldn't stand the fact that this man, whoever this bastard was, died with a name and not having to live with being a number.

Helix shut its eyes as it felt all the memories come back, the pain and burning envy of not having a name, of not being recognized! It hated the monstrosity humans labelled "neglect," the worst kind of torture this creature could imagine. Helix may have been created to be weapon, but it still had a heart, and it was determined to make sure the humans wouldn't fail in seeing that.

Then, the sound of trucks and yelling tingled the entity's senses as it turned to see a mini-convoy of vehicles crawling in the distance where the spring was located.

If a person saw Helix and the face it had, they would say that when the eyes turned blood red and the exoskeleton began *to move like a hundred snakes in a bag*, that is when they'd run!

For the first time in a long time, Helix felt its mouth break into a wide beam, showing the world its bloody maw as it clocked itself.

It was time to spread some carnage.

51

"Hey, look, I only heard something in the springs and maybe – *maybe* -- saw some footprints in the moonlight. You guys are supposed to know about this stuff, right?" Bryan mustered as he tried to reason with the Area 51 operatives.

One of the armored soldier's masks went up against his face in a most uncomfortable way, and he attempted to maintain his composure. Which was no easy task while being confronted by a trio of men armed with deadly hi-tech firearms, to say the least! Unfortunately, these soldiers were a real piece of work and it took God knows how long to even make them feel a sliver of understanding as the black van he was in drove along the desert.

The color of the vehicle's exterior was black, pure black, and inside---well, that's another story. The interior was filled with small screens, and pieces of technology Bryan couldn't even begin to identify was strewn about in small piles. Hidden speakers emitted electrically enhanced voices every minute or so, talking about how to catch "Subject Six."

Bryan was quite aware of the numerous reports of strange activity occurring in and around Area 51, which included a respectable number of UFO sightings. He was convinced that something big and disturbing was going on, and that he had inadvertently found himself slam dunk in the middle of it. And with Bryan's experience in reading people's habits and common signs of lying or otherwise, the young man was also sure his captors were more scared than he was uncomfortable.

"Look!" the militia man in his face said coldly, "we don't care if you're sighting-seeing or what! You have to get out of get out of here or else… our *target* is going to do a deadly 180 on us. This is confidential, and you better keep your fucking yap shut on it!"

"And what is the danger level of this fucking *target* of yours?" Bryan countered, refusing to let his shaking nerves and tingling anxiety get the better of him. "Okay, maybe I'm not the most informed party on this situation, but I can tell you for damn sure you're doing your damned best to get this situation finished. If my little brother was still around, he'd bluntly say 'Belch it up! You are hiding something!'"

"Hawk-3, back off and return to focusing on the operation," a soldier of superior rank told the irate officer who was arguing with the civilian. "We had enough of this stress already; save your aggression for where it's needed."

With a frustrated sigh, the operative acquiesced to the command as he sat back in his seat in silence.

The eternity they all felt was actually a mere three minutes before a beeping came from the front seat. Before Bryan could utter a single word, the three other operatives flew from their seats to the front.

"What's the status?"

"Target is veering toward our position, at thirty miles per hour southeast our direction."

"Shit! Tell the others we need…"

"The hell? It just disappeared right off the map!"

"What? Get the radar up and point it to the sky, all directions! Don't let the sucker get away!"

Bryan's mouth dropped when he realized what was happening. *The target, whatever in God's name it might be, is coming right here! What the hell should I do? If only I didn't let them confiscate my bag!*

Then, the shit hit the fan hard. The glass on the van shattered and the worst nightmare Bryan ever saw came smashing through the otherwise tough exterior of the armored vehicle.

52

Every person present in the van looked on in horror as Helix tore through the heavy vehicle's exterior armor, its metal appearing like nothing more than cardboard to the artificially created grotesquerie. The van immediately derailed off the road and tumbled into the desert, its metallic composition crunching and squealing with each thud. Helix shrieked in fury as it saw the operatives fall out the vehicle, and it immediately swung its pincers at the nearest operative.

The soldier barely had time before the scythe-like claw ripped through his chest. He cried out in horror and agony just before Helix lunged forth and bit clear through his neck, immediately decapitating the hapless military man. Blood painted Helix's jaws like Satan's version of paint and drops of blood dotted all around the van's gray interior.

"Shoot the bastard!" cried one of the other soldiers. Within minutes, a rain of gunfire erupted within the van and pounded the creature's thickly-coated hide like a thousand pebbles hitting a tank. Helix sneered at their attempts to harm it. *They really haven't learned anything*, its resultant stare seemed to convey.

Only a few seconds had passed before the rest of the soldiers' heads were severed from the bodies and rolled grotesquely about the monster's feet.

Hearing a cry, Helix turned to see its next victim: a man who witnessed it all. Bryan stood shaking in his seat while holding a photo of his dead brother, having witnessed the brutal massacre of the soldiers and thus horribly aware of exactly what fate awaited him during the next few moments.

Helix saw terror in the man's eyes; yet it also saw something else within the shuddering and terrified man.

Forced determination.

53

Bryan had heard the word "fear" all his life; he could remember as a kid being afraid of what lurked outside the house and under the bed. It felt horrible, gut-twisting; yet somehow *familiar*! Of course, he was weirded out by the strange feeling, who wouldn't be? After growing up, he began to research phobias, why people fear the things they do, as well as monsters in general.

He never thought he would ever feel that same fear again. That gut-grabbing and squeezing feeling that left one so afraid they'd vomit after.

But staring into the eyes of whatever the hell this thing was… he was feeling that fear all over again!

The monstrosity took two steps towards Bryan and leaned forward towards him, nearly pressing its eyes against his own while blood mixed with its saliva. The beast's eyes squinted, scrutinizing the fragile human as if it didn't quite know what to expect from him, and the neck moved around in unearthly fashion as it observed the cornered young man. The beast's front left foot hit its quarry's chest softly yet firmly, causing Bryan to experience the sensation of a large amount of pressure pushing down on him. The man could feel a bit of the creature's rough but deformed hide as it sniffed at him, like some devil dog from Hell sent to pull its possible victim to its twisted underworld lair.

"What is your name, *person? I can smell you are not one of* them, *but you are not supposed to be here… am I not right?"* The voice reverberated through Bryan's head like a deep-toned, warped, growling echo of the most nightmarish of sorts.

Bryan could not control his heart rate and his sweat glands were practically working over-time. He could tell this creature had some sort of vendetta against the men who held him hostage; and judging by the sheer brutality of the attack, it was more than just bitter at them.

Bryan's eyes opened wide as he came up with the worst idea he ever had.

"Name's Bryan Corner... and why should my name be of any interest to you?"

"You have a name...whereas I was just a number! The same with the rest of my brethren. And I am going to find my name, if it means killing the entire facility that kept me caged and unloved!"

Bryan frowned. This was interesting; a creature that had just murdered an entire military squadron now claimed it was unloved and wanted a name? Well, that was--

"Ridiculous, you say? You humans take nearly everything for granted; my brethren and I have been created as weapons."

Then he saw the creature becoming visibly upset and riled as it took a moment to remember something it didn't like remembering.

"That wretch... the one who always watches from his little seat... Hudson. He will give me a name... even if I must soak him in his own blood first! My brethren and I only wanted to have a companion, a friend, someone to care for us. But no! They had to treat us like weapons... because, of course, Hudson" --the beast spat the name as if it had a terrible taste to it-- *"believes we deserve no other existence but what they have created us for."*

The beast finished off a growl that punctuated the silence like the clicking of a gun barrel.

"So, you mean you've never been loved or named?" was all Bryan could muster saying from the tense silence wrapping his body like a snake coiling around its prey.

"It means we should have been treated better! That is why we escaped! I can feel my brethren's fury.... .and it will not be long until we get what we want... no, deserve!"

The creature's right claw drove straight into Bryan's gut and all through until it pierced through the bottom of the van. Because of the agony inflicted upon him, Bryan almost failed to see the bright orange fluid seep into the puncture wound. The skewered young man screamed as the mysterious fluid started to flow through his veins with an awful, acid-like burning sensation. It felt as if fire in liquid form was burning his arteries and every one of his internal organs from the inside out.

Finally, the invasive orange fluid hit the brain. Oh, how it hurt! In fact, it hurt so badly that all Bryan wanted to do was to crawl back to where he belonged.

Then, came the illusions. And the twisting of the memories; at first, the memories of his childhood started cascading through his mind as he remembered them. Nothing was wrong. Nothing was wrong. Until he picked up his pet cat... *with the creature's head on it!* It only got worse when the young Brian dropped the cat and ran screaming to his parents. He found that they had the creature's head too; and so did the neighbours.

Soon, the head appeared on everything living, and like a scene out of some movie about demonic possession, these multiple monstrous heads began tearing out the walls while simultaneously yelling, "*Let me have your name! Let me rip it from your body!*

After Bryan finally lost all control of his consciousness, everything went blank.

54

Bryan was woken up by a shaking of his shoulder and he wrested himself out of the repeating memory loop he was trapped within. The nightmare he had was still fully fresh, but he was glad to be out of it.

However, he wasn't so glad to see a man looking down at him with a gun in hand. He looked around as his vision cleared. Bryan found he was still at the site where the creature attacked him, and the van remained laying on its side off the road. Now, though, he could see a bunch of black suited soldiers surrounding the site along with jet-black helicopters cavorting high in the air. He then witnessed suspension wires lifting the van into what looked a holding station of some sort. Nevertheless, he didn't know what had transpired during the interim between his blackout and the moment he awakened.

"You alright?" he heard a deep male voice ask him. "You seemed banged up. And in more ways than one, unfortunately."

Bryan turned around to see a black-clothed figure coming towards him, followed by another man who had a grim expression on his face.

"And who are you?" the newly conscious young man asked the two strangers. "I just had the worst mind-fuck I ever had in my life, and…"

Bryan groaned as he felt his head ache. He reached up to his forehead where the pain was emanating. It felt damn awful and he hoped whoever these guys were, they planned on taking care of his headache and the damn beast that caused all of it in the first place.

"Don't worry. We're looking for the thing. It's sly and wily but we'll find it. We have just the thing for you back at the base and…"

"Wait! You knew what attacked us--I mean, *me*--tonight? How do you know about it?"

"Well, you could say I'm the director of Area 51's Project Hydra operation… which just failed miserably," the grim-faced man said as he pulled his mask off.

"The name's Hudson. And may I ask you to never tell anyone what you saw tonight?"

55

It was about four hours since Helix finished off the guy in the van and became bored with screwing with his mind, so the creature figured it was best to turn its attention towards other things.

The creature laid still as it saw the car roll towards it down the road and readied itself for the anticipated attack. It heard the joyful scream of a young woman, and the chuckle of the young man that followed it. Then a declaration of "I love you!" came from the male voice; the young lady said the affirmative as the vehicle kept on driving.

Helix merely sneered as it saw the headlights come into view. The beam pierced the darkness as the monstrous beast got ready to pounce. This wouldn't be the first time it preyed on humans for their names, nor would that be the last place it would continue its morbid journey. For the creature now smelled a city nearby... a city it definitely planned to visit.

This was only the beginning of its reign of terror. Hudson should have known better than to be so casual as to allow Experiment Subject Six to continue roaming free like it now did.

As the car came into view, Helix pounced from its position and into the air, its glowing eyes staring down onto the sports car below. It released a monstrous screech that drowned out the simultaneous screams of terror emitted by the two people below it. As the abhorrent monstrosity came down to rip and shred its latest victims, one thing was decided by the creature:

It would keep the name Helix for now. That is, until it eventually found a better one. And it wasn't concerned where its spree of slaughter took it next... as long as it got its name.

THE CULT OF VINE

Zach Cole
Robert Galvin

56

Subject Four had gone dark. No sightings or reports of the experiment could be verified for months since its unprecedented escape. Tracking the beast proved to be a much more difficult task than previously expected. Due to the appearance of the creature, any reports of demons or sasquatches could potentially be a lead. Yet, there are thousands upon thousands of sightings of these cryptids and paranormal entities, and it could be any one of them.

What the government needed was a specific case. They needed one lead with one little piece of evidence or information that could confirm it was what they were hunting for. Strangely, despite Subject Four being designed as a cunning and brutal killing machine, there were indeed no reports of anything killing as it did. It was possible that its intelligence and stealth were so great it would slaughter without being caught. However, a scarier possibility could be that it was anticipating a murder spree, waiting for the right place and moment to strike.

What would be discovered about Subject Four would turn out to be a lot stranger than anyone could have imagined.

Orange seeped through the forest as the sun was gradually slipping away from view. An army of trees stood proudly together to make this beautiful forest, glimmering in the sunlight. The day was slipping away, and the night was preparing to take over the sky.

A man walked through the forest with his head down. He was dressed all in black -- trench coat, pants, boots, etc. The exception was his white gloves. A slight chill breezed through the air, causing the man to shiver briefly. It became harder to trudge through the thickening slimy, muddy ground as he approached his destination. He was ankle deep into the mud and kept on forward. Eventually, a pathway appeared, the ground hardened.

It was close. A wretched odor emitted from the area. Deer corpses were scattered about. Some were strung up to trees and transformed into grizzly displays. Flies and maggots were still feasting on many of them. Hanging about the trees by strings were sticks and twigs tied up into bizarre symbols. Another breeze passed, the wind letting them dance in the air.

The man raised his head, scanning the area briefly before looking to the structure before him: an abandoned building of stone with two large wooden doors. Three gargoyles guarded it with care, two on opposite sides and one in the center. They stared down at their visitor, as he stared them back. The figures on the edges were your average cliché gargoyle, with one wearing a smile and the other a frown. The center looked more demonic than the others, not even bearing eyes, and featuring a gaping hole for a nose, as if it was carved down to the skull. A long stone tongue extended from its tooth-filled mouth, like it was screaming into air.

Dead vines covered portions of the place, only adding to the creep factor. The darkly clad man walked to the door and paused, making one last scan of the area with his eyes. No one seemed to be near. He dug his hand into his pocket to pull out a pair of keys. Plugging one in and twisting, the door opened. Quickly, he slammed the creaky door, locking it just as fast. A staircase stood before him, and down its steps would be yet another entrance for his other key. Past it was yet another hallway, this one adorned with a red carpet beneath and its walls of stone bearing lit torches. It was filled with a crowd of people, dressed very similarly to the one man. Some greeted him, and he waved back.

This would lead to a special place of worship. The walls were stone but chipped and colored with red and black. Deer heads were hung between torches parallel to each other, which led up to a center display. They all stood in what was akin to a big mosh pit, awaiting the arrival of a priest.

There it was, centered before the crowd upon a platform so it could look down on those as they stared back in awe at its horrific majesty. The flickering flames gave brief glimpses of the abomination. Thick chains connected to the wall behind were locked tightly around its wrists, thus keeping it in place. Its eyes glowed brightly with a dark-toned red.

The priest pulled back his hood, revealing a horribly scarred visage. He remembered the encounter that left him disfigured more vividly than any other memory of his life.

57

Two months ago…

It was a warm summer night. He had just left the small town of Yuma, Nevada when he spotted a family pulled over to the side of the road. The father, a short man with round glasses and scraggly brown hair, wearing a tank top and shorts, was standing at the front of the car. The hood of the vehicle was pulled up. He stopped, rolling down his passenger-side window to speak with the man.

"What seems to be the trouble?" he asked.

The father scratched his head, a deep frown on his face. "The damn thing overheated."

"Need some help?"

"Unless you have some water, I don't think there is much you can do."

He reached behind the passenger seat and pulled out a bottle of water. He waggled it before the man.

"Just got a full case."

"Well ain't I lucky?" the father said, looking relieved.

The man smiled as he stepped out of his car and whispered to himself, "Indeed you are."

He held his hand out to the father. "The name's Gray."

The father took Gray's hand. "Nice to meet you, Gray. I'm Arthur."

Gray cracked a smile. "Your last name wouldn't happen to be Pendragon, would it?"

Arthur gave Gray a look he was all too familiar with. A look of judgement. Of ridicule. He internally sneered at the look. He had dealt with that look all his life.

Gray forced the smile that had slipped away back onto his face. "It was a joke… about King Arthur."

Arthur's face lit up as he exclaimed, "Oh!" Then he began to chuckle.

"Anyway," Gray said and held out the bottle of water in his hand.

"Right," Arthur replied, taking the container from Gray.

As Arthur turned to pour the water in the radiator, Gray pulled an object out of the pocket of his jacket. He brought it down on the back of Arthur's head. The father dropped like a rock, unconscious. The act made Gray grin. His heart hammered with excitement, flooding his system with adrenaline. He loved the rush.

"How's things coming up there?" came a woman's voice, the wife of Arthur and mother of his children, killing his buzz.

Gray frowned, stepping around the car to the mother, the gun he used to knock out Arthur pointed at her face. The woman was pretty and blonde, almost having a supermodel figure. She wore a sundress, her cleavage catching Gray's eye. The mother gasped. Her two children, a boy with scraggly brown hair and the body of an Oompa Loompa that looked about ten -- he'd make a good snack for his dogs; and a girl that looked like a younger version of her mom -- he had a few ideas of what to do with her -- being maybe sixteen, were both cowering in the back seat.

"Get out," he growled.

The mother complied but began to ramble, continuously asking about the fate of her husband. Gray remained quiet, letting her think the worst.

He smiled fiendishly, saying, "The children, too."

Tears filled her eyes as the mother saw the predatory look in his eyes.

"Come on, children," Gray called. "Get out here with your mommy."

When the children didn't budge, he lost his temper. Gray thrust the gun's barrel against the mother's head and yelled, "Get the *fuck* out here!"

Their sobs grew to a fever pitch, but they complied, taking a position next to their mother, who was crouched before the man with the gun.

"W-wh-what are you g-go-gonna do with us?" the mother stammered, her voice shaky with fear.

Gray loved the sound of terror in a person's voice. It was almost like a drug to him.

"Well," he said, answering the terrified woman's question, "we're all going to go for a little ride in my car. Now… *get the fuck up and get moving!*"

The family squirmed under Gray's raised voice. Oh, how he loved to watch them squirm! Still, they complied, getting off their knees and making their way toward his car.

As they neared the front of the vehicle, the hapless trio caught a glimpse of their unconscious father. They began to weep again and call out for him. Gray laughed at them, pushing the family toward his car. They climbed in, their movements shaky and sluggish.

Gray leaned in close to the mother, who he forced in the passenger seat, and whispered, "Can't be having any witnesses. He saw my face and my car."

The mother's eyes widened in horror, knowing what he was planning. Gray leveled his gun at Arthur's head. The mother and children squealed as he did.

"I prefer knives, but… a gun kills people just the same," Gray chuckled.

His grin grew wickedly wide as he began to squeeze the trigger of his weapon.

Click.

The family in the car behind him squealed in horror.

Gray giggled, looking back at them.

"Oops. Forgot to chamber a round," he laughed.

He pulled the hammer back with his thumb, his index finger tightening on the trigger once again. But instead of the loud report of a gunshot filling the night air, it was that of an unearthly roar.

The family slammed the doors to Gray's car shut and pressed the locks down. He didn't much care as he had the keys. There were no worries of the family driving away or keeping him locked out.

Gray looked around frantically, trying to locate the source of the animalistic howl. But all he saw around him was open desert and the distant cities. He scratched his head in confusion.

The sound he heard came from something big. Something that couldn't easily hide. Yet... he saw nothing.

Suddenly, a hint of motion caught his eye. Gray slowly turned his head to the spot of movement. His eyes widened, and he stumbled back, flattening himself against his car. The mother tried to lean around him inside the vehicle to see through the window he blocked.

Arthur stood suspended in the air... four feet off the ground. His eyes were wide in pain and terror. Blood gushed from his throat.

Then the beast appeared.

Its fangs were sunk into Arthur's throat. Its face was that of a demon, skull-like with eyes sunk in deep sockets. Curved, ram-like horns jutted from the sides of its head. Its eyes glowed a sinister orange. The rest of the creature looked like the abominable snowman, with a broad, stocky body and thick limbs ending in clawed digits. Its body was covered in a thick, red-brown fur. The skin that showed was a maroon color. On its left hand, he spotted the number "five" tattooed on it.

The creature's fangs slipped from Arthur's throat as it sighted in on Gray. Blood splashed across the fur on its neck as it did. Arthur's body flopped in a pile on the ground at the beast's feet, blood still gushing from his throat.

Gray shook out of his stupor, raising his gun and firing off a few shots at the demonic beast. The creature snarled at him, the bullets having no effect. Realizing his gun was doing nothing to the beast, Gray jumped over the hood of his car and pulled his keys from his pants pocket. He slipped the key into the door and unlocked it easily and quickly, his hands not shaking a bit despite how scared shitless he was. Gray then yanked the door open and jumped in. The three others in the car squeaked in terror as he did so. They were just as scared of him as they were of the creature stomping toward the car.

Gray slipped the key into the ignition and started the car. Despite their terror of the dangerous man, probably due to him still having his gun in his hand, the family made no attempt at getting out of the car. He would have let them, however, since this would have slowed the beast down, allowing him to get away.

Gray put the gun in his lap, shifted the car into drive, and pushed the pedal to the floor. The tires squealed and smoked before the vehicle jolted forward. The demon beast roared in anger at his fleeing prey. It pursued, keeping pace with the car, but at a distance of about eight feet behind it.

Impossible! Gray thought as he glanced at his speedometer and seeing he was going a little over a hundred miles per hour.

The creature pursuing them dropped to all fours, picking up speed as it did so. Gray was surprised at the beast's agility despite its seemingly bulky form.

The fur must make it look bigger than it really is, his mind rationalized.

Not that it really mattered. It was about to kill him, along with the family trapped in the car with him. The mother's terrified eyes darted back and forth between her captor and the creature gaining on the car. The two kids in the back had their eyes locked on the demonic beast that refused to give up.

"Can't this thing go any faster?" she screeched.

Gray shook his head. "I'm afraid not."

Once it got close, the creature leapt into the air. It crashed down on the vehicle's trunk, the force flipping the front of the car into the air. Shouts of terror echoed around Gray, none of them his own. He just froze.

The car crashed down onto its top, Gray hitting his head. The pain was excruciating. His vision spun, the edges black. Then the blackness consumed it all.

Gray groaned as he returned to consciousness. His head hurt like hell; in fact, his whole body did. He felt the seatbelt digging into his chest, the only thing keeping him in his seat... which he was upside down in. The smell of blood filled his nose. Some of it was his, he knew, but some wasn't. He realized this as he smelled it all around the inside of the car... and he wasn't the only one in the vehicle.

Gray looked to the passenger side, where the mother was… only she was missing. The door was ripped away, and she was gone. Then the sound ofr crunching and tearing reached his ears. He knew the sounds well, when he had fed undesirable victims to his dogs. It was the sound of a person being eaten.

The creature had taken her.

Gray craned his head around, peering into the back seat. The children laid crumpled on the roof of the car, bloodied, bruised, and unconscious. He fought back a chuckle, knowing the fat boy would likely be the next on the creature's list.

The man fumbled with his seat belt, reaching for the clip. After a moment of stretching, he found it and pressed the button. He held in a shout of surprise, unprepared for what happened next. Gray fell from his seat head first. His head banged against the roof, sending blazing hot pain through his body, before his body hit. He groaned in agony, not caring if the beast heard or not.

Until he heard a growled "hrmph" outside.

The sound of a body hitting the ground came next. Gray began to panic as the creature's clawed feet appeared in front of the missing door. He ignored the pain wracking his body and started fumbling for his door's handle. Then he looked back to the passenger side to find the creature crouched down, its hideous face peering inside the car at him. It squinted its orange eyes at the man, sighting in on its next meal.

Gray's panic became horror as the creature shifted and began reaching a hairy arm into the car. He found the handle and kicked open the door, rolling out onto the pavement just before the creature's clawed fingers reached him. Then he stumbled to his feet as the monster stood up from its crouch, glowering at him with its sinister eyes.

Gray searched himself for his gun, his eyes never leaving the monster's, but came up empty. Then he remembered he put the gun in his lap before he began to drive, meaning it was thrown somewhere in the car when it was flipped.

Shit.

Gray quickly checked his jacket pockets, finding something. He reached in and pulled out the objects as the monster began skirting around the front of the overturned car. Subject Five's next intended prey looked away for just a moment as he pulled an item from his pocket, but it was too long to be a firearm. The beast had closed the distance between them and slashed at Gray.

Pain unlike anything he had ever felt rocketed through his face as the monster's claws dug into his flesh, then through it and his right eye, which erupted in red and white gore. Gray cried out in agony, hurling the bottle he produced from his jacket pocket into the demon's face. The bottle he had found was chloroform, a substance he used for knocking his victims unconscious. This, of course, made them more manageable while he… transported them. He planned to use it on the family, but shit went sideways.

Through his left eye, which went untouched by the creature's assault on his face, Gray saw the great beast stumble backward, grabbing at its face which steamed from the chloroform. The creature fell onto its back, gasping and clawing at its face. Then it fell still, the noxious chemical doing what it does.

Gray stared at the fallen beast, feeling the blood gushing from the gashes the creature left on his own face. As he did, he thought. Thought about what to do next. With the creature.

An idea formed.

58

Gray transported the beast by… borrowing a moving truck that he found in Yuma. He was surprised how light the beast was and how easily he could drag it up the ramp and into the back of the large cargo vehicle. Subject Five easily stood ten feet tall, but only weighed a few hundred pounds. He would've thought the creature to weigh a fourth of a ton. After the creature was aboard, he threw in Arthur's and his wife's corpses. Next, he pulled the still unconscious children from the wrecked car and threw them in the back with both the sleeping beast and their parents' cadavers.

Gray took one last look at the teenage girl and shook his head in disappointment. But he pushed aside his personal desires and focused on what she would provide in the long run. He grabbed the strap and pulled down the sliding door, locking it.

Before departing the scene, he took the license plate and anything linking the car to him out of the automobile. He also grabbed the first aid kit he kept in the car, because, yah know, people fight back when they're taken against their will. Then, he got into the driver seat of the truck. Gray took a moment to bandage his wounded face with gauze taken from the first aid kit. Once he was done, he started the truck, and drove off, leaving the decimated car surrounded by blood behind.

Minutes after driving off, he heard the screams of the children surrounded by their dead parents and a sleeping demon. Their shrieks, however, had awoken the beast. The truck shook as the creature pounced on its prey, which first wailed in terror, then in agony. Gray cringed at the sound of tearing flesh and crunching bones.

He continued out of Nevada, driving tirelessly, not stopping for more than a few minutes to use the restroom or to acquire food and gas. He ignored the questions and looks his gauzed-up face got.

Before he knew it, he was back home in Chicago, Illinois. Gray realized he couldn't take the creature back to his house. So, he continued driving around the city, pondering his options.

"The old church!" he exclaimed aloud. He knew there was no one in the cab of the moving van with him, but he needed to speak after being quiet for so long.

The church he was referring to was located in the heart of the Camp Pine Woods. No one knew its name or what happened to it. The structure just stood there, abandoned. It was the perfect place to hide a monster.

Gray stopped at a nearby store to get supplies. Chains, clamps, and bolts, plus the tools to install them. The cashier gave him a inquisitive look, but never voiced his questions aloud. They could have been his bandaged face, blood seeping through the gauze, or the supplies he was buying. Gray didn't care either way.

After getting the supplies from the store, he stopped at his house and grabbed more chloroform. He knew he'd need it to get the creature into its new home.

The conniving man drove to the edge of the woods, making sure there was no one around. The fact that the area was shrouded in the darkness of night certainly helped. It wasn't late, but his actions would be masked by the dark. Once he was sure no one was watching, Gray unlocked the back and threw open the door.

The creature turned toward him, eyes squinted, teeth bared. Its face was coated in blood. The remains of one of the family members was clutched in its clawed hands. It squatted, surrounded by gore. Gray's grip tightened on the bottle of chloroform he clutched in his hand as the beast began to rise from its squat. The man reeled the arm holding the bottle back, then shot it forward. The chloroform-filled glass container smashed into the demon's face, shattering and covering its monstrous visage in chemicals. The creature squealed in agony as it clawed at its steaming face. Then it was out, thumping to the gore-slathered floor of the truck's cargo hold.

Gray set to work. He pulled the furry beast from the vehicle and strapped it to a sled he bought to haul the monster through the woods.

The trek through the forest was a struggle. The beast was heavy and maneuvering it and the sled around the trees was tricky. But he managed to do it. And before he knew it, he was standing before his destination.

Gray wiped the sweat out of his eye. His clothes and the gauze covering his wounded face were completely soaked with the stuff from hours of effort dragging the unconscious beast through the timberland. Luckily, the chloroform kept it that way for so long.

Let's hope it stays that way a little longer.

The gauze-faced man made his way to the lowest level of the church and got to work bolting chains into the stone floor of the building's basement. He frowned at his next task, which was dragging the monster to the basement and chaining it up.

After a brief rest, Gray returned to the first floor, the demon still unconscious and strapped to the sled. The task was much easier than dragging it through the forest. However, this would make for a bumpy ride for the monster. Gray cringed at the thought, fearing the beast might awaken while *en route* to the basement.

Luckily, it didn't.

So, he set to work. He unstrapped the beast from the sled and replaced them with iron shackles and chains. Once done with his chore, Gray curled up in the corner as exhaustion took hold of him. He pushed it away long enough for him to replace the blood-soaked gauze with a fresh set. Upon completion, he pushed the first aid kit away and closed his eyes.

Before he knew it, he was in a deep sleep.

59

Gray awoke to the sounds of snarling, growling, and rattling chains. His eyes fluttered open to reveal a horrifying sight. The creature stood just several feet away, at the edge of its iron restraints, staring at him with hungry eyes. He felt fear at first, pushing himself as far as he could into the corner he fell asleep in. After a few moments, seeing that the chains were holding, he relaxed.

"Don't worry. I'll find you some food," he said to the monster.

The creature growled in reply.

Gray made his way out of the church, leaving the snarling beast behind. He shut the door to the basement, dampening the creature's hungry cries. Once he exited the church's front doors, he shut them behind him and applied a padlock he had also purchased at the store. He tried the doors, and left the building satisfied that no one would be getting back into the church except for him.

He made his way out of the woods. It didn't take as much effort as the previous night, but he was still exhausted from hauling the beast through the forest.

Gray cringed as he stepped from the woodlands, covering his eyes from the bright afternoon sun. He sighed in relief as he found no one around. The backdoor to the moving truck was still open, with its gory contents revealed for all to see.

"Shit," Gray muttered to himself, quickly closing and locking the door.

He then made his way around the truck and got into the cab. His first thought was to pull out his phone and open his Internet browser. Gray wanted to know what the creature he had just captured was, so he navigated to the Google search engine and typed in "list of demons." He was redirected to a relevant Wikipedia site and scrolled through the list, reading each linked article until he came across one that fit the beast he captured well.

Vine.

A weird name, for sure, but it fit. According to the article on demonology, Vine was a King of Hell. He was the trickiest and deadliest demon under Satan's command. He had the power to take a human's soul without permission, as according to spiritual teachings, a demon had to acquire Satan's approval to take a soul. And Satan had to ask permission from God.

However, that wasn't what interested Gray the most. It was the fact that Vine had the ability to tell the past, present, and future, to discover hidden things -- treasures came to his mind -- and bring down walls. He associated that last part with immense strength.

While the description of the demon didn't match, as Vine was described as a lion holding a snake in his hand and riding a black horse, but everything else fit. The creature was certainly tricky. Gray could see the monster's intelligence in its eyes. It was also deadly, as he had seen that first hand. Its strength was also immeasurable, surely able to bust through a wall.

The more Gray read about Vine, the more he was certain the creature he had just captured was the demon in the flesh. He surmised that ancient texts got its description wrong. Either that, or they were too terrified of what it really looked like to describe it properly.

And as the leader of a cult -- for which young, virgin girls, like the one he fed to Vine, were his favorite sacrificial prey -- it was his duty to preserve a live demon. He dialed up the other members of his cult and told them the news. They were excited about what he had accomplished and made plans to come to the church.

Gray hung up the phone after speaking to the last of the five others that comprised his cult. He leaned back in the driver's seat of the moving truck with a sigh, still exhausted, despite having slept for hours the night before. That sleep, however, was on a hard, concrete floor and his body still ached from it. He closed his eyes, intending to drift off to sleep, when a knock sounded on his window.

Gray slowly swiveled his head toward the driver's side window. A bearded man's face stared back at him, eyes full of worry upon seeing his bandaged face. With a sigh, Gray rolled down the window to see what the man wanted.

"You alright, mister?" the man asked.

"Quite," Gray replied.

"What happened to your--"

Gray cut the man off with a quick, "I rather not talk about it."

The man nodded, muttering an apology.

"Is my face the reason you came to bother me?" Gray asked, doing his best to mask his annoyance.

The man's reaction suggested he did a poor job. He then shook his head and motioned toward the cargo bed of the truck. "No, I came to ask about the smell coming from back there. You hauling some manure or somethin'?"

An idea formed in Gray's mind, perking him up. He turned to the man excitedly, which caught his visitor by surprise.

"No," Gray replied, "not manure. I actually just delivered a very rare animal."

"Out here?" the man asked.

Gray nodded, grinning ear-to-ear. "Want to see it?"

The man's brows creased in thought for a moment. Gray could see the gears moving behind the fellow's eyes. But soon, the man's curiosity got the better of him and he nodded, replying with a "sure."

Gray stepped out of the truck and headed for the woods. "This way."

The man looked reluctant for a moment, but soon followed.

With a wicked grin on his lips, Gray led the gentleman through the woods and to the church.

"You delivered an animal to the old church?" the man asked, doubt in his voice. "No one has been here in a very long time."

"That's where you're wrong," Gray said as he slipped the key into the padlock and turned it. "You see, I live here now. It's the only place I can keep… my new pet."

The man's only reply was silence.

With the padlock off, Gray opened the doors to the church and motioned for the man to enter. He could see the chap's skepticism alongside the curiosity in his eyes. It was the latter that Gray took advantage of.

"Trust me," the cult leader said. "This is something you don't want to pass up seeing."

The bearded man hesitated for a moment, but soon relented, allowing his curiosity to get the better of him. Gray lead the man down the stairs, and through the sloping hallway that led to the church's basement. He made sure he was positioned in front of his guest, so the visitor didn't see what was in front of him. The growling and snarling noises were hard to mask, however.

"What kind of animal is it?" the bearded man inquired. "I've never heard anything like it before."

That was when Gray stepped out of the way, revealing the chained-up Vine. The man stumbled back at the sight of the demon. He tripped over the red rug that covered the hallway floor, which sent him sprawling.

"W-what the h-hell is t-th-that?" the man stammered, his bottom lip quivering in fear.

"This," Gray said, motioning toward the chained monstrosity, "is the great demon Vine!"

The man's eyes widened as Gray pounced, his fist connecting with the visitor's forehead. The guest's body went limp and he fell to the floor unconscious.

Gray grinned wide as he dragged the man's insensate form toward Vine, whose teeth chattered excitedly. The demon-like beast dug into its meal with gory gusto. The cult leader watched excitedly as it did so.

60

It was days before the other cult members arrived, which they did one-by-one. Gray didn't allow them to see Vine until they had *all* arrived. Once they had, they all gathered at their leader's house before setting off to the church.

Gray stood in the middle of his living room while the others sat on the various couches and cushy chairs available to them. They all wore street clothes. Their leader had just finished telling them his story of how he had come across the great demon Vine.

"Extraordinary," Brother Nick said. "It's almost as if it were fated to happen."

"I couldn't agree more," Brother Samuel said, nodding his head.

"And now that we are all together… we get to see him, don't we?" Brother Ross asked excitedly.

Gray smiled. "Of course, my brothers. I shall take you there right away."

The cult members filed out of Gray's house and piled into his SUV. No one said a word as they drove to the edge of the Camp Pine Woods, lost in their excitement. Upon arriving at the appointed destination, they exited the vehicle and Gray led them through the woods to the abandoned church.

"This is where you keep it?" Brother Joe asked, skeptical.

"It's the safest place I could think of," Gray said as he opened the padlock.

His fellow cult members nodded behind him. Gray threw open the wooden doors, revealing their new place of residence.

"With a little work, this place could be a great place of worship," Brother Jack said.

Gray and the other four members nodded their agreement.

The quintet followed their leader down the stairs leading to the sloping hallway that in turn led to the church's basement… and Vine. About halfway through the hallway, a groan echoed from behind Gray.

"That smell is horrible," Brother Jack said.

The others mumbled their agreement while holding their noses.

Gray stopped, turning toward them.

"Vine is a living creature," he told them. "He eats …and defecates… just like us. What you are smelling is probably both."

"What have you been feeding it?" Brother Samuel asked.

Gray grinned. "I'm sure you already know the answer to such a question, brother."

Samuel returned Gray's smile, figuring it out. The others nodded, knowing the answer as well.

"You'll get used to the stench," Gray promised. "And we can keep the smell down by… cleaning up after him. I've done my best thus far, but it is a very strenuous job to keep up with by myself."

His fellow cult members nodded their understanding again. Then Samuel motioned for their leader to proceed. Gray gave his chief acolyte a smile and continued down the hallway to where Vine was chained up.

The quintet gasped in astonishment as they laid eyes upon the beast for the first time. Gray couldn't blame them. The creature filled him with awe each time he saw it. Vine was crouched in the middle of the room, surrounded by corpses. Some were half consumed, while mere bloody chunks were all that remained of the others. They were still recognizable for what they once were, however.

Some were human. Others were deer and other wild animals Gray was able to capture.

Aside from the corpses, there were also piles of shit and puddles of piss.

Vine rose from his crouch, eyeing his visitors with hungry eyes.

"He is… magnificent!" Samuel exclaimed, thrusting his hands toward Vine.

"Exquisite," Jack said.

"Extraordinary," Ross said.

"Unbelievable," Joe said.

"Beautiful," Nick said.

"Indeed, he is all of those things," Gray concurred, his eyes never leaving Vine.

After a few moments of staring, the cult set to work cleaning the place. This included carting away the remains Vine didn't eat and mopping up the demon's feces and urine.

It was a weekly chore for the next couple weeks. Though, surprisingly, people that were intended to be meals for Vine actually joined the cult. They saw the creature the same way Gray and his cult did.

61

Five days before the raid…

Agent Alexander Gordon sighed as he stared into the darkness of the Camp Pine Woods. He was in the city of Chicago investigating a lead on Subject Four. There had been reports of people going missing around the city. While that may have seemed like a job for the local police force, the big bosses at Area 51 believed it was possible that Subject Four was responsible for the number of missing people, which was close to sixty.

Alex was at the woods because it was the most logical place that Subject Four could successfully hide itself from the human population.

The real question is: how the hell did it get all the way here from the Area 51 facility in Nevada? he wondered.

Little did the agent know that he was soon going to find out.

Darkness surrounded as he peered into the forest. Alex decided to scour the woods at night, mostly so he wouldn't scare anyone who happened to spot him walking around with a AA-12 shotgun (loaded with explosive rounds) and in full body armor.

The agent stepped into the woods, shotgun leading the way. He searched the forest, looking for any sign of Subject Four. It wasn't very long into his search that he caught a whiff of death and decay, which he followed to the abandoned church.

He shivered at the sight he beheld upon reaching the area. Maybe it was the animal carcasses strung up in horrific displays. Or the twigs and sticks tied together to form symbols Alex couldn't identify. Or the gargoyles that guarded the church.

The fuck is this? A cultist hideout?

He stepped up to the wooden doors of the church, feeling in his gut that it was a clue to finding Subject Four. The soldier tried the doors, and was unnerved to find them easily push open, creaking as they did. The noise only fueled his freaked out feeling. Something didn't seem right.

Alex radioed his location into base before stepping inside the abandoned church, with his weapon leading the way. He searched the worship area, finding it strangely untouched. The armored soldier then made his way back to the door and was about to leave the church and continue his search in the woods when he spotted another door. Alex tiptoed toward the entrance and eased it open. This one creaked, too, sending another shiver through his body.

Beyond the door was a staircase that led to another door. Alex slowly crept down the stairs towards this other entrance. He hesitated a moment before pushing open the door with the barrel of his shotgun. Beyond the door was a sloping hallway with a red carpet that led further under the church.

The agent slowly stalked forward, shotgun in the lead. As he neared the end of the hallway, noises registered in his ears. Snarling. Growling. And voices. Hushed whispers. Then the smell hit. Death and decay, like that outside. There was also the hint of animal waste.

He was sure he had found Subject Four even before he exited the hallway and saw the creature chained up and surrounded by people in black cloaks. Subject Four lifted a dismembered torso in its clawed, almost human-like hands and took a bite out of it. The cult members watched as it did, saying nothing.

Alex backpedaled into the hallway he had just peeked out of. He turned back the way he came and began retracing his steps. The soldier realized he had to get out of the woods and call for back up… but he only made it to the top of the steps before a fist connected with his temple. The blow sent the agent rolling down the steps before falling into unconsciousness.

When Alex awoke, he found himself on his back, the ground beneath him freezing. In fact, the surrounding air chilled his whole body. He groggily looked down at himself, finding his clothes and armor gone. Above the hapless stood the cult members, staring down at him.

One of the cultists pulled his hood back, revealing a scarred face and a missing eye. He kneeled next to Alex's naked form.

"You came to take him away from us," Gray said.

"You have no idea what that thing is. It's dangerous!" Alex rejoined, trying to talk some sense into the man.

"I know exactly what he is. His name is Vine! One of the Dark Lord's many servants. We are keeping him safe from those who wish to hurt him, like you, until the Dark Lord comes for him."

Alex couldn't help but laugh at the man's insanity.

"You find my words funny?" the cultist growled.

"You're damn right I do," Alex spat. "That thing is not Vine. It has no connection to your Dark Lord at all. It's a weapon designed by humans to use against other humans. An instrument for war."

The agent knew the information he was giving out was top secret and not something he should be speaking, but he was desperate to save his own life. If they didn't listen to him, he had no doubt they'd feed him to Subject Four.

Gray stared at him for a long moment with his one eye. Alex quivered with anxiety about what the man would do. Then the cult leader spoke.

"You're a non-believer," Gray said.

Alex's heart hammered in fear.

"And non-believers are fed to Vine," the cultist finished.

"Nooo!" the agent screamed as Gray's followers began to roll him toward Subject Four. The creature hopped excitedly in anticipation of its next meal. Then Alex was in the creature's clawed hands, weeping and pleading. The soldier felt Subject Four's fangs slip into his neck and rip a chunk of it out. The pain was immense. Blood gushed from the wound, numbing him as Subject Four took another bite out of Alex.

Then the inky blackness of death took him.

Area 51, Nevada...

"Sir."

Director of Operations Mark Hudson looked up from the paperwork that was piled on his desk. They were reports of various creature sightings that could be potential leads on Subject Four. Standing before his desk was Jacquelyn Gonser, a communications officer and the current handler of Alexander Gordon who was looking into a possible lead in Chicago.

It had been hours since the director received any news about Gordon. Last he'd heard, the agent had found a cultist hideout. He figured that the cultists were to blame for the missing people and that Gordon had been ordered to return to base.

"What is it?" Mark asked.

"I've... not heard from Alex -- er, I mean Gordon," Jacquelyn said.

Mark stood up, his chair rolling hard into the wall of his office. That Gordon had gone missing meant one of two things. One: he had found Subject Four and had lost his life trying to subdue or destroy the beast. Or two: whatever cult he found had managed to subdue him and used him in whatever sacrificial rituals they conducted.

There was only one way to find out.

"Get a raiding party together," Mark said. "I want it ready by the end of the week."

Jacquelyn nodded, turning and making her way out of his office to go about the task she was ordered to carry out.

Mark sat back down in his chair, thinking.

62

The night of the raid...

Mark Hudson pressed himself up against the outside wall of the church, a AA-12 tactical shotgun -- loaded with explosive rounds -- clutched in his hands. The seven other men with him were armed with the same ordinance. The explosive rounds had already proven effective against Subject One. And if Subject Four wasn't in the building, it'd work just as well against the cultists.

He looked across from him, on the other side of the wooden doors of the church, to his second in command, Cody Bratsch. Cody nodded to him. Hudson nodded back.

The team leader tried the door and was frustrated to find it locked. He motioned for two soldiers carrying a battering ram to move in. They did, and three tries later the door broke open. Hudson then beckoned to the rest of the squad to move in. Once one of the soldiers called "clear" over their throat mic, Mark and Cody moved in.

Hudson looked around, scanning the inside of the church. He creased his brows in confusion at the untouched worship area.

If they're not in the worship area, then where are they?

His eyes widened in realization.

If they had the creature... they'd want to hide it.

Hudson walked back to the entrance, finding another door. He pointed it out to the rest of his team. They nodded, aiming their weapons at the door as he opened it. The mission leader jumped out of the way once it was open. They gave him the all clear. He nodded, motioning them down the stairs.

The task force stormed down the stairs, the lead soldier's rifle shouldered. They ended up at another door. The lead soldier tried the door, finding it unlocked. Hudson spurred the man forward. He nodded, throwing the door open and quickly sweeping the hallway with his shotgun. The lead man gave the all clear and they continued forward.

A few moments later, they came upon yet another entrance. Hudson motioned for the lead man to try the door. He did, finding it unlocked. They pushed through the last stretch of hallway without incident, coming upon the end of the corridor. The smell of defecation and death made them cringe.

The lead soldier peeked around the corner. A few moments later, his voice came through Hudson's earpiece. "Uh… sir. You're gonna want to see this."

Hudson pushed his way through the group to the lead man. The soldier moved aside, letting his leader peek around the corner.

Hudson gasped at what he saw.

He witnessed the cult they were hunting gathered around a bound naked man. A scarred figure stood above him, his palms raised to the ceiling.

"Don't worry, my friend. Your sacrifice is for a good cause. And the Vine will reward you for it in the afterlife!"

Mark Hudson could tell this scarred man was the leader.

The man tried to plead with the cult leader but the gag in his mouth prevented it. The tears in his eyes told Hudson the man was begging for his life.

The cult leader, however, all but ignored his weeping sacrifice. He motioned to two of his fellow cult members surrounding him. They nodded while making their way toward the naked man lying on the floor. The leader stepped aside, revealing something that widened Hudson's eyes even more.

Subject Four was crouched near the floor, bound in chains, one for each of its limbs. At the premise of a fresh meal, it stood to its full height. The creature made strange gurgling noises as it did so.

Two cult members singled out by the leader approached the intended sacrifice. The bound man squirmed, his muffled pleas reaching a fever pitch as the two cultists reach for him. Their hands grasped the prisoner, beginning to shove the man toward Subject Four.

Hudson acted on impulse, breaking from cover and shouldering his shotgun while shouting "Hold it!"

Every eye in the room turned toward him, including Subject Four and the man that was to be sacrificed to it.

The cultist leader put on a friendly, yet creepy smile. "I wasn't expecting company."

That's a good thing, Hudson thought.

"Let the man go," the task force commander ordered.

The smile faded from the cult leader's face. "I'm afraid I can't do that." He motioned to the bound prisoner at his feet. "This man is a sacrifice to the great Vine. And you do not want to deny Vine a meal."

Hudson shook his head in frustration and growled, "You have no idea what that thing is!"

The cult leader's calm demeanor suddenly shifted. His brows furrowed, and he gritted his teeth, obviously infuriated.

"How dare you assume what I do and do not know!" Gray shouted, thrusting a hand toward Subject Four. "This is the great demon Vine!"

"No!" Hudson shouted back. He was incensed at the man's cluelessness. "That thing isn't a demon! It's a government created biological weapon designed for war."

Gray scoffed at Hudson's words. That was when the latter's patience wore thin.

"Take them out," Hudson said into his throat mic.

His team broke from cover, shotguns shouldered. The loud booms of gunshots filled the space as the men opened fire. Hudson joined in, sighting in on the cultist leader and pulling the trigger. The cult leader dove out of the way, and the explosive round ripped through one of the chains that bound Subject Four.

Son of a bitch!

Hudson's attention then shifted to the carnage happening around him. Cultists dropped with every trigger pull. Some fell with holes in their chests, and others with missing limbs.

It didn't take long for the unarmed cult members to surrender. The task force gathered the survivors in one corner of the room. Hudson's brows wrinkled in confusion. The cultists' scarred leader wasn't with them.

Then the snap of a chain called the team leader's attention. In the time it took him to turn toward the noise, another chain snapped. Gray suddenly appeared and raised a fire axe above his head, ready to cut through another of the chains that bound Subject Four.

"Stop!" Hudson shouted, shouldering his shotgun.

The cult leader glanced in the direction of the task force leader's voice just as he was about to bring the axe down on the last chain. Hudson pulled the trigger, but the scarred cultist was already gone… again.

"Fuck," Hudson muttered as an exploding bullet tore through the last chain, unleashing the monster that is Subject Four.

63

Subject Four roared to announce its freedom to everyone in the room. A few of the soldiers turned toward the newly unfettered beast with weapons aimed. One of them was brave enough to fire off a round. Singed fur and chunks of flesh flew from the monster's shoulder, triggering the beast to wail in agony.

Subject Four turned toward the puny human that dared harm him and swiped out its claws. The man was flung through the air with blood spraying from his slashed throat.

As Subject Four tore into the other soldiers, Hudson looked around for the second threat: the leader of the cult. But the man was nowhere to be found. The team commander looked back to his teammates who were locked in combat with Subject Four. He locked eyes with Cody, who nodded to his commanding officer.

"Go!" Cody shouted. "We got this ugly sonuvabitch!"

Hudson nodded back and disappeared down the hallway they came from. Before he knew it, he was back outside the church. He scanned the forest, easily spotting the cloaked cult leader scampering off into the trees.

Hudson chased after the man. He found it easy catching up with his quarry, and he figured it had something to do with the cloak the cultist leader wore.

Hudson threw himself at the scarred man, tackling him to the forest floor. Gray's hooked fingers clawed at Hudson's face. The soldier felt the man's fingernails digging into his flesh and drawing blood. Hudson ignored the pain and brought a fist into the cultist's 's side. He heard the air leaving Gray's lungs a moment later. Hudson leaned up, straddling the now gasping man while breathing hard himself.

"This… is not… the way… it's supposed to… be," the cult leader said between gulps of air.

Hudson glared down at the man and said, "No, it wasn't."

The task force commander pulled out a pair of handcuffs and manacled the cultist leader. Gray snarled and fought as he did this, albeit to no avail. Hudson got to his feet and pulled the man up with him.

"This isn't over!" the cult leader yelled. "Vine is free now and the world will know his hunger for flesh!"

The soldier ignored his prisoner, but something in the back of his mind told him that what he was saying was true.

Hudson dragged the cult leader back to the church's basement. What he saw made him stumble. Bodies, of both the cultists and his teammates, laid about in bloody heaps.

One of the dead cultist's bodies moved.

Hudson acted on instinct, shouldering his shotgun and aiming it at the body as it began to roll over. Two armored hands shot up from beneath it, a wide-eyed and bloody face that Hudson recognized staring back at him.

"Don't shoot!" Cody exclaimed.

"Shit, man," Hudson said, lowering his shotgun. "The hell happened here?"

Cody shook his head. "After you left… things took a turn for the worst. The cultists… they… they threw themselves at us. Holding us down for Subject Four to feast upon. I don't think they were expecting to be caught in its bloodlust too, though."

"And how did you survive?" the handcuffed Gray asked, a smug smile on his scarred face.

Cody frowned but answered, motioning to the carcass he rolled off himself. "One of the bodies fell on me in the creature's rampage. I just went with it. Acted dead. It didn't touch me."

Hudson frowned. "So… it's gone then?"

Cody averted eye contact with his commander. "I'm… afraid so, sir."

"Shit!" Hudson growled.

"What do we do now?" Cody asked, sliding the rest of the way out from under the body. His leg was a mess, but he was able to get to his feet. He winced in pain, though the wounds were only superficial.

"Now," Hudson said, looking the cultist leader in his only remaining eye, "we report back to base. There is nothing more we can do now."

After a brief inspection of the forest to be certain the creature wasn't still around, they did.

AFTERMATH

Zach Cole
Christofer Nigro

64

Mark Hudson leaned back in his cushy office chair rubbing his temples. He was beyond stressed. Two experiments had slipped through his grasp. Then there were the reports of more creatures popping up out of nowhere.

Area 51's director of operations sighed in frustration before looking up as a knock sounded on the door to his office.

"Come in," he called, but the men who stepped in were not who he had expected.

The door opened and Alfred Stenze, the director of Area 51, walked in with Logan beside him.

Righteous anger flowed through Hudson. These two were the assholes who unleashed those monsters upon the world. But he held his tongue.

"Hudson," Stenze said in a friendly voice, a pleasant smile on his face.

Hudson maintained a poker face, not falling for the man's charms. "What do you want?"

"Straight to the point, I see," the director replied.

"It's not been the best of times for me."

Stenze nodded. "I've read your reports."

Hudson frowned deeply at the mention of the reports that described his past failures.

"They're even craftier than we predicted," Stenze said, making no mention of Hudson's fiascos. "I have a team on Six. Another is trying to get a bead on Four."

"And the other creatures that have been reported?" Hudson asked.

Stenze wasn't the one who replied.

"That's why we're here," Logan said with a smirk.

Hudson sneered at the man. Logan just chuckled at his displeasure.

"I want you to put together a team and look into it," Stenze decreed.

"What team?" Hudson asked. "Most of our operatives are either out in the field or dead from the recent ops eliminating our runaway experiments."

"Well…" Stenze looked almost hesitant to speak his next words. "We have plenty of recruits in the brig."

An eyebrow shot up on Hudson's forehead. "The survivors from the experiment?"

Stenze nodded.

Logan chuckled.

Hudson fought the urge to sock Logan in the face and shook his head. "I don't think they'll be very cooperative. They've been locked up down there for two months."

"They've not been treated as prisoners. In fact, they've been treated rather well."

"Not the point, sir. They want to return to their homes. Not held against their will in a government facility."

Stenze grunted, but said nothing, as he was clearly deep in thought.

"If anyone can, I'm sure you could butter them up a bit," Logan stated.

"If you have to… give them an ultimatum. Help us and they get to return to their lives, or… die," Stenze said.

Both of Hudson's eyebrows shot up this time. "Die? You're willing to kill them?"

Stenze's brows furrowed in anger. "You understand the importance of these creatures, don't you? We can't let word of these things get out. Of what we've accomplished! These people jeopardize all of that. They either help us contain this or they are to be silenced."

You're the one who let them out in the world in the first place, Hudson thought with a mental sneer toward his boss.

Moments passed in silence.

"Get it done," Stenze ordered before he started walking out of Hudson's office, with Logan following close behind. They suddenly both stopped in their tracks, but Stenze was the only one to turn back toward him. "Except that crazy cultist fuck. He's already been taken care of."

274

Taken care of? Hudson wondered but didn't dwell too much on it. He knew what it meant. The man had been killed.

Stenze turned away from Hudson and both he and Logan exited his office.

Hudson sighed and returned to rubbing his temples.

65

Tim Greymountain and Billy-Bob Tyler laid atop their respective bunks bickering like a married couple, as per usual. Or as the proverbial odd couple they truly were.

Since they were stuck sharing a single room for the past two months, this became a typical occurrence rather quickly. And just as quickly, these two men from very different worlds unexpectedly became best friends.

This latter occurrence would only have surprised those who were unaware of what these men had all too recently experienced together; and what the two had lost during the same time.

"It just fuckin' figures," griped Billy-Bob, "that no sooner do those cock-sucking government spooks finally agree to give us a TV set, then I gotta find out that you don't like watchin' the same fuckin' shit I do."

"Sorry, my newest friend," Greymountain replied as he lay comfortably on his bunk with both hands folded under his head. "But I refuse to apologize for not wanting to watch John Wayne movies."

"Some newest friend you are, then! Jesus Christ, man! John Wayne was the total shit! Why do you Injuns gotta be so mother fuckin' sensitive for?"

"At least we can agree that your John Wayne was 'total shit,' as you so eloquently put it. And as for why someone may be sensitive about seeing their people portrayed as villains fit only to be slaughtered by gun-wielding occupiers of their land… well, think about that for a minute and try not to strain your brain cells too much while doing so."

"What? Now that was fuckin' insulting!"

"Good. Which means you are now familiar with the feeling."

"Well, fuck you, man! I dunno why I put up with your shit sometimes!"

"We share that feeling too, it would seem."

"You totally suck balls, man!"

With that invective tossed out, Billy-Bob hurled a pillow at his friend. Greymountain simply grinned in satisfaction as he pulled the plush object off his rugged tan face.

The two men suddenly turned towards the electronically locked door leading into their quarters as they heard a familiar buzzing sound. That sound being the very brief forewarning the two unlikely roommates received just before an agent of the Area 51 facility was about to enter what passed for their joint domicile.

"Shit, here we go again," Billy-Bob complained.

Mark Hudson strolled through the doorway as if he owned the quarters (and, in a sense, he did) with Logan stepping in directly behind him. The director of operations bore a scowling expression on his square-jawed countenance as he sauntered in the adequately furnished residence and fixed his gaze on the quarter's unwilling tenants.

Logan's visage, by contrast, simply bore its usual jovial but nevertheless unsettling – and decidedly unfriendly -- smile.

"Gentlemen," Hudson said in a calm and professional tone. Neither of the two tough-as-nails lodgers returned the curt salutation. "This is Logan. He is one of our… other agents."

"To what do we owe the displeasure of this latest visit, Mr. Hudson?" Greymountain asked with evident sarcasm.

"Are we finally gettin' the fuck outta here?" Billy-Bob queried sharply as he stood from his bunk and approached the two government employees.

"Well, kinda sorta," Logan answered, his patented sardonic smirk never leaving his face. "And let's just say that like most good things in life, it comes with a catch."

"I fuckin' knew it!" Billy-Bob exclaimed while slapping his hands against his hips in frustration.

"That's life, sir," Logan said. "Did you seriously expect the good folks here at Area 51 of all people to be an exception to that rule?"

"Fuck you, ya little overpaid, tax-dodging punk!" the large redneck yelled while stepping closer to the crafty espionage agent.

Logan didn't flinch, nor did he lose his smile, despite the very intimidating presence of Billy-Bob directly in his personal space. Hudson took a step forward and intervened before the looming confrontation went any further.

"Back off, Mr. Tyler," Hudson said with all due seriousness. "This is a matter of grave importance."

"Likely with the word 'grave' being the operative term. Am I correct, Mr. Hudson?" Greymountain lamented while sliding off his bunk and walking to Billy-Bob's side.

The mighty Amerindian warrior knew it was fortuitous for him to intercede here as well. He gently put his hand on his friend's shoulder, which caused Billy-Bob to quietly go silent in deference to Greymountain's greater diplomatic ability.

"Something like that," Logan responded to Greymountain's ironic query as his smirk grew wider.

"Please stop, Agent Logan," Hudson ordered through clenched teeth. "You're not helping matters any with your ill-timed flippancy."

"What does our esteemed Agent Logan mean, Mr. Hudson?" Greymountain enquired.

"What he means," Hudson replied, "is that your debriefing period is almost over. However, due to the very sensitive nature and national security issues surrounding the… situation you both recently survived, I'm afraid the degree of freedom we can allow you must come at a price. And it's a price you have both proven well-suited for 'paying' even without formal government training, and under the most hazardous possible conditions."

"I sure as hell don't like where this is goin'," Billy-Bob said with concern.

Logan smiled again as he remarked, "It would seem our resident redneck might actually be smarter than he looks and sounds, Mr. Hudson."

"Mother fucker…" Billy-Bob retorted while raising his fist.

Logan moved into a defensive stance as Greymountain grabbed his friend's upraised wrist. "It's not worth it, Billy-Bob. Do not let men like him bait you into worsening our situation."

"... but still not as smart as his red-skinned homie," Logan continued. "Eh, Hudson?"

"Don't make me warn you again, Agent Logan," Hudson said firmly.

"Can you get to the point, so you can conclude this less than cordial visit, Mr. Hudson?" Greymountain asked, as not even he was certain how long he could effectively restrain Billy-Bob. Or himself, for that matter.

"Yes," Hudson replied, "and pardon the tactless behavior of my associate."

Logan released a sarcastic "pfft!" through his lips. "As if that label doesn't apply to Billy-Boy here..."

"That's Billy-*Bob*, asshole!" the rural hunter corrected.

"Whoops! My bad," Logan quickly replied with a less than sincere tone.

"As I was saying!" Hudson decisively interjected. "We anticipate the problem of other... experiments like Project Hydra going similarly awry in the future. Accidents... can happen."

"Accidents? From you guys?" Billy-Bob said with an ironic roll of his eyes. "Who could imagine that?"

Logan began to chortle before pointing to the redneck and saying, "I'm actually starting to like this guy. He really grows on you. Sort of like athlete's foot between the toes, only funnier."

"My cousin and a good friend died because of this 'experiment gone awry,' Mr. Logan," Greymountain said with a biting tone. "As did Billy-Bob's closest friend. As did many other innocent civilians. As did several soldiers of this very agency while bravely attempting to clean up the mess their employers caused. So, I strongly suggest you lose the quips and show us, along with the victims who didn't survive, all due respect.

"Because you need to understand this, Mr. Logan. The people who both cleaned up your mess and suffered greatly because of it are not the only ones who will have to pay for the folly of your agency. Heed my words."

Hudson then quickly realized the importance of reining Logan in, as he knew how much the very angry Goshute warrior was hoping for an excuse to take a shot at any and all employees of Area 51; and that Billy-Bob would certainly follow his lead if he did. Despite the military training that he and Logan possessed and the obvious "home field advantage" provided by the government facility, Hudson knew that two men who battled Subject Two and emerged to tell the tale were hardly individuals to be needlessly trifled with.

"Agent Logan, I am preemptively telling you to shut up again!" Hudson ordered. "Do not push it any further, as I am now through warning you without acting on that warning!"

The director of operations of the god-forsaken facility then turned back to Greymountain and Billy-Bob. "You two have indeed earned my full respect, and I apologize again. Both for my associate's behavior and for having to put this stipulation on your freedom in the first place."

"Describe this stipulation, if you would, Mr. Hudson," Greymountain said with his full attention focused on whatever the director of operation's next words would be.

66

One day later, Greymountain and Billy-Bob stood in a special training room deep inside the darkened byways of the extensive Area 51 facility. There they were reacquainted with the hearty Kenna Sazuki and the newly promoted Lieutenant Terrance "Tee-Bone" Morrison, all survivors of the bloody encounter with Subject Two in the Goshute National Wilderness. All were clad in combat armor specially tailored for each. Beside them was the similarly attired Bryan Corner, a survivor of a different encounter with another experimental organism spawned by Project Hydra, the vile multi-limbed Subject Six.

Standing in front of the quintet was Mark Hudson and Logan, who were explaining to them the specifics of the "stipulation" the director of operations mentioned to Greymountain and Billy-Bob twenty-four hours earlier.

"So, you want us to work for this agency?" Kenna asked. "I mean, seriously?"

"I couldn't be more serious, Agent Sazuki," Hudson replied in a no-nonsense manner. "Lt. Morrison will be field leader of the very special task force you five will comprise the nucleus of."

"You just gotta be shittin' us here," Billy-Bob said.

Greymountain didn't speak, as he instead continued to inspect the specialized body armor designed just for him. He couldn't help but admire its resemblance to a Kevlar-reinforced Native American buckskin. This included how it provided full freedom of movement despite the degree of protection it afforded its wearer.

Bryan remained strangely silent and looked a bit pale and shaky. Why this was so would soon become terrifyingly evident.

"No shit whatsoever, Agent Tyler," Hudson replied. "In addition to that individually tailored armor, each of you will be given generous government wages and benefits, as well as access to an appropriate expense account and manufactured identification as required whenever you are out on a mission. Recreational, emergency, and medical leaves in addition to periodic paid vacations will be allotted to you."

"I mean, you seriously expect us to work for you?" Kenna reiterated with even more incredulity. "After what your asshole little 'Project Hydra' took from us? And all the other innocent lives it took? My girlfriend and two of my best friends, all good people, died because of your douchebaggery!"

Bryan continued to quiver in seeming discomfort before coughing a few times.

"Consider what I am about to tell you, Agent Sazuki," Hudson said. "This is a chance to personally see to it that as few other innocents as possible will suffer due to future... errors of this agency."

"You mean, you expect more errors like this in the future?" she retorted angrily.

"Considering the shit hole government agency this Area 51 is," Billy-Bob said, "of course there's gonna be more! And they want us to put our asses on the line to clean up their messes! After the mess they made of our lives!" The irate redneck pointed at Hudson and Logan. "Why aren't any of you assholes goin' straight into the hoosegow for this shit! Why do we gotta pay and keep on paying for your shit?"

Tee-Bone then stepped forward. "Billy-Bob, I understand that you're pissed," the newly promoted military man said. "The fellow soldiers I lost to Subject Two were friends of mine. And a few of the soldiers in the other task forces who were lost to other subjects of The Experiment were also friends. I know the government can be nothing short of ape shit crazy sometimes, but it's still the only government we've got. And as long as we're on the inside here, we find ourselves in the perfect position to make sure things never get too out of hand again."

"I understand what you're saying, Lieutenant," Hudson interceded, "but do not overstep your bounds here."

"Only if things truly get out of hand, sir," Tee-Bone replied. "There has to be checks and balances on the government, or more innocent lives could be lost. And more bad decisions can be made and gotten away with."

"Uppity little thing, isn't he, Mr. Hudson?" Logan said with a strained version of his patented smirk. "Maybe he should join the Black Panthers instead of our agency. I hear they're making a comeback in the current political climate of… unrest."

"Agent Logan, did that dig of yours just imply that seeing to it that the government stays on the straight and narrow is somehow unpatriotic or an act of civil disobedience?" Tee-Bone asked.

"It simply meant, Lieutenant, that we all need to grow up and respect the chain of command even if we disagree," Logan advised. "That, my esteemed soldier, is a fact of your job, as well as a fact of life. Do you let your kids discipline you if they happen to disagree with one of your orders?"

"Orders need to be governed by rules and principles," Tee-Bone replied. "The powerful must protect the powerless, not walk all over them."

Logan rolled his eyes in exaggerated fashion. "Very lofty, soldier-guy. And even more naïve."

"I think I need to say it again," Kenna said. *"Ser-i-ous-ly?"*

"Seriously fucked up is what this all is," Billy-Bob added with an exasperated sigh.

"There are codes of conduct, Agent Logan," Tee-Bone spat back. "Soldiers have to live by them. And so do… people like you. At least if I have anything to say about it."

"People like me?'" Logan said with an upraised eyebrow. "Care to elaborate, Lieutenant?"

"I think he mighta' meant that even fucked up government spooks like you need to be not so fucked up every once in a while," Billy-Bob interpreted. "And slapped down on your ass if you stop givin' a shit about the little guy."

Greymountain greatly disliked the situation he now found himself in, but he could not help feeling some degree of respect for Tee-Bone. Despite never imagining he could ever have a single iota of respect for a dedicated soldier of the establishment, what he had recently been through with Lt. Morrison had begun changing the Goshute warrior's thinking. After all, if he could warm up to a rural white redneck like Billy-Bob, and vice-versa, then just about anything was conceivable.

"We will follow your game plan for now," Greymountain finally said. "But only for now. And only so long as this task force does as you say it will do. Because if we must clean up a mess, we're going to clean it up *entirely*. I'm sure you get my meaning."

Both Hudson and Logan shuddered involuntarily, as they each understood what was likely to happen if this new task force found out the full truth. They were barely amenable to this situation with what they already knew about Project Hydra. But if they were to discover that Director Stenze hired Logan to deliberately sabotage the facility so that the Project Hydra subjects would be set loose on the public as part of an experiment beyond the original experiment that first created them…

"I want the whole lot of you to focus on the good you can do as part of this new task force," Hudson said, trying to sell the idea to them and suppress any lingering doubts. "In addition to the compensation I mentioned earlier, along with your individually tailored armor you will be provided further training designed to enhance the talents you already have. Furthermore, you will each be equipped with specially designed weaponry that will likewise be tailored to the skills each of you have displayed.

"Agent Greymountain, I think you will really appreciate the specialized longbow and hi-tech set of arrows our team is developing for you. Agent Tyler, you will love the plasma-firing shotgun we're now in the process of constructing for you. Agent Sazuki, you will be delighted to receive a paint gun whose liquid ammunition spheres do a lot more than simply dye a target. All of you will be well prepared for the tasks ahead of you, and it will all be entirely on the government's dime."

Suddenly, Bryan began coughing again, this time louder and more intensely than before.

"Yeah, and what about this guy?" Billy-Bob asked, pointing his thumb at the now uncontrollably hacking Agent Corner. "What the hell is his story? He ain't one of our group of survivors. And what the hell is ailing him right now? Somethin' tells me that ain't just a touch of bronchitis he's got."

"Yes, he does seem to be sick," Greymountain agreed.

"We'll send him to the infirmary to get that cough taken care of right after we adjourn in a moment," Hudson promised.

"But what's his story?" Billy-Bob repeated.

"Yea, I would like to know the answer to that," Kenna agreed. "We know next to nothing about him, other than that he survived an attack by one of the other creatures. And that he seems to be in really bad health because of it. How is he in any shape to be part of this task force?"

By that point, Bryan was hacking to a degree that he looked about ready to keel over. Clumps of dark-colored phlegm had now begun flying out of his mouth with each cough.

"Jee-zus," Billy-Bob said as he backed away from Bryan's "line of fire."

"Subject Six injected Agent Corner with some unknown type of fluid during his encounter with the creature," Hudson explained. "He seemed really sick when we brought him here, so we gave him a few... experimental drugs that we hoped would remove extreme pathogens from the human system. Instead, those drugs seemed to combine with the creature's fluid to... change him."

Bryan was now coughing so hard he was on his knees.

"What do you mean by 'change?'" Kenna enquired curtly.

Logan tapped the director of operations on the shoulder. "Hudson, maybe you shouldn't..."

"No, Logan, they're going to find out soon enough anyway," Hudson said. "We had best tell them now. The combination of Subject Six's bio-chemical injection and the experimental drugs had... mutagenic effects on Agent Corner."

"Muta-gentric what-sis?" Billy-Bob queried through a confused expression. "Is that some kinda gentrification?"

"Mutagenic," Greymountain clarified. "That means, he was mutated... transformed... into something... different than human."

"Oh, fuck," Billy-Bob whispered.

As if on cue, the incessantly hacking Bryan Corner suddenly stood up and let out a piercing scream. His tongue extended over two feet from his mouth in a writhing, lizard-like fashion before the altered young man forced himself to pull it back into his mouth.

"Oh, fuck!" Billy-Bob exclaimed much louder this time. "Did you fuckin' see that?"

"Oh… my… god…" Kenna muttered.

But the grotesque display wasn't over yet. Bryan began gritting his teeth while an intense spasm overcame his body, as if he were fighting against an increasingly drastic re-alignment of his entire physiology.

The young man appeared to at least momentarily lose that battle when he reached his right arm in Greymountain's direction and a long, pink tentacle-like appendage shot out of a cavity in the palm of his hand with tremendous speed and force. The formidable Amerindian was struck in the chest by the tentacle and pushed up against the cement wall directly behind him.

"Fuck shit!" Billy-Bob hollered.

"I'm sorry, Mr. Greymountain," a still trembling Bryan said through a raspy throat. "I'm – I'm trying to control it, but…"

"Get the fuck offa' him!" Billy-Bob yelled as he ran and grabbed the center of the extended tentacle in his bulky arms and attempted to yank it off his friend.

"Kenna, you help on that end!" Tee-Bone commanded. "I'll try to subdue Bryan!"

Kenna ran beside Billy-Bob and added her feisty strength to the redneck's own rather considerable might in struggling to wrest the tentacle off Greymountain's chest. The Native American warrior was himself working on the very same task, using his own impressive strength in attempting to pull the aberrant appendage off him from directly where it was attached. The tentacle seemed to have four half-inch long sickly yellow talons extending from its slightly bulbous tip that was embedded in the outer layer of his armor.

It hadn't yet penetrated into his flesh, and the Goshute athlete wanted to remove it from his person before that had the chance to happen. Since he had no idea as to how strong that appendage and its talons actually were, Greymountain was making due haste in the removal effort. As was his friends and teammates.

Tee-Bone rushed Bryan and punched him in the side of his face. The strong, expertly placed blow stunned the young mutate, but didn't succeed in knocking him off his feet. Nor did it cause the tentacle to detach from Greymountain's chest.

"Bryan, let him go!" the lieutenant ordered. "Get control over yourself!"

"I'm trying, sir…" Bryan said through a garbled voice. "But… I can't seem to… stop myself…"

"Then sorry, but I gotta do this!"

Tee-Bone hit Bryan even harder, this time in the solar plexus. That fearsome blow knocked the wind out of its target, weakening the grip of his appendage just enough to enable Greymountain – aided by Billy-Bob and Kenna's added strength -- to pry the talons at the tip of the tentacle out of the armor covering his sternum.

Bryan quickly recovered from the blow to his plexus and surprised Tee-Bone by extending a tentacle out of the palm of his other hand towards the attacking soldier. He appeared to be acting more out of some sort of primal, bestial instinct than actual cognizant choice.

Tee-Bone's trained reflexes proved true as he used his armored forearm to block the talons at the end of it from embedding into his forehead, where the projected appendage was aimed. However, the sheer strength of the ropey tentacle took the lieutenant off his feet and slammed him up against the wall on the other side of the room, stunning him as its talons embedded themselves half an inch into his grayish-white gauntlet.

By this time, though, Greymountain was recovered enough that he could act to help Tee-Bone. Since the Amerindian warrior was still holding the other tentacle in his grasp, he used all his might to pull on the appendage and use it as a makeshift tether to swing Bryan up against a portion of the wall. The impact of that slam succeeded in momentarily dazing the young mutate.

"Billy-Bob! Kenna!" Greymountain shouted. "We need to pile on and pummel him until he's out! Hudson, get help from the medical crew!"

The large-bodied redneck and lithe but tough young woman quickly did as Greymountain commanded and the trio slammed into Bryan in unison. They then beat him to the floor with a combined deluge of punches and kicks. Bryan was now down, but still not out; the mutated human, acting on an instinct he could not currently control, resisted the onslaught with an inhuman degree of strength and resilience.

Within moments, Greymountain and Billy-Bob each used their full strength to attempt to hold one of the two gyrating tentacles from being brought to bear on them again, while Kenna repeatedly drop-kicked him in the face. She couldn't help noticing that the blood dripping from Bryan's split lip and nostrils was an ochre-ish hue rather than the normal red.

"Someone do somethin' before some other weird thing comes out of him!" Billy-Bob yelled while doing his best to keep one of the two writhing flagella-like appendages from hooking its talons into his flesh.

"You had best heed that suggestion!" Greymountain exclaimed while struggling in the same fashion with the other tentacle.

"Damn it, I'm trying to knock him out!" Kenna lamented as she continued kicking the out-of-control mutate in the face and chest.

It was at that point Bryan again extended his thick, serpentine tongue and wrapped it around Kenna's attacking leg between her foot and the knee. It constricted her limb with a strength reminiscent of a small anaconda, thus preventing the girl from delivering another kick. It then pulled Kenna off her feet, and the young woman landed directly on her buttocks. Thankfully, the armor she wore prevented the extended tentacle-like tongue from damaging the skin or bone beneath, but considering the degree of force it exerted, she was unsure how long that would last.

"Aw, shit! Somebody better fucking do something now!" Kenna demanded as she kicked repeatedly at the constricting tongue with her free foot (albeit to no avail).

Tee-Bone had by now recovered, and he had quickly removed the gauntlet of his armor where the tentacle's talon was embedded before it could penetrate through to his skin and muscles.

All according to plan, Hudson thought. *Now that they subdued him...*

"Lieutenant!" Hudson shouted, quickly getting Tee-Bone's attention. "Hit him with this! Quickly!"

Hudson pulled a long cylindrical syringe from one of his coat pockets and threw it to the soldier. Tee-Bone caught it skillfully, and saw it was filled with a bluish liquid. The armored militiaman knew what had to be done, so he swiftly ran towards the violent pig pile before him.

"Greymountain, Billy-Bob, hold those tentacles good!" Tee-Bone commanded. "Kenna, keep that tongue occupied!"

The three did as bade, and Tee-Bone leapt up against Bryan with his full weight. He then plunged the syringe into a bulging vein located on the struggling mutate's neck. The pallid young man began screeching again for a few seconds before going into spasms. His two arms then went limp and fell to the floor, with the tentacles quickly retreating in whip-like fashion back into the cavities in his palms. The cavities then seemed to self-seal, leaving a barely visible slit in their place. At the same time, his long tongue released Kenna's leg and retracted back into his now tightly closed mouth.

Bryan began taking several deep breaths, as if he were hyperventilating. "I'm... I'm sorry. I just need to get it... under control."

"All is forgiven," Greymountain said gently. "This wasn't your fault."

"It sure as fuck was *somebody's* fault!" Billy-Bob bellowed. "What the fuck was this shit all about?"

"What did that thing do to this poor guy?" Kenna demanded to know as she ran up to the director of operations. "And what further shit did *your people* do to him? Talk, Hudson!"

"As Agent Corner said, he still hasn't gotten it fully under control," Hudson noted, while Logan looked on from a few feet behind him, that perplexing smirk once more in evidence. "His physiology has undergone a rapid morphological alteration at the genetic level. Once he does get it under control, with further drug treatments and training, he can serve the task force as an invaluable living weapon. Agent Corner can enable us to fight these creatures with some of their own organic weapons; sort of like fighting fire with fire."

"Further drug treatments?" Kenna lamented. "Look what those fucking drugs of yours helped do to him already!"

"Right!" Billy-Bob concurred. "And what we just saw shore didn't look like they was helping him none!"

"We just need to find the right formulation and dosages," Logan proffered. "The lab boys and ladies will get it right eventually."

Kenna cocked her head and upraised the left side of her mouth. "Eventually? You mean, hopefully before he loses it too many more times and ends up killing more than just a few people in the process? Including, maybe, one of us? Like he just almost killed Greymountain?"

"You aren't helping, Agent Logan," Hudson said. "Let me handle this. Like you wanted me to in the first place."

"As if you're doing any better yourself," Logan snarked.

"Allow me to handle it as well," Greymountain said as he approached Hudson and Kenna. "This man was hurt, infected, and changed by forces that were not of his control. He needs a lot of help and support, despite how dangerous he now is. We, of all the people in this world, should understand his need. We were all affected by these same forces, even if in a different way than he was. We all lost people we cared for. But he lost his very humanity."

"Well, if you say so," Billy-Bob grudgingly acquiesced. "But I'm gonna be keeping an eye out on him. Two eyes, in fact."

"Yes, Agent Corner is very dangerous now," Tee-Bone said. "But it's our job not only to help him control his mutation, but also to make certain he is only dangerous to the right targets."

"Can't say I liked the sound of that," Logan muttered almost inaudibly.

"Are we all in accord with this, people?" Tee-Bone questioned his new team.

"Without a doubt," Greymountain answered.

"Yea, totally," Kenna replied. "We all need to look out for each other."

"Yeah, yeah," Billy-Bob said. "I do sorta feel sorry for the little guy. I mean, did you see that fuckin' tongue?"

"Thank you," Bryan choked out. "I really mean it. I will… learn to control… this." With that said, he let out another weak cough before passing out entirely as the metabolic suppressant took full effect.

"All right," Hudson said. "Let's get Agent Corner to the infirmary, and the rest of you off to your quarters for sleep. Your training starts tomorrow, and we need to have you all out on the field within a month or two."

Greymountain fixed a heavy glare on Hudson and Logan before they all adjourned as ordered. The thoughts that filled his mind at the time were poignant.

Do not think for a moment that this is how it ends, with us in your permanent servitude. You all have much to answer for. And the mysterious Director of Area 51 more so than anyone else. One day, he and I shall meet. When that day comes, the true reckoning will commence. This I swear to the Great Spirit, and to the memories of Shaun and Marcus. And to all others, both alive and not, who have suffered — and who will suffer in the future — from the actions of these fools.

THE EXPERIMENT

67

A few days later…

Gray sat in his small cell looking straight ahead with no sign of emotion. This wasn't too unusual for him. After all, he was incapable of displaying many feelings other than anger and the type of exhilaration one derives from the thrill of dominating or killing another person. Or, the euphoria one experiences due to religious zealotry.

Nevertheless, the fallen leader of the Cult of Vine wasn't exactly comfortable in that cell. Unlike the other survivors of the Project Hydra massacre, Gray wasn't allotted a space that combined a prison cell with a reasonably comfortable apartment-like setting -- complete with heating, plush furniture, coffee table, refrigerator, private bathroom, and television set. This was strictly a prison cell, with no amenities or accouterments beyond a simple cot with a thin blanket and flat pillow. The walls were a dull gray in color, lacking any type of décor. He wasn't held in by bars, but a heavily padlocked door with a small barred window and a thin rectangular opening at the bottom where a tray of food or meds could be quickly slipped under. Much like what one would find in an asylum for the violent mentally ill.

Still, the dangerous killer had been forced to reside in worse dwelling places in the past. And he was forced to eat much worse than the swill served to him three times a day from the facility cafeteria. So, he could grin and bear all this. Without actually grinning, of course, save for the brief beams that crossed his scarred countenance whenever he relived the dark memories of torturing and otherwise harming others, starting with animals when he was a child. This was the closest he could come to doing one of the very few things that elicited any type of deep emotional response for him, even though joy, happiness, and love could never actually be one of those feelings. The deeds that elicited one of the limited emotions he could experience would have to occur strictly within the realm of his twisted imagination from now on.

Or, so he thought. Because Fate was about to smile upon this vicious man. Sort of.

Gray's ruminations and dark reminiscences were interrupted when his cell door was opened, and Mark Hudson stepped in. The displaced cult leader looked at the intruder into his new "home" with an impassive expression. His single remaining hazel eye was as dull as the surrounding walls; the gaping hole where his other eye once existed was covered by a leather patch.

"Hello, Mr. Gray," Hudson said without hiding the contempt in his tone. "Feel free to take a lunge at me, if you are so inclined. I am really hoping you do. As I would like nothing better than to have a reason to finish what we started back at that fucked up church of yours. I am not exactly pleased with these scars you left on my face. Not that they compare to the ones Subject Five left on you, however."

Gray didn't make the play Hudson was hoping for. Instead, he remained on his cot and responded in a completely emotionless tenor.

"I have no interest in that, Mr. Hudson," he said. "Did you just come here to try and bait me into making an escape attempt through you? Or, is there something else I can do for you?"

Hudson huffed to himself, almost appearing to be disappointed. But Gray chose not to make the action, so Area 51's director of operations proceeded with the intended business at hand.

"I have a deal for you, Mr. Gray. I encourage you to decline the offer, because I would very much like to carry out the alternative. Personally. Because you are among the worst scum I have ever encountered on this planet. And considering my line of work, that is truly saying something."

Gray squinted and glowered at Hudson with his single gleaming eye. "I am intrigued. I would like to hear your deal before I grant you the alternative measure you are hoping for. Your straightforward capacity for bloodlust is refreshing, considering how many people try to deny that side of themselves. I actually like that about you, Mr. Hudson. So please, do not ever change." Gray's expression came close to forming a smile with that last statement.

Hudson gritted his teeth and clenched his fists before taking a deep breath and laying out the proposition.

"As I was pointing out, Mr. Gray, you are a horrid, remorseless piece of shit. But the fact remains, you're a *tough* piece of shit. One of the few people to actually survive an encounter with one of the Subjects. Let alone put one of them out of commission on your own."

"The great Vine wanted me spared. So I could bring his glory to the world!"

"So you could make the world his feeding ground, you mean! And judging by those scars on your face and that missing eye – which are suitably fitting to your personality, by the way -- I highly doubt that bastard intended to leave you off the menu."

A nasty scowl suddenly permeated Gray's disfigured face. "You dare besmirch the great Vine!"

"That's just *the beginning* of what I dare, Mr. Gray. So, get used to minding your manners for the first time in your putrid life, or I will take the deal off the table. Which I am fully authorized to do at my discretion. Or, I can simply take the matter out of your hands by reporting that you made an escape attempt. And no one in this facility or elsewhere in the government will give enough of a shit to question me on the matter. I doubt even your own parents – assuming you didn't kill them – would give a shit either. Can you dig that?"

"Rest assured my parents *deserved* to be killed, Mr. Hudson."

"No doubt they did, simply as penance for bringing *you* into this world."

Gray's angry clenching of the teeth slid from his torn features. "As I said before, Mr. Hudson. I am listening to your offer."

"Then listen good. As awful a specimen of humanity as you are, it seems you might be an unusually useful one. Because you have two striking attributes that this facility is quite interested in. Neither of which has anything to do with your manners or your looks, mind you."

"And those two attributes you believe I excel in would be what, exactly?"

"First one: Your surviving an attack by Subject Five and even managing to subdue the creature and use it for your own purposes, however fucked up those reasons were, makes it clear you are one tough and resourceful son of a bitch. I kicked your ass, of course, but I didn't get where I am today by being a wuss, so no shame in that. And getting to the top of that depraved cult of yours is further testament to these skills of yours.

"Second one: As tough as the other survivors of an attack by one of Project Hydra's creations happen to be, you have something none of the rest of that lot do. Or, more specifically, you *lack* a crucial attribute displayed to some degree by the others that could make them a liability in some cases. Unlike them, you have no conscience, no empathy for other human beings, and no feeling of remorse or responsibility to anyone or anything other than yourself. Your pretensions to caring about some religious bullshit notwithstanding, since I think that is just your rationale of choice to wreak bloody hell on others."

Gray winced only slightly at the last comment before replying. "One… might argue that my lack of conscience could likewise be a liability. Though I am guessing that would only be the case if you were planning to set me up with your sister or proposing I adopt a child or take in a puppy. But not if I was offered a position on the executive board of a big corporation. Nor if I was offered a place in some black ops government program. Am I getting the gist of the offer, Mr. Hudson?"

"You are indeed, Mr. Gray. And since you wouldn't look good in a suit and tie, I am going to give you a position as a 'secret' member of the special elimination task force I am now putting together to hunt down and destroy the remaining offspring of Project Hydra. Along with any future… mistake that may come out of this or other programs conducted here, or in other black ops programs."

"This task force you mention would consist of the other survivors of your Project Hydra, correct?"

"You got it. But know this if you accept the offer and deprive me of what I am hoping to do (at least, as of today). Though the rest of the task force is aware of who you are since I gave them access to files explaining the basics of all the Subject massacres, I told them we had you killed, because I was told you were. But I was soon informed you were alive, and the higher ups were interested in using you. When I found out you weren't, I was planning to do so myself, but I haven't done it yet because... as much as I respect those other survivors, they may present a problem for the program."

Gray raised his right hand. "Let me guess, Mr. Hudson. You worry the conscience they each have may cause them to rebel against some of your orders. And you need someone on the sidelines ready to, shall we say, put them in their place if need be. In the way that I do best, but secretly, so they would not see me coming first."

"You just earned another gold star, asshole. Lacking that conscience, you will be an ideal elimination agent in many ways. You won't give a shit about anything remotely related to ethics. The only reason you would ever disobey an order, *any* kind of order, is if it somehow didn't benefit your own selfish interests to follow through.

"And you *will* follow through with all my orders, because that is the only thing keeping you on this planet for another day. It's the only thing keeping my hands off your filthy throat. And if you tried to disobey me on the field for any reason, know that I will have no less than ten different ways to kill you instantly, at any moment and from any type of distance. Some of them are quite agonizing and rather prolonged; and the method of your disposal will be at my discretion, and contingent upon my mood that day. And with this job, I am not in a good mood very often, Mr. Gray. And certainly not when it comes to you. Not after all the horrible suffering you inflicted on innocent people."

"So quick to judge. As if you never committed a fucked up act in your life, Mr. Hudson. Both before and after you entered the military."

"I won't lie to you, or to myself, and say I haven't done some fucked up things in my time. But I didn't do them gladly. At least, not often. And I always did it for the greater good."

"Your interpretation of such, I should point out. As if saying you did this or that for the stars and stripes was any less of a rationalization than what I say I did for the great god Vine. The people in the White House and the 'fat cats' in those big munitions corporations are *your* gods, Mr. Hudson. And it was your gods that gave my god a physical vessel to operate on this world. So, maybe we really are aligned in holy purpose after all, eh?"

Hudson again gritted his teeth and clenched his fists. The skin on his hands was beet red before he regained his composure and managed to avoid doing what he wanted to do more than anything else in the world. He reminded himself that he was a soldier first and foremost, and sometimes horrible things had to be done for the greater good. Then, his fists slowly unclenched.

"I've had enough conversation with you for one lifetime, Gray. So, let's just get down to it. Do you accept the proposal… or not?"

Gray's response was immediate. "I accept. I think I will grow fond of being called *Agent* Gray from this day forward."

Hudson's expression was now as impassive as that of Gray's, as if he didn't quite know how to feel about the news.

"Very well. Let me give you a final warning, though. I told the other members of the task force that you're dead, and to all intents and purposes, from this day onward you *are* dead to the world. You will interact with nothing or no one save for me, any other government authorities of rank, and anyone else *only* if I give you explicit orders to do so. When you are out on the field, you stay away from any civilian unless I say different.

"You will have plenty of opportunities to… indulge your proclivities and exercise your skill set. But they will all be coordinated by me, or another government official of rank. Otherwise, that eye will not be the only part of your anatomy that you will lose before you exit this world in a most unpleasant fashion. Do you understand me?"

"Yes, I do, *Director* Hudson." Gray beamed a most unpleasant smile.

"That is all. Your training will begin tomorrow. Maybe. If I feel like looking at you again that soon."

Hudson turned, still hoping that Gray would try something foolish. When that didn't happen the director of operations exited the room, slammed the cell door shut, and locked it securely.

Gray then went back to his silent repose on the cot. His expression went as blank as it was prior to his conversation with Hudson. Only this time, a grin was readily discernible on his scarred face.

Did you hear that, Great Lord Vine? I will soon be able to see you again. To help you and your fellow deities. It will not be easy, and I may have to… damage your earthly vessels if need be to retain my freedom to help. But your will has spoken again, and Hudson could not deny it! Worry not, I will ensure that the government agency that provided you and your fellows with physical vessels continue to work in your favor.

In the meantime, I will quite enjoy the new line of work I am now starting. The world will yet belong to us…

NOTES FROM THE AUTHORS

If you hadn't pieced it together after reading my story, *Horror at Stone Hill*, it exists in an alternate reality version of my book *Tsuchigumo* where Dustin Dreyling survives, and Derek Dawson is the one who sacrificed himself to destroy the nest.

In the process of writing this story, I realized the personal connection I inadvertently wrote in. The main character, Gabriel Gregory, is basically me when I was in school. I liked things people considered "weird." I got bullied for it, even. And the secondary character, Alaina Phillips, is how I wished people treated me. Without judgement. Some people actually did. But not a lot.

As for *The Cult of Vine*, it was another fun story to do. Though, I had Robert to collaborate with. The story was his idea, but due to other things getting in the way, he couldn't write a lot on it. Ninety-five percent of the first chapter was him. The rest was me, but I tried to keep the story as close to his original idea as possible.

I also wrote both *The Escape* -- which sets up the subsequent stories -- and *Aftermath* with the help of Christofer Nigro -- which is basically the epilogue to the book. I had a lot of fun with everything I wrote for this project and love how it turned out overall. All the stories are exceptional. I hadn't given the authors any specific criteria for their stories. Other than that, it needed to be near Nevada (with the exception of *The Cult of Vine*, as it takes place months after the escape of our monsters) and there were to be no survivors. However, the last rule didn't really take effect. There were survivors in the stories. And I let it go, because I loved how the stories had turned out. And I think the fates of the survivors will be awesome to expand upon later.

Anyways, I hope you enjoyed this anthology! Share it and leave a review so we can do a sequel!

--Zach Cole

I had fun writing this little story. I can't really say there were any major inspirations besides years and years' worth of horror movies and novels with the story formula I used, and the original artwork provided by Zach Cole. I did fictionalize the town of Alamo, Nevada quite a bit, so don't go thinking you can go visit Sherman's Truck Stop!

Thanks to Zach Cole for giving me the opportunity, and Kevin Jones for being my advanced reader. And of course, to the real Aaron and Johnny for being the inspirations for the characters in this story. I hope you enjoyed reading it as much as I did writing it.

--Dustin Dreyling

I was first approached with a brief of "do pretty much whatever you want with the creature, as long as it fits the framework of the anthology." So, after thinking for a while I hit on the idea of "what's worse than being eaten alive by a monster? Staying alive." The first person transcripts allowed for a looser, improvisational feel that emulated certain creepy pasta tales I am a fan of and hid the big reveal for the very end. I really enjoyed getting into everyone's heads pace as each character met Subject Five in increasingly grisly circumstances. The alien race that Subject Five got his nerve tissue spinnerets from may show up in one of my horror novel ideas down the road as well...

--Alex Dumitru

Mommy, Where's Fluffy?
(With Complete Apologies to Metallica!)

My tale's titular monster was officially christened "Fluffy" by this tome's esteemed project head, Zach Cole – so, I couldn't resist the above title for my notes/essay!

Anyway, did I have some interesting thoughts while composing *Fluffy Fury*? Did I have a purpose in mind, messages to project, values to espouse? Was there a method amidst the gore and mayhem ensuing on the printed (or digital) page? Though I am more than happy to let the reader glean whatever they may out of my words, I will nevertheless point out that I did indeed have a purpose in mind. I may have developed it as I went along, but hey, it's there!

My first feeling, of course, was being flattered and honored beyond measure to have project developer, editor, and coordinator Zach Cole ask for a chapter/story contribution from *moi* for what I consider to be an awesome hybrid of novel and anthology. Once I fully acclimated to this excitement, I did have my share of messages that I hoped to convey among the actions of the characters who had the misfortune of crossing paths with the dreaded Fluffy (you gotta love a tremendously deadly beast with a deceptively benign and even "cutesy" moniker!).

The main theme I conjured up was the following thought experiment: How do you get several disparate parties of people -- all of whom are predisposed to dislike each other for various reasons -- to overcome their mutual antipathy in favor of working together for joint survival when extraordinarily dangerous circumstances presented themselves? Those circumstances being personified by a deadly, genetically engineered predator whose deadliness is matched only by its impressive stealth; an utterly overwhelming combo of blatant, over-the-top slaughter and a subtle manner of approaching its prey that makes it simultaneously loud and quiet.

Could these different parties not only work together and pool their various strengths to help at least some representatives from each group come out of it alive and triumph over a common foe that presents a far greater danger to them than they do to each other? Not only that, but might each party find themselves forging very unexpected and unlikely friendships and levels of mutual respect in the process of dealing with shared tragedy? And as a natural consequence of watching each other's' backs when they needed their backs watched more than ever before in their respective lives?

I've always been fascinated by the way fate, in both fictional and real-life contexts, can throw so many individuals together under unusual circumstances that demand cooperation rather than competitive and antagonistic behavior if all concerned – or as many of them as possible – are to come out of a situation intact (or reasonably so). In that sense, despite how unpredictably capricious fate can be, it's also one of the greatest motivators and instructors our species can have.

Finally, I had to consider this: Which characters to I allow to survive Fluffy's rampage, and which do I sacrifice to the creature's lethal claws and jaws?

It was quite clear that drama and a full realization of the dangerous circumstances these disparate parties found themselves in would not allow for all of them to survive. Or even for *most* of them to end up on the right side of the grave. So, it was a question of how many from each party would live to regret the incident, and which of them it would be (well, one of them constituted a party of *one*, but yanno what I mean).

Originally, I planned for there to be only a single survivor, with this intended to convey the full deadliness of Fluffy's rampage. But, as I continued to type words on the monitor, some of the characters started to grow on me more than I expected. They seemed to cry out "future potential" and "sorry, but I'm going to survive whether you, the omnipotent author of my fate, wants me to or not."

Needless to say, the "god" behind the word processor was successfully defied in the end. As writers of fiction will often attest, some of our characters will insist upon being *more* than merely characters, and to actually become *people* on the page, with wills and purpose of their own. Or, at least to all intents and purposes!

These characters may not be real, but authors do seem to imbue them with a form of consciousness that can act of its own accord at times, as if they are struggling for a degree of independent existence within the context of the strange fictional worlds we create for them. Possibly you have to be there, and to have worn this proverbial tee shirt, in order to get the complete gist!

It also occurred to me somewhere along the way that perhaps at least one representative of each of the four separate parties (the redneck hunters; the paintball gaming crew; the traditional Native American warrior; the armed Area 51 elimination task force) who crossed both paths and fates in that bleak forest area in the boonies of Nevada should be spared. Overall, I wanted to find a balance between displaying Fluffy's full level of deadliness and what can be accomplished when various parties of people who are not fond of each other manage to overcome their differences and competently combine their efforts to survive the most trying circumstances one can imagine. It certainly will not guarantee survival for everyone, but it can at least insure that those who lose their lives in the process do not do so for nothing.

The readers will also likely note that these characters are, by and large, my favorite type of character to work with: morally *gray* characters. They are flawed individuals, and not always pleasant to be around, but they are nevertheless *all* human. Hence, each of them possesses the capacity to display *real* feelings for human beings other than themselves despite their various personal prejudices. None of them are sociopaths or outright villains (as is Zach's character Gray from *The Cult of Vine*) despite their foibles and attitudes. I am therefore hoping all of them can be readily identifiable, either with the individual readers or with other people you, the reader, knows or has known at one time or another.

I decided to strive for this because I disagree with the notion that all heroes need to be flawless and near-perfect paragons of ethical morality in order to be admired or looked up to. Those whom we can more readily identify with because of their real human flaws are not necessarily incapable of inspiring others. To the contrary, they show us that despite the lows we can all sink to when we're not at our best, we all nevertheless possess the potential to rally for the greater good, overcome whatever prejudices may compromise our personal fortitude, and cooperate with others to overcome the most dangerous and intractable of obstacles.

It may take some work, or maybe even the appearance of extraordinary circumstances, to bring out our best at times, but we *can* do it if need be. And therein lies hope for humanity in general.

Now, what can be more inspiring than that? I'll be content to allow the readers to figure out the answer for themselves, and I thank every one of them for being along for the ride. I hope you had as much fun riding on this metaphorical train as I had driving it!

--Christofer Nigro

THE EXPERIMENT

Pt. 1: Before the Terror

So, since Zach wanted me to write something up for my story *Dark Helix* I have decided to let you all in on how I came up with (hopefully) what you found as an entertaining little tale, as well my first Area 51-related story. I could go on and on about how great this idea is, etc., but since I'm not an arrogant, prideful bugger, I decided to just tell you the story as clearly as I can remember it. (WARNING: Unreliable Narrator at work here, so please enjoy it however much you can!)

So, it was the beginning of what would be my first term at a local university and aside from getting assignments left and right my writer self wasn't terribly active (for those wondering, university is a commitment not unlike that of a strict girlfriend - - a nice girlfriend, but demanding nonetheless) and honestly, my "writer mode" was all but active! With the chaotic bed-time schedule, walking to and back from the bus-stop in the early morning and evening, I just was not motivated/alert enough to write a story that I thought would be of any worth! (Some of you may not have liked *Dark Helix* and thus have questioned what stories would be worth my time, but we won't get into that, shall we?).

To be honest, I was frustrated all the while because story ideas keep popping into my head even during university, and some of them -- which I was absolutely, God(zilla) sure were golden -- poofed into oblivion. For a writer who spends 90% of the time cranking out ideas for new stories, my inner writer was frustrated more than before.

Then one night, I saw Zach's announcement for a new anthology dealing with Area 51, one of the most controversial and mysterious places on Earth. I heard a lot about Area 51: everything from the Roswell Crash, to the stories about dead gray aliens being carried away, the military experimenting with alien technology, and many others in between. Even though I was interested in mysterious cryptid creatures like Sasquatch (yes, I'm referring to Bigfoot as Sasquatch -- deal with it!), the thought of two worlds and their respective intelligent species involved in dark cahoots was more than enough for my imagination to get frenzied and excited

Especially with the author/project head involved with this newest project. This anthology was proposing multiple scenarios branching off from a single incident in which horrific experiments broke loose and were terrorizing the surrounding areas.

Zach Cole is a kaiju and horror aficionado since he was a child; growing up on daikaiju films like *Godzilla vs. Megaguirus* and other monstrous media (like *Critters*), he too had an imagination for the monstrous, terrifying, and unspeakable! He had recently been the author of a couple of kaiju novels (*Tsuchigumo* & *Kaiju Epoch*), *Blue Moon: A Jeremy Walker Thriller,* and as of this writing, is now editing his newest terror novel, *The Legion.* He was a fellow author who submitted a kaiju story to Matthew Dennion's *Attack of the Kaiju Vol. 1: Age of Monsters* anthology, which concerns a post-apocalyptic, *Pacific Rim*-esque story but with titanic monstrosities named after the Four Horsemen of the Apocalypse (check that story out; it's really cool!). Having my name appear in a project from an accomplished author of monstrous fiction was quite an honor... and so, when I heard he'd be helming this project I had to gobble up the opportunity.

But, next came a challenge which I had not previously experienced before: how to approach a story about Area 51, or at least tied to it? I hadn't done a whole lot of research into the mysterious military base in a while at the time, and I needed a bit of a tune-up as far as UFOs and reported extraterrestrial phenomena. So, I watched and read quite a bit in the way of Area 51; I also listened to stories of the Dugway Proving Grounds, as well the rumored underground alien base in Dulce, New Mexico. Research wasn't a big issue for me. If anything, I do research every day to a degree, especially when it came to university! What happened next made me rethink my strategy.

Sometime after Zach announced the project, he posted the rough, PDF draft of what is supposed to be the inciting incident of the collection. For those of you who are confused about how this is structured: what Zach brilliantly created was a mode of storytelling that combined the basic gist of an anthology -- but with a twist! What happens is that after the very first story, the tales we publish will take place right after the titular Experiment Subjects' escape and proceed to commit whatever monstrous acts they plan on doing. The result is a storytelling mode that has a similar format to an anthology, but also has stories that are connected to another and all have the same origin story.

The advantages of this mode of writing are: 1) A more coherent, unified story than other anthologies; 2) The beginning of a shared universe without it feeling too disjointed, gratuitous, etc.; and 3) our monstrosities have a world already in place that feels interesting yet sinister. And because our monsters were in a centralized area, we didn't have to worry about our creatures being in places where it didn't make immediate sense in the anthology. (I use "immediate" here deliberately, because our stories take place directly after the break-out of our terrifying creations).

So, what is the unforeseen problem I mentioned earlier? Well, the flip-side of this decision is, to me, ending up feeling somewhat restricted in terms of monsters, their origins, the setting, etc. I initially had my creation stalk Area 51 militia in a labyrinthine section of the military facility., This was supposed to be a nod to the first *Alien* movie with a very tense atmosphere, brutal yet slightly unseen deaths, and occurring within setting was dimly lit.

Also, Zach had several preconceived descriptions of the monstrosities beforehand -- which was fine, but I also wanted to know if I had even a sliver of creative liberty. Luckily, Zach said I could create my own monstrosity but followed-up saying I must have a numerical designation tattooed on the terror. I agreed to those terms and with that, I was ready to write (Assignments, be damned -- no, just kidding!)

But, like other circumstances I run across as an author, I now had to think about connecting the story to Zach's prologue yet still making it the best to my ability.

Pt. 2: Designing the Terror:

First on my author hit-list was to fully read the rough draft of the introductory story to get a sense of what I'll be going into -- if you didn't notice by now, I kind of take the old saying "Know thy enemy" to an interesting level. As you have already read, the introductory story introduces Director of Operations Mark Hudson, who is in charge of the biological weapons and genetic testing section of Area 51's weapon development. After a mysterious individual mucks with the electronics systems keeping the beasts trapped within containment domes, the monstrous creations escape and go on a bloody rampage before breaking loose from the facility. As I read the story, I took careful note of the tone, the origins of the monstrosities, the terrifying presence they had, the intensity of the situation, and finally, their would-be proximity to the military base.

I also had to keep in mind the numerical designation each monstrosity had because Zach wanted us to make sure we had the numbers correct so as to not let anyone be confused about which monster was which. My creature had "6" tattooed on its back, so that was not a problem. But, since I don't stop at writing the creature's description, I decided to draw the monster before starting the story. And yes, I am an artist and I design each creature for each of my stories myself and always will (with exceptions). So, the next thing that came at me was: how am I going to make this design work?

Then a brainwave hit me, and I re-read a particular section where Subject Six (as Zach described it) massacred a number of militiamen with terrifying ease. I noticed a few traits in the description, but one of them was the feeling of a psychological aspect inherent in the creature's design. Described as being like a praying mantis but much more terrifying, given the Area 51 aspect, that gave me the basic gist for drawing the creature. After a couple of weeks of drafting, detailing, and inking, the result was a terrifying being combining the traits of a snake and mantis, with a nod to the ahuizotl (a water monster of South American myth) thrown into the mix.

Pt. 3: Writing the Terror to Come:

After finishing the drawing of the creature, then came the writing. After doing some preliminary research of the setting as well as getting the tone right, my fingers flew across the keyboards as much as my schedule permitted. Mind you most of the week I was hard at work with assignments and other immediate academic priorities, so I elected to write on the weekends where I was cut a bit of slack.

I remember it being quite difficult to keep pace with university and trying to write things here and there for *Dark Helix*. But, while I was writing, I found myself deeply intrigued by this world; and because of that, I found it much easier to write the story as it came along. Just to let you all know, I usually start with a basic "here's the beginning and this is the how it ends…" type of assumption, but everything in between is 50/50. I know what's going to happen, but not too sure *how* it will happen. Mind you, I don't write all my stories that way, but with a few I sometimes feel that when I'm stumped I just let sit for a while until something comes to mind.

Now for the nay-sayers who think that's lazy, I need to point-out something: The reason I do it is to maintain a level of unpredictability. Anytime I read a story with a saggy middle (yes, you have done this too and don't deny it!) I get an impulse to jump to the next page. So, how I fix the problem is by having a generally faster-paced middle and my attitude is, "Well, the reader has come this far, so why not give them even more incentive to keep going?"

Now with *Dark Helix*, as I was trying to balance my academic workload and the story at the same time -- which I'll never do again -- I felt that some parts might be too fast or, "Well, I have to write in something," at times. (Yes, I'm self-critical too, so any haters wanting to spew any blind hate towards my stories, let me say this: I know, I've seen quite a few of the rough edges!). Suffice it to say, I did do my best. And believe me, university is very demanding of work ethic and focus; anyone who has gone to university would tell you as much!

Now, before I finish up, here are my answers to some questions you may have for my work.

The weird, freakish, and *Evangelion*-esque sequence where the main human protagonist (Bryan Corner) is to highlight a special ability in Helix's gruesome repertoire of attack and kill techniques. That ability is called Hysteria and is hinted to be used as a way of letting the target kill him or herself! The next most common capability is an unnamed cloaking ability which Helix uses to watch its targets without being seen; if it gets really bloodthirsty, it will go into "Blood Mode" in which even the slightest drop of blood will make it go nuts!

For Bryan's inclusion: While I knew the story should still tie back to the incident at Area 51, I knew the readers must have a reason to be invested in the scenario -- and unless they're fans of monster stories, it is at best an uphill battle. Hence, I wrote Bryan in there as a sympathetic individual who is grieving and wants the best for his now deceased brother. This was partially autobiographical on my part; I had a best friend whom I considered a brother die years ago and believe me, no one should ever have to go through that. So, I hoped that including Bryan would keep the audience even more invested in what's happening. Whether I achieved that goal, or failed, or even mildly succeeded is up to the readers and yourself for debate.

The rant Bryan had against the militia about the cover-up at Area 51 is simply keeping with the theme of Area 51. Because this isn't a daikaiju story, I had to make sure I kept in tune with the anthology and with Zach's vision. Now, that was a very odd choice, but I felt it was semi-appropriate based on the fact that the militia were acting unusually bossy and tense to a commoner who has no idea what is happening. Along with the fact that Area 51's secrets really had broken loose. Bryan may have been a mourner, but he certainly is not stupid either! Being an Area 51 and UFO/alien enthusiast, he knew full well of the stories of a potential cover-up; to him, this was smoke to fire (if you will!)

Also, I titled this story *Dark Helix* to 1) reference the sinister nature of the genetic research of Area 51, led by Hudson, but also 2) to inference something particularly dark and potentially nightmare-inducing about the origins of Helix/Subject Six. Helix, to my own horn, is especially terrifying because there is an especially unnatural aspect to this monster, even if it has predominantly extraterrestrial genes flowing through its veins.

Those are my answers for these topics! I hope I could be of help. Needless to say, it was a very fun experience to write for this anthology, especially for an already accomplished author of numerous novels. To this day, I still look on my experiences writing *Dark Helix* fondly and I honestly cannot wait to see what anthology Zach has in store next.

Pt.4: The Terror Has Ended:

So, after weeks of writing I finally managed to complete the story for Zach to edit. Afterwards, I found myself once again wondering what the reception of the story will be; to which I said to myself: "Hey, you gave it your best shot given the circumstances! If some don't like the story, fine. But, for those who like it, I'll be sure to thank them." Which leads me to this final part of my retrospective for the writing of *Dark Helix*: for those who have read the story, thank you. For those who've read it and liked it, thank you so much!

For those who have read it and didn't care for it, thank you for reading but please do enjoy the works of the authors featured elsewhere in this anthology. You don't have to like my work and please do not feel like you must. You have your preferences and I have my own. Let's leave it at that.

And despite the task I had to achieve, writing the story while completing my university term, and through basically the hardship of pumping out this horrifying, thrilling, and monstrous story, may I say this: I kind of miss doing it. It was my first non-daikaiju story to be published by anyone, and I think that's part of the thrill. I was also having fun, yet it was a different sub-genre of monster story. Plus, I hope Helix provided you with plenty of chills and shocks. Hopefully I didn't scar your mind too bad!

So, does that mean Helix has met his end? Does this mean Helix's future as a terrifying, half-alien thing is dead in literature?

Well… perhaps not!

A while ago, there was talk and speculation between me and a few other authors that a sequel to *The Experiment* could be where our monstrosities are captured and as punishment, are forced to go where cryptid creatures are purported to live. Also suggested was an idea where our monstrosities are fighting an actual war against a certain group of assailants. I certainly hope so; it'll be cool to see a pseudo-Avengers team of Area 51 terrors scaring the hell out of the world. (Boy, I am so twisted!)

That is my retrospective. Enjoy the story and I do hope this answers some questions you might have had concerning its genesis. This is only the beginning...

--Breyden Halverson

ABOUT THE AUTHORS

ZACH COLE is the author of the novella *Tsuchigumo*, his debut work, *Kaiju Epoch,* and the Jeremy Walker thriller series. He was born in Wooster, Ohio, beginning his love of monsters at the age of two with *Mothra vs. Godzilla*. He became a writer around the age of ten, writing Godzilla stories and even comics containing his own monstrous creations. His love of books started with the *Goosebumps* series, reading anything that has to do with monsters, big or small. He lives in West Salem, Ohio.

ALEX DUMITRU is a weird fantasy writer from the Midwest. He has written several short stories for volumes of the *Attack of the Kaiju* anthology series, but *The Experiment* is his first published foray into sci-fi horror.

BREYDEN HALVERSON is a young author, part-time yet active cryptid researcher, and all-around monster nut! He lives near Okanagan Lake in British Columbia, Canada, where a sacred creature of the water is said to live -- and breeding! "Dark Helix" is his fourth short story to be written, in what is hopefully a long line of monstrous adventures for readers to enjoy (he hopes!) While not writing stories, he can be sighted at one of Canada's top forty universities stalking the library shelves for new monstrous info and conquering assignments.

DUSTIN DREYLING is an avid fan of science fiction and horror, with a soft spot for all things kaiju, originally hailing from White Bear Lake, Minnesota. He also likes proofreading novels, playing video games both old and new, and taking care of his planted freshwater aquariums. This is his first published story, but hopefully it won't be his last.

CHRISTOFER NIGRO is an author and freelance editor native to the state of New York. He is a lifelong fan of sci-fi, horror, fantasy, pulp adventure, comic books, and video games. His published work includes short stories for Black Coat Press, Pro Se Press, Sirens Call Publications, Grinning Skull Press, Horrified Press, and Local Hero Press. He has had two novels (with a third in the works) for Severed Press. Wild Hunt Press is his first foray into the indie publishing business on his own.

ROBERT GALVIN is an aspiring horror/kaiju writer from Illinois who's written for the kaiju anthology series, *Attack of the Kaiju*. He grew up with many monster movies. Robert has researched countless dinosaurs and cryptids and continues to have much love for them. He can be reached at:: Robertgalvin125@gmail.com

www.ingramcontent.com/pod-product-compliance
Lightning Source LLC
Chambersburg PA
CBHW022136170626
46807CB00005B/1963